BLACK LIGHT: DEFENDED

GOLDEN ANGEL

Published by Black Collar Press

Black Light: Defended
by Golden Angel

e-book ISBN: 978-1-947559-15-8
Print ISBN: 978-1-947559-16-5

Cover Art by Eris Adderly, http://erisadderly.com/
Editor: Maggie Ryan

First Electronic Publish Date, September 2019

First Print Publish Date, September 2019

THANK YOUS!

I have a lot of people to thank for helping me with this book:
My amazing beta readers, who are invaluable in helping me catch mistakes, continuity issues, and working through problems with me. Katherine, Nick, Marie, Karen, Marta, Annie, and Jessie – you all make these books so much better! Thank you for being such great cheerleaders, helping me with mistakes, continuity issues, and constantly asking questions.
Eris Adderly for the absolutely stunning cover.
A special thank you to Ellery and Lisa, who were happy to answer all my many texts and emails about being a lawyer and a PhD student.
Livia and Jen for taking a chance on me and including me in Black Light.
My husband for his continued loved and support.
And, as always, a big thank you to all of you for buying and reading my work... if you love it, please leave a review!

CHAPTER 1

*M*elody Williams was in so much trouble.

The judge presiding over her case sent her a dirty look as she started to sink down in her seat, and she quickly straightened up again, trying to appear responsible and innocent. Because she was both. She was also a victim of circumstances, not that she'd been able to convince the police of that.

Her attorney, Mr. Park, glanced over his shoulder to see what the judge was looking at. Melody tried to give him a smile back, but she was pretty sure it came out more like a grimace. He turned back to the officer he was questioning.

"At any time, did Ms. Williams indicate that the drugs were hers?" Mr. Park asked the cop on the stand. The same cop who had searched her bag and found the drugs before arresting her.

"Well, no, but—"

"And she did admit that she had left the bag unattended?"

"Well, yes, but—"

"Did she show any indication of being high?"

"Well..." The cop's voice trailed off as his cheeks reddened and he glanced at her. Melody immediately dropped her gaze, not wanting to face him. She still felt the shame and fear from having her hands cuffed behind her, all while she protested that she didn't know how the drugs had gotten into her purse. A little tendril of anger curled in her stomach when she remembered his mocking disbelief. She'd been tipsy, not high and he knew it. The cop coughed. "No, she did not appear to be high."

Watching Mr. Park tear the case apart using the cop's own testimony was more than a little satisfying.

Somehow she'd gotten an attorney who looked more like he belonged on screen in *Crazy Rich Asians* than here in this small courtroom, arguing that her case should be dismissed. She was pretty sure that being totally turned on by her lawyer had to be breaking some kind of rule.

Weren't lawyers supposed to be sleazy slimeballs? She was willing to bet they weren't supposed to be six feet of pure muscle packed into a gray suit, have jet black hair that waved away from a movie-star handsome face, and a deep voice that sent all sorts of reverberations through her lower body. Her first lawyer hadn't been sleazy really, but he hadn't seemed particularly competent or interested in her case.

Actually, until Mr. Park had shown up this morning in his tailored suit and told her that her lawyer was no longer available and that he'd be defending her in court today, she'd been convinced that she was going to jail.

From the moment he'd introduced himself and told her that he was taking her case, she'd been an uncomfortable mix of anxious and aroused. Strangely, something about him had also made her feel protected, like everything was going to work out, even though he'd made no such promises. Or maybe she was just fooling herself because she was so desperate for some kind of reassurance, any reassurance, that she hadn't irrevocably ruined her life.

Her life had spiraled pretty wildly out of control since the night when she'd been at a party that had been busted up by the cops. Some asshole had gotten high out of his mind and then run out into the front yard and peed in the middle of the street right as the cops had shown up thanks to a noise complaint. What was supposed to be a much needed night off, a break from the stress and pressures of trying to earn her PhD, had turned into the most stressful situation of her life so far.

All because she'd been dumb enough to set her purse behind the couch and someone had tucked a bag of drugs into it, presumably to hide them when the cops showed up. She hadn't checked it when she'd tried to leave and had willingly handed the bag over to be searched.

Mistake... mistake... mistake...

Never willingly hand anything over to be searched. Never say anything once you've been arrested. She knew that now, thanks to her incredibly attractive lawyer.

"Look at me, not Ms. Williams, please, Officer Linc." The directive was respectful but said in such a firm tone that Melody had to press her thighs together. She'd always had a thing for authority figures. Then again, she'd always thought cops were pretty hot too, until one was ignoring all her protests as he handcuffed her and then shoved her into the back of his car. Definitely not how her cop fantasies had ever played out in her head, and she was pretty sure she was done with those now.

Lawyer fantasies on the other hand...

That was another reason she was in trouble.

"In summary," Mr. Park said, sweeping his hand back at her. Melody started paying attention, sitting up straight and trying to look as earnest as possible as the judge glanced at her again. "Ms. Williams is a model student with no previous record—in fact, she doesn't even have a record of parking tickets. She attended a party where her bag was placed in a manner that anyone could have gained access to it. She immediately offered her purse up for a search when it was requested, was shocked to discover someone had placed drugs inside, and has been consistent in her story throughout. Officer Linc followed procedure, as necessary, but there is not enough evidence to try my client, much less convict her. While she made a mistake in leaving her purse unattended, such mistakes should be learning experiences, not cause for jail time. I move for immediate dismissal of the charges."

Judge Kneupper's gaze was indifferent, but not condemning. He turned to look at the prosecutor, who sat there for a long moment, as if thinking about how she wanted to respond, before standing up and nodding.

"The prosecution agrees and moves for acquittal."

Melody's lungs burned, but she couldn't seem to take a breath, waiting for the judge to speak. It felt like every cell in her body was straining in anticipation of his verdict—a physical impossibility, yet she *felt* it.

"Motion granted." The judge swung his gavel, the resounding wooden thunk seeming to echo through her brain as Melody sucked in the sweetest lungful of air she'd ever breathed.

Her head whipped to the right to look at Mr. Park, who was turning back to her with a slight smile on his face, confirming that she hadn't misheard... the case was dismissed. Walking back to where she was sitting behind the table, he didn't exactly loom over her, but he certainly cut an imposing figure. Especially as his lips curved down to a more serious expression.

"Congratulations, Ms. Williams," he said in a low voice.

"Thank you," she whispered and then cleared her throat, because she hadn't actually meant to whisper, her voice had just caught. "Thank you so much, Mr. Park."

"I hope you've learned your lesson about leaving your belongings unattended," he said, giving her a stern look that made her want to melt into the floor... and it made other parts of her feel all melty too.

～

"Yes, Sir," she said, answering his admonishment, her cheeks blooming with color as she answered in a higher voice than normal. Her tone was almost girlish and he bit back a groan. The combination of her submissive, repentant answer and embarrassed, little girl tone was like something straight out of his fantasies. "I won't do it again."

Little Miss Doe-Eyes was killing him.

She's not a sub, she's not a baby girl, stop wishing she were...

No, she was just an embarrassed woman, relieved to no longer be facing drug possession charges.

He cleared his throat, trying to settle into his normal post-trial client routine. "It was very nice to meet you," he said, holding out his hand to help her up. "Although, if we ever cross paths again, hopefully it will be under better circumstances."

"Um, yes, um... yes." She blushed. She was staring at him like he'd hung the moon, her lips slightly parted and her soft brown eyes so wide that she almost resembled an anime character. Kawan's brain supplied him with a mental image of her dressed up in something soft and ruffled instead of the navy dress suit she was currently wearing, and he shoved it away.

Seeming to realize that she was still holding his hand, she blushed even more brightly and abruptly stood without giving him time to step back, and for one long moment they were nearly chest to breast. Her breath hitched and her head tilted back again to look up at him. The attraction between them was hard to deny, but Kawan made himself step back.

Technically she was no longer his client, but he had a strict rule about playing with vanillas—he wasn't allowed to. It never ended well. But he shoved that thought away too because it reminded him of everything he'd lost.

He wasn't even supposed to *be* here today.

But Paul Standish, the managing partner from his old firm, had called and begged him to help out. His daughter was Ms. Williams' mentor in her PhD program and she'd called her

5

father, frantic with worry that her mentee was going to be rail-roaded in court. She was absolutely certain of Ms. Williams' innocence, but also knew the young woman couldn't afford anyone other than a public defender.

Since Kawan had left Standish and Stanton on good terms and wasn't starting his new job until tomorrow, he'd made a few calls and then come in to defend Ms. Williams. Even though he was a civil defense attorney and not criminal, it hadn't taken more than a glance at the report and a quick conversation with her to realize she was innocent.

Not just innocent. *Naïve.*

If she'd been his...

But she wasn't. And he'd learned his lesson about riding in to be a seemingly innocent woman's white knight. Hadn't he?

"Let me help you with your coat," he said, giving himself something to do that was professional and distracting from the tension rising between them.

"Thank you," she said softly. His fingers brushed against the back of her neck as she shrugged the coat on, and for a moment he thought about breaking his rules. But no, he'd put them in place for a reason.

After helping her into her coat, Kawan beat a swift retreat. There was no reason to hang around torturing himself over a woman he'd just met. This weekend he'd be going to Black Light, as a member rather than a guest for the very first time, and there would be plenty of submissive women there who were kinky. Women who would hopefully want what he had to offer. Women who knew what they wanted and wouldn't... He pushed away that line of thinking again. Krissy had already taken up too much of his thoughts over the past year.

Besides, he was running late.

While his official first day at Lambert, Urbanski, and Reed wasn't until tomorrow, he'd been planning on going in and getting the lay of the land. Sure enough, as soon as he checked his phone, three messages from Alexander Reed—a friend from law school and the 'Reed' in the firm's name—popped up on the screen.

Let me know when you're done being a hero and are coming in.

Sienna saved you a donut for when you get here. It's chocolate.

Never mind. I ate the donut.

Chuckling, Kawan texted back that he was on the way now and immediately got a thumbs up in return from Alexander. He'd be willing to bet that Sienna had another donut tucked away for him somewhere. She was thoughtful like that.

The two of them were an interesting pair, since Alexander, like Kawan, was a Daddy Dom, whereas Sienna hadn't seen herself as a baby girl at all when they'd first met. They compromised though, switching back and forth between who was taking care of whom, so Sienna's need to submit through service and Alexander's need to take care of her in the manner of a Daddy Dom were both satisfied. They were good for each other and they made it work.

He wanted something like that. A real relationship. Between two partners who both knew what they wanted.

Even though he'd been burned, he had to believe it was still possible. Going to Black Light and watching the two of them scene together, watching their relationship grow and progress... well, when Alexander had proposed and Sienna had said yes, Kawan had realized what he needed to do.

A fresh start. Away from Richmond. Away from Krissy and from everyone who had listened to her bile.

And straight to unfettered access to Black Light. The fees were expensive but entirely worth it. Alexander had taken him there more than once as his guest, and Kawan had thoroughly enjoyed every visit. Surely he'd be able to find a submissive within the club's exclusive walls. A baby girl he could have a real relationship with. If not there, then he might visit Overtime as well, and if he found a baby girl there, then he'd bring her to Black Light.

Kawan made himself focus as he entered the offices of Lambert, Urbanski, and Reed. This was not the place to be thinking about his social life. The receptionist sitting behind the desk, Mrs. Connelly, looked up and smiled at him in welcome.

"Good afternoon, Mr. Park," she said. "Mr. Reed asked that you go straight back to his office."

"Thank you," he said, giving her a smile.

"Also, Ms. Davis asked me to give you this." The older woman's eyes danced with amusement as she held up what looked very much like a donut wrapped up in a napkin.

Kawan grinned as he took the offering from her. "Thank you *very* much, Mrs. Connelly."

"Ah, there's our resident knight-in-shining armor." Alexander's voice preceded him into the lobby. His eyes twinkled with mirth as he shifted the files in his arms so he could hold out his hand in greeting to Kawan. "Walk with me, talk with me. How is the damsel in distress? Did the dragon eat her?"

Kawan scoffed, walking alongside Alexander down the hall toward the other man's office. "Of course not. The only thing being eaten is this donut." Holding it up, he took a healthy bite. Mmm. Sugary goodness.

"I knew she hid one from me," Alexander muttered, shaking his head. Putting the files down on his desk, he took a seat in the leather chair behind it, leaving Kawan to sit in the comfortable armchair across from him. "I should spank her for lying to me."

"I'm sure she'll enjoy that." Kawan shook his head, his mind going back to Ms. Williams. "My client this morning could have used one."

Alexander shot him a sharp look, and not because he was worried that Kawan might be unprofessional with a client. They knew each other better than that. "Submissive?"

"No idea," Kawan said, and even he could hear the wistfulness in his tone.

Which was why, despite his strong attraction to Ms. Melody Williams, he wasn't truly interested in her. Just because she had instinctively called him 'Sir' didn't mean she was submissive, and it definitely didn't automatically make her a baby girl. And that was what Kawan wanted. He'd learned his lesson with Krissy—he *needed* a submissive who was also a baby girl, not just someone who enjoyed playing the part every so often. Definitely not someone who would only pretend and use the role to manipulate him.

He liked fulfilling the Daddy role. Loved the total control it gave him. Loved seeing the woman under his care unwind, relaxing into being able to just enjoy herself while he managed everything. Loved setting down rules and meting out discipline for broken ones. Loved the pretended innocence that usually masked a very horny little girl.

While he wasn't a 24/7 Daddy Dom, he definitely wasn't just an in-the-bedroom Daddy Dom either. But with all the submissives available in the city, and hopefully no gossip following him from Richmond, surely he'd be able to find a good match for himself. He hoped.

"We'll find you someone," Alexander said, looking more serious. "Black Light is your best bet to find what you're looking for."

"I know." He just couldn't help but wish that Ms. Williams had been what he was looking for.

"Now, enough about the pathetic state of your love life," Alexander teased, leaning back in his chair. "We've got work to do."

Shooting him a glare, Kawan took another huge bite out of his donut.

CHAPTER 2

*F*reedom!

The warm spring air felt especially good against her skin as Melody took a deep breath, not sure that she'd ever take being outside for granted ever again.

"Oh my gawd, Mel!" Peggy, Melody's best friend and roommate squealed as she threw her arms around Melody. She'd been just coming up the courthouse stairs as Melody exited the building. "I'm so sorry I'm late, but you're here! You're out!"

Red curls bounced and one of them got in Melody's mouth as she hugged Peggy back and spit it out. She'd been looking for that orange-red hair all morning. If she hadn't been so distracted by her hot lawyer, she probably would have been a lot more upset about Peggy not being there... although she wasn't exactly surprised either. 'Reliable' was not one of Peggy's virtues. She was flaky, self-centered, and impatient, but she could also be a really good friend.

Case in point—even though they'd drifted apart after high school, when Peggy had found out that Melody needed a place to live while she was working toward her PhD, she'd immediately insisted that Melody move in with her. Rather than paying half the rent, which Melody wouldn't have been able to afford, Peggy took the bulk of the financial burden while Melody worked off her half by keeping the apartment clean and cooking their meals. It was a win-win since it meant Melody got to live in a nicer apartment in a much better neighborhood than she'd have otherwise been able to afford, and Peggy no longer had to clean or cook, both things she hated to do anyway.

Sure, sometimes Melody wished she could just come home and relax instead of having to pick up after both herself and Peggy, but if she'd lived alone she would have had to do the same thing. And if she was really too tired to cook, which did happen because the long days in the lab could be exhausting, Peggy never minded ordering out. She had a cushy job working at her father's company, which gave her an enviable paycheck.

She'd also been the one to pay Melody's bail, putting Melody even further in her debt.

"So are you done?" Peggy asked, pulling away. Her green eyes scanned Melody up and down, her nose only wrinkling a little as she took in the outfit Melody was wearing. She considered herself a fashionista and she didn't always approve of Melody's clothing choices, but today Melody was going for 'responsible' looking, not stylish. The outfit might be boring, but it had served its purpose. "You're free to go?"

"Free to go!" Melody confirmed, nodding, feeling relief flood through her all over again. Peggy squealed and hugged her tight once more, looking just as relieved as Melody felt.

"Let's go get lunch to celebrate!" Peggy said, grabbing Melody by the hand.

She resisted the tug, digging in her heels slightly to keep Peggy from pulling her off balance. "I can't. I'm already behind on all my work and everything because I had to be here today. And I need to check in with Katherine."

Katherine Standish was her mentor and the only other person she'd dared call about her court appearance today. The rest of the research team knew she wasn't coming in but they didn't know why.

As usual, when she said Katherine's name, Peggy made a face. The two of them had met, but had definitely not hit it off. Sometimes Peggy could be jealous of Melody's other friends, and Katherine had definitely become one, as far as a mentorship allowed. Between working on her dissertation and trying to keep up with the social demands Peggy made of her, she didn't really have time for many other friends. Just Katherine, since she was both a friend *and* mentor.

Well, and the others on her team, but she didn't see really them outside of the lab. She didn't even *want* to see some of them outside of work.

"Ugh, fine, Miss Responsible," Peggy said, rolling her eyes, but she gave Melody's hand a squeeze to take the sting out of her derision. "We're going out this Saturday night to celebrate though. Elliott's taking me to Black Light again and this time you *are* coming."

Just the name of the premier BDSM club made Melody's insides clench tight. Peggy had been talking about nothing else since she'd started dating Elliott a month ago. Before Peggy met Elliot, neither she or Melody had ever done anything but read about BDSM. Now Peggy had real life experience, and raved about it, but Melody still wasn't sure how she felt about making her own fantasies a reality.

She pressed her lips together, thinking about how she was going to answer.

"Uh uh." Peggy pointed her finger at Melody, giving her a look of warning. "You're going. You don't have to do anything, but you need to see how cool this place is. I was right about how awesome Runway is, right?"

Runway was the regular club that operated above Black Light and was also where Peggy had met Elliott. They'd gone last month at Peggy's insistence to see DJ Elixxr, the hottest new

DJ on the scene, and it *had* been a really great night. Unfortunately, between the drinking and the late hour they'd finally come home, Melody had been dragging for the entire week after. Something that Peggy didn't have to worry about. She'd just called out sick on Monday to finish her recovery, an option that Melody hadn't had.

"You were," Melody conceded. Anxiety warred with excitement. Could she really go to a BDSM club? Part of her really wanted to, but the rest of her wasn't too sure it was a good idea.

"You're going," Peggy said, in the bossy tone that indicated she was putting her foot down. The same tone that had made Melody agree to go to the party where she'd been arrested, to Runway last month, and to a ski weekend two months ago. When Peggy used that tone, Melody knew there was no arguing with her. Granted, only the party had turned out *really* badly.

She groaned, but she couldn't deny that the little bubble of excitement in her stomach was already growing in anticipation. Besides, she should celebrate not having to go to jail, right? YOLO and all that. "Okay, fine. But I'm not going to do anything but watch."

Squealing, Peggy jumped up and down, clapping her hands. "Yay! I knew you'd give in. You go to work; I'm going to go home and pick out your outfit for Saturday. We might have to go shopping."

Now Melody really felt like groaning, but she hid it behind a smile. "Fine, do what you will. Does Elliott know how bossy you are?"

Because she'd definitely gotten the impression that Elliott was a Dom. Not that she was an expert on spotting Doms. But she couldn't see him submitting to someone else; he had too much of an air of unthinking authority. A lot like her lawyer this morning, in fact.

Peggy smirked. "Nope. He thinks I'm sweet and submissive. It's fun."

Oh yeah, fun. Melody hoped Peggy wasn't getting her into anything she couldn't handle.

~

LUNCH at the Blue Duck Tavern with all three senior partners of his new firm was only slightly intimidating. Alexander had brought Sienna with him, with no objections from anyone, and Kawan had also spent time with Connor Lambert at Black Light his last visit, so Urbanski was the only partner he hadn't spent any social time with.

He doubted he'd see Urbanski at the club any time soon. Alexander had told him that the older gentleman and his wife were strictly vanilla, and more amused than intrigued by the standing membership all three partners had to Black Light. They'd never visited the club.

In respect of that, conversation didn't turn to Black Light until after Urbanski excused himself, needing to get back to the office to meet with a client.

"You're coming to the club this weekend with us, right?" Alexander asked. He was playing with Sienna's long braid while she finished the duck fat French fries she was eating slowly, obviously savoring them.

"That was my plan," Kawan said, grinning widely.

"I won't be there," Connor said, leaning back in his chair, only sounding slightly regretful. "Ella and I are going to New York for the weekend." Ella was his fiancée, a sweet and sassy spitfire whose masochistic streak matched Connor's sadistic one perfectly. They'd known each other for years, but got close after being matched at Black Light. Although, now that Kawan thought about it, both couples had come out of the yearly Valentine's Day roulette game the club held.

Well, if he hadn't found a match for himself by next Valentine's Day, maybe he'd take a spin at the wheel and give himself over to the hands of fate.

"I'm sure this won't be Kawan's only visit," Alexander said, giving him a sidelong look. He knew all about the implosion of Kawan's last relationship and what Kawan was hoping to find with this move. "Even though he has his own membership now and doesn't need either of us to get him through the door."

"It *is* the best perk of moving here," Kawan acknowledged mildly.

Connor chuckled and elbowed Alexander in the side. "I told you that's why he agreed to come work for us."

"It wasn't the only reason, but it definitely helped," Kawan said, winking at Sienna when she looked over at him. She giggled and Alexander mock-scowled at him.

"Stop flirting with my fiancée," he admonished, although it was clear to anyone who knew him that he wasn't actually bothered by it. Although he and Kawan could be competitive with each other, they'd always kept their competitions to grades, moot court, and mock trials during school. Their relationships were hands off, other than meaningless flirting, something that Sienna had at first been startled by, but which she now often played into in order to tease her dom.

"You're only engaged; she still has time to change her mind and come let Daddy Kawan spoil her." Kawan winked again and Sienna giggled harder, ducking her head when Alexander turned his gaze to her. "I promise to be a much nicer Daddy than Alexander is."

"Don't listen to him," Alexander instructed her sternly, but his blue eyes were dancing with amusement. "His girlfriends think they're going to be pampered and spoiled, and the next thing they know they're in a diaper with a bottle in their mouth."

The smile on Kawan's face froze in place as he forced back the memory of Krissy's accusations. That *was* exactly what he was looking for. But he wanted someone who would enjoy it. Who would thrive under those circumstances. Fortunately, Connor didn't notice anything wrong.

"Nothing wrong with that," Connor murmured, a little smile spreading on his lips, but they all knew that for Sienna, that kind of baby time would be more of a punishment than a pleasure. Not that Alexander couldn't make it enjoyable if he wanted to, but 'baby time' wouldn't be Sienna's preference.

"Shhhh, Sir," Sienna said, holding her finger to her lips as their server approached, her cheeks bright pink from the conversation. She gave the young man a brilliant smile as he cleared their plates and offered the dessert menu.

Alexander really was lucky to have her.

Watching them gave Kawan a familiar pang of envy. Visiting Black Light was definitely going to be a priority. Hopefully he'd be able to meet someone who wanted the same things he did. Someone who wouldn't feel the need to deceive him.

The wide, soft, doe-eyes of Melody Williams flashed through his mind again, and he pushed the image away. Their instant attraction aside, she wasn't what he was looking for, what he needed. He was sure by the time he got to the club this weekend, he'd have forgotten all about her.

No changes.

Sighing, Melody sat up and stretched, her back aching from all the time she'd spent bent over the microscope this afternoon. Comparing the new cultures to each patient's bacterial profile was tedious but necessary work. Even a small change in their gut microbiome and blood sugar could be impactful to the research, if it were the right kind of change.

As much as she wanted her PhD, she also wanted her research to mean something. To make a difference. Her mom struggled with both diabetes and depression, which was what had drawn Melody to this particular study.

Not that her mom really understood how looking at her poop could affect her mental health, but the important thing was that Melody understood it.

All my reading material has butt stuff.

The thought made her smile.

Glancing at the clock, she winced as she realized it was actually no longer afternoon, it was almost evening. Everyone else had already gone home and she was the only one left in the lab. She needed to get her butt in gear if she was going to make dinner for herself and Peggy and then get ready to go out to Black Light tonight. Thankfully, she was almost done—and had almost caught up on everything she'd fallen behind in this week.

It had meant pulling some longer hours than normal, but it was worth it. For once, Melody didn't mind at all. Long hours were a hell of a lot better than being in jail.

Not for the first time, her mind wandered to Mr. Park again. She had found her thoughts straying to him quite often over the past few days. Every time she had to put down and pick up her purse.

I hope you've learned your lesson about leaving your belongings unattended.

The memory of his stern look and deep voice had worked their way into her dreams more than once since her day in court. Dreams that had woken her up feeling achy and needy. The same way she felt after reading the naughty books she loved so much. Dreams that made her feel more excited than apprehensive about going to Black Light tonight.

Because she *was* tired of dreaming. She wanted to *do*.

And after this week, she definitely wanted to just escape for a little bit.

Sighing internally, she cleaned up. She was just finishing wiping down her station when she felt a presence behind her.

"Miss Williams, there you are." The deep voice interrupting her was nothing like Mr. Park's had been. No, this voice was low, oily, and made her feel uncomfortable the moment she heard it.

Pasting a smile on her face, she turned to see Professor McCready behind her, and she nearly stumbled back because he was standing so close to her—invading her personal space, the way he always did. She thanked her lucky stars every night that he hadn't been assigned to oversee her and that she had Katherine instead. McCready was the definition of skeazy, and she'd heard rumors about female students unfortunate enough to have him as a mentor.

The university seemed to have caught on because this year he didn't have any women in his sphere of influence... but he still had his job. Katherine had told Melody to let her know if he did anything to her, but so far he just made her uncomfortable. Standing too close, speaking too familiarly, but nothing that Melody felt like she could actually report.

"Hello, Professor," Melody said, holding her bag in front of her chest like a shield. She could feel her heart racing from being startled... and it didn't slow when she saw who it was. Anxiety prickled through her.

"You're here late. Hope to run into anyone in particular?" The question was completely innocent, but his tone made it clear he was fishing. He winked at her, like he thought she was there for him.

Again, nothing she could actually report, because it was just small talk, but she felt acutely uncomfortable and more than a little grossed out. Not that she let either emotion show on her face. Sometimes she thought he enjoyed making the women in the department uncomfortable.

"Nope, just lost track of time. I'm actually running late." She gave him an insincere smile. "If you'll excuse me." Gingerly, she stepped around him. He didn't move to stop her, but he didn't move out of her way either, and she felt her skin crawl as she hurried away.

"Until next time, Miss Williams," he called after her.

Melody pretended she didn't hear him. Yup, she definitely needed to get out and away tonight. Hopefully she wouldn't hate whatever outfit Peggy had finally picked out for her.

CHAPTER 3

*T*ugging on the top of the corset Peggy had squashed her into, Melody tried not to feel totally out of place as she followed Elliott and Peggy into the psychic shop. She found Elliott intimidating, although she didn't know why. He was being incredibly nice to her, but there was an aura of authority that seemed to hang around him. She didn't understand how Peggy could be so relaxed with him. The psychic shop confused her enough that she managed to find the courage to speak up anyway.

"Why are we in here? Runway's around the corner." She whispered the question, unsure of why she was doing so. Peggy had told her that Black Light was underneath Runway, so she'd expected to go there. This shop wasn't even on the same street.

Elliott looked over his shoulder at her and winked. "Welcome to the secret entrance to Black Light."

Turning her upper body around, Peggy reached back for Melody's hand, her eyes sparkling with glee.

"Isn't this awesome? We're going to have so much fun!"

"Totally awesome," Melody echoed. It really was, but she was becoming more and more nervous with every step she took.

When she saw the big dark-haired man at the back of the store, she felt like covering her half-exposed boobs. The corset made her waist tiny and propped her breasts up like a platter, but it wasn't comfortable and *she* didn't feel particularly comfortable in it. But, as Peggy said, it made her look a lot skinnier than she was and really showed off her assets.

She just wished it maybe didn't show them off quite so much.

As if she could hear Melody's thoughts, Peggy looked at her right as Melody was trying to pull up her corset again.

"Stop messing with it," Peggy hissed, letting go of Melody's other hand to slap the one fiddling with the corset. "Your boobs look amazing."

Elliott glanced over his shoulder but Peggy shoed him on ahead to Melody's relief. She did not want to talk about her boobs with Elliott.

"I hope so, since everyone will be able to see them," Melody muttered, but she dropped her hands to her sides as Peggy glared at her. Her bestie had no problem prancing around in her corset and short leather skirt. If only she was more like Peggy, slimmer and more confident, she'd feel sexy instead of silly. Or maybe if she had more confidence she would have insisted on wearing clothes she actually liked and felt comfortable in, instead of letting Peggy dress her like a doll. But it was too late to bemoan all of that now.

At least she'd let Melody wear a slightly longer skirt, rather than a mini-skirt like the one showing off Peggy's legs.

"I told you, we had to cover your legs, so we needed to show off your boobs," Peggy whispered. Oh right. It wasn't that Peggy had *let* her wear a longer skirt, she'd insisted on it. Because of Melody's chubby thighs. Melody smoothed her hands over the skirt. Somehow her thighs being covered made her feel almost as uncomfortable as her boobs being out. Peggy had no patience for her hesitation though. "Come *on.*"

Elliott was waiting for them, talking to a Hispanic guard at the entrance to the back hall of the shop.

The scar down the side of the guard's face made him look pretty threatening, but he gave her a little wink, his lips curving up in a smile that softened his expression. Melody gave him a little smile back before scrambling after the two.

Ugh. She totally felt like a third wheel.

And the sparse, not-very-well-lit hallway was not making her feel any better either. Peggy was hanging off of Elliott's arm, taking all of his attention, although he did glance back to make sure Melody was behind them a couple times. She gave him a little finger wave.

Yup, still here.

When they finally reached a door that led to a reception area, Melody couldn't help but stare at the the ceiling. The combination of black lights and recessed lamps bathed the room in a purple glow that bounced off the wall of small lockers.

"Melody." Elliott's amused tones interrupted her perusal of the ceiling, and she blushed as she brought her attention back to him. He and Peggy were standing in front of a desk where a security guard was seated, and all three of them were looking at her. "Come over here, sweetheart, you need to sign some forms."

"Right, sorry," she said, feeling her cheeks blush even brighter. Who got distracted by pretty lights?

Me, that's who.

Moving over to them, she saw a woman behind a window to the right of the security guard's desk, also watching with amusement. She'd been hidden by Elliott at first. Startled, Melody nearly tripped, making Elliott reach out to catch her.

"Careful, sweetie," he admonished, although his smile was kind. "If you have trouble walking in those heels, take them off and go barefoot, okay?" Peggy rolled her eyes at the clumsiness and Melody gave her a little shrug of apology for taking her boyfriend's attention before looking at the sheets Elliott handed her.

Holy mother of all non-disclosure agreements...

"Read and initial each page and then sign on the last one," the woman behind the window said, her instructions audible through the small opening at the bottom of the glass.

"Right," Melody murmured, acutely aware of everyone's eyes on her. She read it as quickly as possible. Nothing in it looked surprising considering all of the secrecy, and she initialed and signed with the pen Elliott passed to her. As she put the last flourish on her signature, she could feel her heart hammering in her chest.

Anxiety? Excitement? A too-tight corset?

An overwhelming combination of all three?

Probably that last one, if she were being completely truthful with herself. "Have a good night," the security guard said as she passed over her papers, giving her a broad grin. Somehow his welcoming expression made her feel a little less nervous. Too bad he was behind the desk and not inside the club.

"She's just going to be watching," Peggy said, leaning into Elliott again and giving his arm a squeeze as she arched her back to give them all the best view of her cleavage. "But we're definitely going to have a good night."

"I'm sure Melody is too," Elliott said, turning his head to smile reassuringly at her and making Peggy frown, her eyes darting back and forth between Melody and her boyfriend. "Watching can be a lot of fun at Black Light."

"Well, of course," Peggy said, her slightly irritated tone conveying that she didn't like being rebuked.

"Probably not quite as much fun as doing," Melody said, smiling at Peggy. Her best friend beamed back at her, obviously happy that Melody was smoothing things over for her. Melody was used to Peggy's little comments; they could be thoughtless, but she didn't mean them the way they sometimes sounded. She knew better than to take them personally. Elliott would learn too if he and Peggy stayed together for any length of time. "But I'm still looking forward to it."

A locker popped open for them, breaking the tension to Melody's relief. Although letting her phone out of her grip felt strange to Melody. She hadn't realized how connected she was to that little device until now. It was a safety net, but now it was gone. Elliott had reassured her about all the safety measures in the club though. She didn't need the phone if she was in trouble. All she had to do was yell the club safe word, 'red'.

"Good." Elliott flashed her a friendly grin. "Don't forget, you're under my protection while you're in here, so no one should bother you. Unless you want them to." He winked at her. "Let's go in, ladies."

Arm wrapped around Peggy's waist, Elliott ushered her into the club, checking over his shoulder again to make sure Melody was right behind them. He slowed once they entered, so that she could come up beside them.

Wow.

That was her first thought. Leather laced with vanilla... that's what the club smelled like. And sex. Could a place smell like sex? Or maybe it was just her imagination supplying that, because *my goodness* there was a ton of sexy in the air. Melody felt her jaw dropping slightly as her eyes attempted to look everywhere all at the same time.

Spanking benches, stocks, leather floggers falling through the air in a cascade of black tails striking pinkened flesh. Lots of flesh. Oh so much flesh... She suddenly felt overdressed instead of underdressed.

"Steady there, sweetheart," Elliott said, chuckling, cupping her elbow to help keep Melody on her feet as she tried to turn too fast and nearly toppled over again. Peggy laughed at Melody's reaction.

"Told you it was incredible," she teased, snuggling up to Elliott's other side. "Aren't you glad I made you come out tonight?"

"Yes," Melody murmured, although it felt like her eyes were about to pop out of her head. This was... it was so much more than she'd ever imagined. So much rawer, so much more shocking, and so much hotter.

"Come on, let's go over to the bar and get you a drink, then we'll give you the tour," Elliott said. It wasn't quite a command, but it was more than a suggestion.

Thankfully, he kept his hand on her elbow, helping move her through the club, while his other arm was around Peggy. Melody needed that steadying hand to keep her from veering off course as her head swiveled around, still trying to see everything and everyone they passed on their way to the bar. She felt flushed, all the way through her body.

Was a full body blush a thing?

Her nipples itched inside of the corset, desperate to be rubbed, and she could feel how slick her pussy had become with every step she took as her wet lips rubbed against each other. Everywhere she looked was sin and seduction and sadistic sexual fantasies being meted out.

"What do you want to drink?" Elliott asked her kindly when they reached the bar area.

Melody let out a long breath. "Um, dirty Shirley Temple, please? Uh, Sir?"

His blue eyes sparkled with amusement, but he didn't chastise her for the belated honorific that she tacked on to the end of her request, even though he'd told her before entering that she needed to call him either Sir or Master Elliott.

She looked up at the alcohol bottles displayed above the bar while Elliott and Peggy turned away to order their drinks, giving herself something to focus on other than all of the... well, everything. While she could still hear moans and the smacking of leather and flesh against flesh, at least she had something else to look at while she tried to wrestle her wayward hormones under control.

And that was when it happened.

"Ms. Williams? Is that you?"

Her insides clenched because she could not, *could not,* be hearing *that* voice *here.*

The world seemed to slow as she pivoted, the air thicker than molasses, dragging her movements, drawing out the awful moment. She wasn't imagining things... it was him. Standing beside a tall, handsome man in a suit and a petite brunette wearing a school girl outfit, looking like he'd stepped right out of her fantasies in a button-down shirt with the sleeves rolled up to his elbows, it was her sexy lawyer, Mr. Park.

Hide! Her brain shrieked. Except there was nowhere to hide.

So she just reacted and, of course, made an even bigger fool of herself.

Ms. WILLIAMS MOVED SO QUICKLY that Kawan jerked forward, trying to catch her, before he realized she'd dropped on purpose. He stared down at the figure now curled up in front of him, crouched into a ball with her arms wrapped over her head. It reminded him of when his nephews were still young enough to think that if they couldn't see him, then he couldn't see them.

The woman was definitely his former client, Melody Williams, although he'd barely been able to believe it when he first spotted her being led through Black Light. With her curves now fully on display in the tight-fitting corset and skirt combination she was wearing, she definitely didn't look like the buttoned-up twenty-something she'd appeared to be in the courtroom.

Not that he could see them at the moment.

The woman and man she'd walked in with turned to stare down at her, and the redhead burst out laughing when she saw Ms. Williams' position. "Mel, what *are* you doing? You look like an idiot."

Kawan shot her a dirty look as the little ball that was Melody Williams shook, because that was not going to help the situation. Thankfully, the Dom she was with immediately took her in hand, literally wrapping his hand around the back of the redhead's neck and whispering in her ear. From the stern look on his face and the way her mirth immediately faded, he was handling her.

Which left Kawan to handle Ms. Williams.

He shot an apologetic glance at Alexander and Sienna. They were both still watching curiously, but didn't move to intervene.

Crouching down, Kawan settled with his elbows on his knees, close enough to the mortified young woman that he could speak without anyone else being able to hear him. She flinched slightly when he cleared his throat.

"Ms. Williams?" He kept his tone gentle. "May I give you a hand up?"

He was pretty sure he heard her moan. "Could you just pretend you haven't seen me at all?" she asked in a small voice.

Despite himself, Kawan chuckled, hoping she realized that he wasn't laughing *at* her. At least, not in a mean way. He actually found her reaction completely adorable. She turned her head slightly, peeking at him through her arms. Even with her face partially obscured, he could see that her cheeks were bright red.

"Now why would I want to do that?" he asked, instinctively using his Daddy Dom tone, as if he were addressing a baby girl who was playing with him. It wasn't until after the words were out of his mouth that he realized what he'd done.

Fortunately, she didn't seem to take issue with his manner.

"Because you want to be nice to me?"

He wondered if she realized that she was very much using a 'little girl' voice to answer. All week he'd been looking forward to coming to Black Light and hopefully finding a submissive to play with. Now, right in front of him, was the woman he'd been pushing out of his mind ever since he'd met her... except it seemed he didn't need to anymore. She was here and, he assumed by the way she was behaving, submissive.

Possibly even a baby girl?

Slow down. Stop getting ahead of yourself.

"I think I have a different idea of what being nice to you would entail," he said, holding out his hand where she'd be able to see it as she peered at him. "Be brave, Melody, and stand up with me."

She stared at him for a long enough moment that he wondered if perhaps he'd read her wrong or maybe she just wasn't attracted to him the way he was to her, but then she reached out and put her hand in his. Her fingers trembled, but her gaze never wavered.

"Good girl," he said. This time, he was sure her blush wasn't from embarrassment at all.

CHAPTER 4

*T*he kindness and understanding in Mr. Park's dark eyes were the only things that gave Melody the courage to actually straighten up. She felt like a total idiot. She knew she'd looked like one. Even though Peggy had been the only one to laugh out loud, she knew everyone who had seen her childish reaction was probably laughing internally at her.

"Melody, these are my friends, Master Alexander and Sienna," Mr. Park said, gesturing with his hand, although he didn't take his gaze from hers. Melody was the one to reluctantly look away, because it would be rude not to greet his friends.

"Hello," she said shyly, feeling awkward even though they were both smiling at her—neither of them seemed like mean smiles either. If they thought she'd looked like a twit, they were doing a good job of pretending otherwise. "Um, this is Peggy and El... uh, Master Elliott. This is Mr. Park."

"Kawan, please," he said, giving her hand a squeeze.

"Kawan," she repeated softly, emphasizing the second syllable the same way he did as the others exchanged greetings around them. And he was still holding her hand, which was feeling increasingly warmer.

Was it possible for a hand to be an erogenous zone? Because she was feeling pretty warm and tingly all over even though that was literally the only place he was touching her.

"Are you a member here?" he asked, cocking his head to the side as he looked down at her. "Or a guest?"

"Guest," she said, trying not to squirm. There was something about the piercing look he was giving her that made her feel extremely vulnerable for some reason. Like he could see all the secret thoughts inside of her head—including the vivid ones she'd had about him while she'd masturbated at night. "Um, Peggy wanted to take me out to celebrate you getting me out of jail... I mean, not that I was *in* jail yet, but you getting me out of having to go... anyway, I've read some books about this stuff but that's it, so she thought I'd like coming here and Elliott's a member so... yeah." She finished lamely, realizing that she was babbling.

She pressed her lips together to keep more words from spilling out of her mouth, something that was all too likely to happen since he was just standing there not saying anything. But something about the way he was looking at her made her feel like he thought she was cute, not crazy, so that was a win. Still, better to cut it off now, in case she crossed the line.

"You're not here to play with Master Elliott then?" he asked, glancing at the other man.

Melody nearly sagged with relief as he finally looked away from her. Holy cannoli being under his scrutiny was intense—way more so here at Black Light than it had been in the courtroom!

"No," she said.

"She's just here to watch," Peggy said, right over top of her.

Startled, Melody turned to look at her friend, who was eyeing Kawan—should she call him Master Kawan?—with suspicion and dislike. She could be a little overprotective sometimes. Normally Melody just brushed it off, but right now she felt a well of irritation stirring in her chest.

Next to her, Elliott shook his head, his hand clamping down on Peggy's shoulder as he looked at Melody. "Would you like to spend the evening with Master Kawan, Melody?"

Peggy opened her mouth, probably to answer for Melody as she sometimes did, but Elliott's fingers tightened and he shot her a stern look. The redhead's mouth snapped shut, but she didn't look happy about it. Elliott turned his attention back to Melody, his blue eyes softening when he looked at her nervous expression.

"Yes," she whispered, acutely aware of Kawan's fingers, which were still wrapped around hers. Clearing her throat, she deliberately didn't look at Peggy for fear that she'd lose her nerve in the face of her friend's disapproval, as she raised her voice a little and answered Elliott. "Yes, I'd like that. If, if that's what he wants."

She couldn't think why else he might have asked if she was there to play with Elliott or why he was still holding her hand, but she didn't want to assume either. Peeking a glance at him, she tried to look hopeful, not desperate. That was a thing, right?

"Yes, I do," Kawan answered firmly, enjoying the happy—and slightly relieved—smile that bloomed across Melody's face. Hadn't been sure of him, had she? While part of him liked that she didn't make assumptions, if her reasoning behind that assumption was a lack of confidence on her part, then they were going to work on that.

Well, assuming that things went well tonight and that they wanted to see each other again.

He wasn't sure whether the chemistry between them would

lead to anything, but regardless, he was happy to oversee her first time in the club. So far he hadn't met anyone else he wanted to play with tonight, and even though she was no longer a client, he still felt some degree of responsibility toward her for some reason.

And a *lot* of attraction.

The outfit she was wearing fit right into Black Light, although he'd loved to see her dressed as a baby girl. The dark red corset pushed her breasts up into enticing mounds with deep cleavage between them, the almost knee-length flirty black skirt would be easy to flip up over her bottom, and the high ponytail she had gathered her brown hair in both exposed her neck and gave a man something to grip if he were so inclined. The dark eye makeup and red lipstick completed her vixenish look

How a person dressed didn't always mean that was the only way they were willing to play though. Kawan wondered if she would be willing to give him a chance to show her how fun being a baby girl could be. If she even knew what a baby girl was.

And, his preferences aside, he certainly still appreciated the way the corset pushed up her generous cleavage and cinched in her waist, even if the main thought on his brain was how he'd like to get her into something less restrictive and more comfortable.

"Enjoy your evening," Master Elliott said, giving Melody a little wink. "We'll find you before we leave."

"But—" The redhead—Peggy—started to protest, but Master Elliott was already turning her back around, cutting her off in a low voice that Kawan could barely hear.

"You and I are going to have a talk." The glimpse of his expression was foreboding, convincing Kawan that the other man had her firmly in hand.

Which left Melody with him. She appeared nervous, excited, and maybe a little terrified all at once, a delightful combination that appealed to his Dom nature. The little flick of her tongue, wetting her lips, only made her more adorable.

"Would you like to get a drink?" he asked her, turning slightly so that his body would block any view of her friend from her. It was pretty clear to him that Melody was the more submissive personality and he didn't want her friend influencing her answer. "Or we could jump right into a tour of the club."

"Um." Her eyes darted toward Alexander and Sienna, who were still watching them and not bothering to hide it. Alexander looked amused, while Sienna's interested gaze was bouncing back and forth between him and Melody in turn.

"We'll go get a seat," Alexander said, with a warm smile to Melody. "Feel free to join us, either now or later." Sienna looked disappointed, but she didn't protest as her fiancé led her away toward an empty table, leaving Kawan and Melody completely alone. She gave Melody a friendly wave before turning away.

Melody looked up at him.

"There is no wrong answer," he reassured her and gave her hand an encouraging little squeeze. Her fingers tightened around his.

"A tour?"

"Is that a question or is that what you want to do?" He was teasing her a little, but he was also serious about wanting a firmer answer. Considering she was now under his protection for the evening, Kawan wanted explicit consent.

She straightened a little, looking him directly in the eye, her chin tipping up stubbornly. "I want a tour."

Good, so she could be direct when she wanted.

"Good girl." He squeezed her hand again and she blushed.

When he'd met her in court earlier this week, he'd been pretty sure the attraction he felt for her was mutual, but he would never have guessed he'd actually see her at Black Light. Or that she'd be without a play partner if he did. There was an air of naivete about her. Not innocence exactly, but it was clear she was new to the scene and feeling out of place.

He doubted she would have come here without her pushy friend, so that was one point in her friend's favor.

"Even though we can see a lot of what's going on from right here, a closer look is always more revealing," he said, as he moved them toward the closest scening area, where a woman was already bent over a spanking bench. He kept a tight hold of Melody's hand. "You said you've read some books about BDSM?"

At this point, he wasn't sure if the pink in her cheeks was ever going to subside completely. Not that he minded.

"Um, yeah. A few. They didn't quite prepare me for this, though," she said, her eyes widening as they approached the scene area. The woman being spanked was squealing each time the leather paddle, expertly wielded by her Domme, crashed against her bottom. The Domme's smile was sadistically gleeful as she counted off each stroke, scolding her sub for being naughty.

Melody's eyes widened, immediately zeroing in on the sub's red bottom, which was turning brighter with every thwack of the paddle. The implement was wide and long enough to cover the woman's entire bottom each time it impacted, making both cheeks quiver and dance. After each squeal, her hips were already lifting again, offering up the hot red target for another stroke. The glistening, swollen folds of her bare pussy made it clear how much she was enjoying her punishment.

Letting go of Melody's hand, Kawan slid his arm around her waist, pulling her in front of him so he could hold her there. His hands splayed over her stomach, although the stiff boning of the corset made it more difficult to feel her reactions. But he liked the position anyway, especially as her rounded bottom pressed against his groin.

He'd already been a little aroused, but with her nestled

against him and the flowery scent of her perfume now filling his senses, he was quickly growing even more so.

So was she, going by the way she was squirming a little against him. She kept shifting her weight back and forth, like she couldn't stand comfortably, and her breathing was becoming more rapid as she watched the scene. Kawan wondered if she was picturing the same thing he was—her in the submissive's place, draped over the spanking bench with an increasingly hotter bottom.

"If at any point you feel uncomfortable, just say so," he murmured in her ear. "No need for safe words tonight; I'll stop whenever you want me to."

~

PLEASE DON'T STOP.

She bit back the words. Saying them out loud would be weird, right? Instead, she just nodded.

"I need verbal confirmation, please, Melody." His deep voice was so soft, but firm, and it sent a little shiver down the back of her spine.

"Yes, um, Sir?" She added the honorific, because she was pretty sure she was supposed to. That's what the submissives in books did. Dominants were all called Sir or Master, but Master didn't feel quite right. Although she could call him Master Kawan but that felt formal, and the way he had her leaning against him while they watched the spanking scene felt *far* from formal.

He chuckled. "Sir is fine, for now."

The Domme stopped spanking her submissive, leaving the woman on the bench panting and wriggling. Putting her hand on the bound woman's back, the Domme leaned over to say something to her sub. Melody couldn't tear her eyes away from them. The woman's butt looked painfully red, but she was obviously highly aroused. Just as aroused as Melody was.

Even though she couldn't look away from the two women, she was simultaneously totally distracted by everything about Kawan. She both resented and was thankful for the corset between his hands and her skin. Part of her wished she was wearing something that would allow her to actually *feel* his hands, the rest of her was glad that he couldn't, because then she'd be freaking out about him having his hands on her stomach and wondering what he thought about one of her least favorite parts of her body.

His hot breath on the back of her neck was making all the little hairs on her body stand straight up. The rigid bulge nestled between her butt cheeks had her pressing her thighs more firmly together, trying to get some secret stimulation to her clit, because she was so turned on by feeling the evidence of *his* arousal.

Holy shit, he's actually into me...

At least physically. Evidence like that didn't lie.

"Is this the kind of scene you enjoy reading about?" he asked as the Domme moved back into position, rubbing her submissive's already bright red cheeks before lifting the paddle again.

Melody winced as the leather slapped against hot flesh with a loud *thwack*. "Yes, but..."

"But?" he asked, sounding somewhat amused, pulling her more tightly against him and rocking his hips against her butt. It broke the tension she was feeling, and she giggled, twisting her head around to look up at him. He smiled back at her. The warm feeling that rushed through her in response had nothing to do with sex and everything to do with the look he was giving her. The gleam in his eyes was both indulgent yet somehow authoritative at the same time.

Thwack!

She winced again at the sound.

"But not that hard," she whispered.

"Not if you're a good girl," he agreed. Melody gulped, pressing her thighs together again as the ache between them intensified by a thousand. The hanging threat, that if she was a bad girl she'd get a hard spanking like the one they were watching, was somehow the hottest thing a man had ever said to her.

Maybe that made her a bad feminist, but it's not like she could control what turned her on.

And apparently her hot Asian lawyer hinting that he'd give her a hard spanking if she was a bad girl just flat out did it for her.

THE WAY MELODY was squirming against him gave Kawan all sorts of ideas.

She was enthralled by the spanking. Turned on by his veiled threat. And her lips were slightly parted as though she was begging him for a kiss. So he decided to accept the invitation.

"Remember, your safe word is 'stop'." That was all the warning he gave her before dipping his head, slowly enough for her to read his intention and give her the chance to say something, and taking her lips in a kiss. Her body lifted, leaned, her head falling back to give him better access to her mouth. Her back arched, pressing the rounded curves of her bottom against his cock and thrusting her breasts out.

Kawan kept one hand on her stomach, dragging the other hand up her body, over the swell of her breasts, to curve his fingers around her throat. She whimpered at the touch, shuddering, and he could practically feel her melt against him with the intense sexual heat flaring to life inside of her. His cock throbbed as he deepened the kiss, tasting her, seducing her, feeling her instinctive submission to his touch.

When he lifted his head again, her pupils were so dilated that she appeared almost dazed, her lips still parted as she panted for breath. Still holding her throat, Kawan stroked her soft skin with one finger. If she wasn't so new to all of this, if this wasn't her first night at Black Light, he'd be dragging her off to scene right now.

Unfortunately, he didn't feel comfortable doing that. Yet.

He still needed to know more about her.

"So you like spanking books," he said, keeping his voice low. Intimate. "What else happens in your books?"

Her little pink tongue flicked at her lips as she blinked, gathering herself enough to focus on answering him.

"Um, bondage," she said, her voice soft, hesitant. She gestured around at the club. "Pretty much all of this."

"Any specifics? Medical play?" He kept stroking her throat with that one finger, holding her gently but firmly with the rest of his hand. The slow movement was soothing, hypnotic. She was still blushing, but she wasn't tense. Her eyelashes fluttered, closing.

"Um, I've read some," she admitted. Her head tilted back, resting against his shoulder.

"Pet play?" Not his usual kink but he sometimes enjoyed playing with a kitty-girl.

"Yes." She giggled, adding shyly, "I don't think it's my kink though."

"Daddy Dom?" he asked, careful to ask with the same inflection he had used for his previous questions. Especially with a submissive, he didn't want to accidentally influence her answer. There were plenty of age play books out there though, and he wanted to know if she'd come across any of them.

To his delight, her blush darkened, and another little shiver went down her spine.

"Yes." She dragged her teeth across her lower lip, shifting her weight again. "Um, I've read a few."

That was said in a completely different tone than she'd used for her first answer.

"Only a few?" He slid his finger up under her chin, holding her in place against his shoulder. He deepened his voice, letting his Daddy Dom out to sternly demand the truth. "Answer truthfully, Melody, unless you want to find out what happens to naughty little girls."

Her breath caught in her throat as a shudder wracked her body, her fingers clutching at the arm across her stomach. Fear, lust, eagerness, all flickered across her face.

Maybe she did want to find out what happens to naughty girls.

CHAPTER 5

*A*s much as she'd liked it when he'd called her a good girl, naughty little girl somehow sounded even better.

Because those were Melody's favorite books. The Daddy Dom books. It felt so wrong to love them so much. She was smart. Independent. Had been taking care of herself for a long time. She had loving parents who hadn't ever neglected her. Her own father was a good dad.

She didn't know why she loved the idea of a Daddy Dom so much.

But she did. Just as much as she was loving the way Kawan was holding her right now, with a gentle but firm grip... the authority in his voice... the way he supported her while he was arousing her...

She needed that support. Getting weak in the knees was the least of her body's reactions. Her nipples were so hard they felt itchy. The pulsing emptiness in her pussy made her want to beg to be filled. She felt so swollen and wet that all she had to do was press her thighs together and it stimulated her.

The impulse to turn around and rub herself all over him was

nearly overwhelming. If he hadn't had such a firm grip on her, she couldn't guarantee that she wouldn't have.

For the first time in her life, it felt like her brain had entirely turned off. She wasn't consumed with the thoughts or doubts that usually distracted her. This was an *in*-body experience like she'd never had before.

The heat coursing through her, the emptiness that ached to be filled... the erotic *neediness* obliterated everything else.

She'd never understood until now, just how sexy a hand on her throat could be. The simple brush of his fingertip over her sensitive skin, the strength she could feel in his fingers, it made her feel so vulnerable yet somehow completely protected.

"Um, what was the question again?" she asked. She really couldn't remember.

"How often do you read Daddy Dom books, little girl?" His teeth nipped at her earlobe and Melody whimpered. She was pretty sure she would have melted into a little puddle of sexual need if he wasn't holding her up. As it was, her panties were soaked beneath her skirt and she could actually feel the slick cream now coating the tops of her thighs as she rubbed her legs together.

To be a good girl or to be a naughty little girl?

That was the question.

For the first time, she remembered that they'd been watching a scene, and her eyes flicked to the Domme and her red-bottomed sub. She hadn't even noticed that they'd finished the spanking and the Domme was now using a wicked looking vibrator on the writhing, panting submissive. Melody's insides clenched all over again as the sub cried out with passion, climaxing despite—or maybe because of—the harsh spanking.

"Um... not often?" she lied. It wasn't even a very good lie, but it's not like she was trying particularly hard to be convincing.

She wanted to see what would happen.

The vibration of his chuckle rumbled against her back. "Alright, naughty girl, if you want to play we can play."

That sounded good, but Melody almost wanted to cry when he stepped away from her. His hand slid around her neck, now cupping the back of it, using it to direct her as he began to move to the semi-private alcove lining one of the club's walls. To be honest, Melody was so turned on that she didn't care where he wanted to do whatever he was going to do, but in the back of her head she knew she'd be grateful later.

He let go of her when they reached the alcove, sitting on the couch provided and then patting his knee. Melody knew what he wanted—even without her preferred reading materials she was pretty sure she would have known—but she just stood there, her stomach churning with nerves. She thought he would be angry when he saw her hesitation, but he just smiled.

"It's still up to you, Melody." He held out his hand. An offering, not a demand. "We can sit here and talk or you can go over my knee and get a taste of what happens to naughty little girls." Somehow he made even that sound seductive.

She couldn't help looking around, but no one was paying attention to them. Which was a good thing. She didn't see Peggy anywhere either. That was even better. She felt self-conscious enough without someone she actually knew in sight.

When she turned back to Kawan, he smiled. "Come to Daddy Kawan, little girl."

It was a wonder her panties didn't disintegrate from the sheer heat of her arousal.

Heart hammering in her chest, Melody reached out and took his hand. Stepped closer. As much as she wished he would just yank her over his lap, because that would be so much easier in so many ways, she took heart from the approval in his expression as she bent down to awkwardly position herself over his thighs.

"Good girl," he murmured, and Melody shuddered, sighing

as his hand caressed her upturned ass. She bit her lip as she felt her skirt being lifted, pulled up over her butt cheeks and exposing the thong she was wearing to the world. Her fingertips pressed against the floor, helping to balance her, and she stared down at the carpet fibers beneath her, feeling the shifting leg muscles of the man about to spank her.

Oh goodness... she was actually doing this.

WITH MELODY'S lush curves draped over his lap, her creamy bottom bisected by a pretty pink thong topped off with a little white bow, Kawan reflected that tonight was going so much better than he'd ever imagined it might. Even better than he'd hoped when he'd first seen her here in Black Light. Not only was she submissive, but she was definitely intrigued by Daddy Doms. He'd seen it in her expressions when he'd asked about the books, felt it in her reactions.

He was willing to bet that little Miss Melody had read quite a few Daddy Dom books.

Now it was time to find out how she felt about the reality.

Kawan cupped the curve of one buttock, rubbing it gently, and making Melody squirm. He decided against pulling down her panties since the thong she was wearing gave him all the access he currently needed.

"Have you ever been spanked before, Melody?" he asked. If she'd been reading, she might have been experimenting. He didn't want to give her more than she could handle, but he didn't want to disappoint her either.

Her ponytail flipped over her shoulder as she turned her head, craning her neck to look at him. The expression on her face was slightly disbelieving. "You're asking me that *now*?"

Smack!

The little squeal of surprise as his hand slapped against the soft curve of her bottom was more than a little satisfying. While he was fairly certain she hadn't meant to brat, he wasn't going to let her get away with talking to him like that either.

"Yes, I'm asking you that now," he said firmly, hiding his amusement. "Now seems like the perfect time. So, little Miss Melody, I'll ask again. Have you been spanked before?"

She peeked back over her shoulder at him. "Sort of? Not like this. Just during, um, you know... sex."

Her voice dropped on the last word, turning it into almost a whisper, and Kawan had to clench his jaw to keep from laughing. She was so adorably sexy and he doubted she knew it. That little prudish streak contrasted with her presence here at the club, but somehow it fit her perfectly.

"Alright then. Since you haven't had one like this before, I want you to use the club safe word if it becomes too much. If you need me to slow down, just say 'yellow,' and if you need me to stop then say 'red'."

He really had intended to just show Melody around and get a feel for what she might be interested in. Maybe give her a few small demonstrations if there were any toys she wanted to try, just so she could see how they felt... but then she'd deliberately and obviously angled for a spanking. That she'd done so over his question about Daddy Doms, well... it was like waving a red flag in front of a bull.

"Yes, um, Sir." She glanced at him nervously again, flipping her head so that her high ponytail ended up on the other side of her neck.

"Call me Daddy, sweetheart," he told her, lifting his hand above the spot he'd been rubbing. "Don't worry, I'll go easy on you since this is your first time."

SMACK!

The first slap against her skin was a measured one. It was more sound than sensation, but would definitely sting enough to get her attention. She squeaked, jerking in surprise. Kawan was already rubbing the spot he'd just spanked before lifting his hand again to give her a matching one on the other side.

SMACK!

"Oh!" she yelped, bucking. He grinned in appreciation.

While scening with someone completely new to the scene could occasionally be fraught with potential emotional pitfalls, there was also something supremely satisfying about their first reactions to everything. There was as much shock in her voice as there was arousal, as if she couldn't quite believe she was allowing him to do this.

That she didn't immediately scream for him to stop or try to roll away was a good sign.

Kawan began to spank her with swift, short smacks that would sting as they slowly heated her bottom, but wouldn't be too painful. Every few swats, he paused to rub her warmed skin. The previously pale white was now pink, like her blushes, and she was squirming delightfully on his lap, still gasping every time his palm came down.

THIS IS EASY?

Melody yelped as Kawan's hand came down again, smacking against already stinging, hot flesh. The heat growing in her bottom burned, but not entirely unpleasantly. Each new swat made her wish he'd stop, but then the burn would sink in, making her feel even hotter in a different way.

She knew about the chemical reaction happening in her brain. Adrenaline and endorphins were being released. Epinephrine and norepinephrine were responses to pain that explained the rush she was feeling as the spanking continued, hurting more and yet turning her on more as well. But knowing what was happening and actually experiencing it were two very different things.

"Ow! Ow!" She squirmed, throwing her hand back over her burning cheeks. She could feel how hot to the touch her skin had become when he spanked a particularly sensitive spot.

Without missing a beat, he wrapped his fingers around her wrist, settling her hand down in the center of her lower back, and then his other hand came down again.

SMACK! SMACK! SMACK!

Tears smarted in her eyes as she yelped and wriggled, her pussy gushing in response to his easy domination.

Say yellow, urged part of her brain, *you don't have to do this.*

But I want to! The answer was a wail from deep inside, a part of her that had been wanting a man to come and take control of her, a part of her that loved a bite of pain with her pleasure, a part of her that had been mostly ignored, pushed down, and rarely indulged.

A part of her that was loving every moment of this. A part of her that was mentally recording every second of it, knowing that she'd be masturbating to this memory for the rest of her life.

His strong grip on her wrist. The heavy weight pressing down on her lower back to keep her in place. The firm, stinging slaps of his palm against her butt cheeks. The press of his cock into her side as he spanked her. The shifting muscles of his legs as he moved her forward slightly, giving him even better access to her upturned ass.

The new angle put the top of her mound right against his thigh and Melody instinctively spread her legs a little further, trying to get more contact. *Oh!* It felt like lightning striking, a shot of electricity straight through her pleasure centers, zinging through her body, narrowing the distance between ecstasy and pain.

She finally understood what people meant when they said 'it hurt so good'.

By the time Kawan had both cheeks glowing pink, Melody was rubbing herself against his leg, practically writhing. All semblance of the self-contained young woman he'd met in the courtroom was gone; she'd turned into a creature of pure sexual need, submitting to the spanking, submitting to his dominance over her. His cock ached, but if spanking her hadn't been in his plans, sex definitely wasn't. They hadn't talked about it before-hand, and she certainly wasn't in the right frame of mind to give informed consent.

Right now he could probably suggest whatever he wanted to her and she would say yes. Knowing he'd brought her to that point was satisfaction in and of itself, and it would be enough for tonight.

He squeezed each dark pink cheek, feeling the warmth of her skin against his palm, digging his fingers in enough to make her groan and squirm even more. The small movements against his cock were little teases for him to enjoy.

This time when she turned her head to look back at him, her eyes were filled with pleading need and sparkling tears. Her cheeks were flushed and wisps of hair had escaped her ponytail to flutter around her face. Just that one look made his groin throb in response. That expression was one that every Dom endeavored to put on the face of any sub he was playing with.

Little Miss Melody liked being spanked. And Kawan was thoroughly enjoying being the one to deliver her first.

"Please," she whispered, arching her back, rubbing against his hand like a cat in heat.

"Please what, baby girl?" he asked, and felt her bottom quiver in reaction to the endearment. He traced his fingers over the sodden fabric of her panties, which were clinging to the swollen lips of her pussy. For a moment, it almost seemed as though her eyes were about to roll up into her head. She was so close to orgasming, it wouldn't take much to tip her over the edge. Kawan had something he wanted from her first though.

"Please... I need to... I can't..." she stammered, struggling for the vocabulary to express what she wanted, needed.

"You don't have to find the right words, baby girl. I'll give you what you need." He rubbed the outside of her panties for emphasis, right around her swollen clit, and she let out a little cry as her hips bucked slightly. "But what do you call me?"

"Daddy! Please, Daddy!"

～

SHE'D THOUGHT she'd feel silly saying it.

She *should* have felt silly saying it.

But somehow it fit, somehow it sounded *right,* the same way it had when he'd called her 'baby girl'.

And the reward...

Daddy Kawan moved his finger, no longer circling her clit, but rubbing the little nubbin directly and Melody cried out as ecstasy seemed to explode outward from his touch. Hot waves of rapture billowed through her, assuaging the demanding need of her body, even as her muscles clenched emptily around nothing.

It was white noise and bright fire bursts of pleasure, swamping her senses, and carrying her away.

She writhed, pressing the front of her mound against the hard muscle of his thigh, sobbing out with the sexual rapture that kept going and going as his fingers skillfully wrung every last ounce of pleasure from her overheated body. He didn't stop until she was practically limp and insensate over his thighs, panting for breath, and dizzy from the intense sensations that had wracked her.

When he lifted her up, curling her on his lap, that was when she finally felt the afterburn of the spanking he'd given her. It hurt more now than it had when he'd been actually spanking her, although it still felt good in a way too. She wriggled, trying to get comfortable, and then realized why she couldn't.

He was still hard.

"Oh! I..." She looked down, trying to shift her hips away as she wondered what she was supposed to do. Something, of course, but what?

"Stop that, baby girl," he said sternly, pulling her closer again, one hand sliding up her back to guide her head down to his shoulder, while the other firmly gripped her thigh to keep her in place. "Stay right where you are. I want to cuddle you."

Melody bit her lip and tried to relax. To her surprise, she didn't have to try very hard. It was shockingly easy to just sink into his embrace, especially because she knew that's what *he* wanted her to do. Because he'd told her so. It was so much easier to just let go and let him take control, knowing that he'd tell her what he wanted from her.

She closed her eyes, letting out her breath on a long sigh. Lassitude settled over her limbs, reminding her of how wrung out she was. She couldn't remember ever feeling this satisfied, this *fulfilled* before. Definitely not after sex.

Not that they'd even had sex.

What would sex with him be like?

Melody wasn't sure she'd survive it.

But oh, to make the attempt...

CHAPTER 6

*W*ith Melody snuggled up on his lap, Kawan motioned to one of the passing servers that he needed a water. Once he'd made clear what his wishes were, she'd completely relaxed against him with a little contented sigh, and he didn't want to move her until he absolutely had to.

This was...

Perfection. It was exactly what he'd been missing. What the Daddy Dom part of him had been needing. What he'd hoped to eventually find by being able to attend Black Light regularly. While he'd played since the disastrous end of his last relationship, none of those scenes had felt anything like this. Hell, he'd completely forgotten about Krissy once he'd run into Melody, until now.

When the server brought him a bottle of water, Kawan thanked her before shifting Melody on his lap to stir her. She wasn't asleep, but she might as well have been. The hazy, muzzy headspace wasn't subspace, but a kind of afterglow that could follow a good scene. He'd be surprised if she realized she'd already been snuggling with him for close to ten minutes.

Shifting her on his lap, he could feel the heat from her

bottom through the fabric of his pants. It wasn't the hardest spanking he'd ever given a woman, but for a first spanking it had been thorough and entirely pleasurable. She'd be feeling it for a few more hours, although she should be back to normal by tomorrow morning.

"Open, baby girl," he said, lifting the water bottle to her lips.

Still looking a little dazed, her mouth popped open, and he saw the moment she realized how thirsty she was. Kawan couldn't help but indulge in a little fantasy of doing this with her with a bottle or sippy cup sometime... having a woman so completely dependent on him was just one of his kinks. He didn't know how to explain it. While he'd fed, burped, and changed plenty of actual babies and small children, it never affected what he wanted from a woman.

Kawan was a caretaker, through and through. In some ways, age-play was role-playing, but for him it was so much more than that. He *couldn't* be in a relationship without slipping into a Daddy Dom headspace regularly. Not that that always ended well. Darkly, he pushed those thoughts away and refocused on the present. On Melody.

He thought he'd picked up on some signs that Melody might be a little, or at least willing to play as a little. Hopefully he wasn't just misreading things because of his own desires.

When she finally stopped drinking, she blinked, seeming to come back to herself, and then she immediately blushed when she looked at him. Kawan grinned.

"How are you feeling, baby girl?"

"Good, um... good." She wriggled slightly, her brow furrowing as she felt his erection jerk against her. Glancing down between their bodies, she bit her lower lip. "Um, shouldn't I be doing something about that?"

"Not tonight," he said firmly. The little pout that formed on her lips at his words made him smile. "You weren't planning on playing tonight, remember? So I want you to go home and think about whether or not you'd like to come back, with the intention of playing... hopefully with me."

He tugged on her ponytail as she blushed and ducked her head. When she opened her mouth to answer, he put one finger up to quiet her and gave her a stern look.

"I don't want you to answer me right now. I'm serious about going home and thinking about it once you're away from me and the club. This was your first time, so once you've had some space, you might realize that while you enjoyed tonight, you'd prefer a different partner. Or a different kink. I'm a Daddy Dom and being a baby girl or a little isn't something that appeals to everyone. I want you to take the time to think about what you want." He kept toying with her hair, winding the soft strands around his fingers as he spoke.

As much as he hoped he'd hear from her again, he knew there was a possibility that she might decide she didn't want what he did. Especially since this had been her first time scening. They definitely had chemistry, which was a point in his favor.

"What do you want?" she asked. Her voice was a little bit higher, a little bit softer, a little more girlish. Kawan could very easily see her as a baby girl—his baby girl. But it was up to her.

"I want to get to know you a little better," he said easily. "I want a baby girl to care for, spoil, and punish. I've been attracted to you from the moment I met you, so if both of those wants align, that would make me very happy. But if they don't, I'd be happy to see you here at Black Light again anyway, for an occasional scene if you're amenable."

Her lips formed a little 'o' but she didn't quite seem to know how to respond.

"Here," he said, holding the bottle back up. "Drink."

EVEN THOUGH SHE'D already had a spectacular orgasm, Melody felt her insides clenching a little bit.

Daddy Kawan.

That was definitely how he was now embedded in her thoughts. It suited him so much better than Mr. Park or Sir.

As much as she wanted to tell him that everything he described sounded like exactly what she wanted, she also knew that she was flying high on the chemical afterglow of pleasure. Now was not the time to be making decisions. She was thinking clearly enough to know that.

Approaching movement caught her eye, reminding her that they weren't alone. Somehow she'd blocked out everything else and now it all came rushing back as she looked up to see Peggy nearly upon them. Most of her make-up had been wiped off and she seemed more subdued than usual, although also kind of dreamy. Behind her, Elliott stood back, arms crossed over his chest, a blank expression on his face.

Melody couldn't help but wonder how much of her spanking they'd seen... maybe they hadn't seen any of it or maybe they'd watched the whole thing. She'd been so caught up with Daddy Kawan that she'd pretty much forgotten the rest of the world existed.

She found that she resented the intrusion.

"Excuse me," Peggy said, her gaze flickering between Melody and Kawan, as if she wasn't sure whom she should be addressing, before finally settling on Melody. "Elliott and I are ready to head out. Do you want to stay here or come with us?"

Normally such a question from Peggy would be a bit whiny or posed as a challenge, as if asking Melody to choose between her and whomever Melody was with. This time, she just sounded like she didn't care either way. Wow. Whatever Elliott had done to give her an attitude adjustment had really worked.

But even though Peggy wasn't angling to ensure Melody left with them, she really should go.

She had planned to leave with them after all. And apparently she had a few things she needed to think about, although deep down she was pretty sure what her answer was going to be. But she also appreciated that he wanted to be sure she knew what she was getting into.

Because right now it would be so easy to throw all caution to the wind and beg him to be her Daddy... something she had never ever considered actually doing in real life, because she hadn't anticipated ever meeting a Dom who was interested in her, much less a Daddy Dom. Since he wasn't speaking up to say that she should stay, that pretty much clinched her answer.

She looked up at Kawan, feeling both reluctant and somehow shy. "I should probably go."

A little part of her was disappointed when he nodded, rather than telling her to stay. But she'd expected it too, so it was only a very little part.

She glanced at Peggy, giving her a little smile. "I'll come with you two, just give me a sec."

Nodding, Peggy turned away, trotting back to Elliott, so that Melody could focus on Kawan.

"Think about what I said," he said, giving her ponytail a final little tug that made her scalp tingle. "Do you still have my number?" She nodded. Even though she didn't expect to need a lawyer again, she'd held on to his card, not wanting to throw it away. "Good. Call me when you have an answer."

Melody nodded again and this time he raised his eyebrow at her. She blushed.

"Yes, Daddy," she whispered, blushing even more furiously. Grinning, he used her ponytail to pull her down for a brief kiss, making her squirm a little. He was still hard.

Was he going to play with someone else after she left?

Don't think about that. Not my business. Not yet.

First she had a decision to make. And she couldn't really

protest if he wanted to play with someone else when she hadn't even made a claim. Even though she kind of wanted to.

WATCHING Melody walk away with her friends, Kawan felt deflated.

Letting her go tonight was the right thing to do. Not pressuring her was the right thing to do. Leaving their next contact up to her was the right thing to do. But all of it screamed against his instincts, which said to stake a claim and convince her that being his baby girl was what she wanted. Submissives could be easily manipulated. It was what Krissy had claimed he'd done to her.

His resolve firmed.

That was exactly why he had to let Melody go tonight. He'd given her a taste, now she had to decide if she wanted the full meal and everything it entailed.

It was still harder than he'd thought it would be to watch her walk out of the club.

Once she disappeared through the door, he sighed and looked around for something to distract himself with. There were plenty of interesting scenes going on. He grinned when he saw that Alexander now had Sienna in the hot tub with him. Well, she was partially in the hot tub. She must have said or done something to get herself in trouble because she was bent over the side of it, facing away from the water, while Alexander spanked her wet bottom.

Wet skin always hurt more than dry, so it was no surprise that she was shimmying and squealing as he reddened her bottom.

He wondered if he'd have the opportunity to demonstrate the difference to Melody.

"Excuse me, Kawan, isn't it?" A deep voice at his elbow interrupted his reverie and he barely managed to keep from jumping in surprise.

He immediately recognized Jaxson Davidson, the owner of Black Light, although he was missing his two submissives and lovers. Kawan had met all three of them once before when he was just visiting with Alexander, several months ago.

"Yes, hello again, Mr. Davidson," he said, opting for formality since they were only the barest of acquaintances and he was a client of the firm, as well as this being his club.

The Dom held out his hand in greeting for Kawan to shake. "Just call me Jaxson, please. Now that you're a member, I'm sure we're going to be seeing a lot more of you, although hopefully we won't need your specific services."

Kawan chuckled. Since Jaxson would only need his services if he were defending himself or the club against a lawsuit, he didn't take offense.

"I'd much rather be here for pleasure rather than business," he said, letting his hand fall back from Jaxson's very firm shake. "Are your submissives here with you this evening?" He'd heard that Jaxson was very rarely seen without them, but the Dom shook his head.

"They're at home with our twins, but I needed to come in to take care of a few things. I was going to say hello earlier, but you were busy." Although his expression barely changed, his eyes glinted with appreciation. He'd obviously caught a little bit of Kawan's scene with Melody.

"Thank you for waiting." Kawan's lips quirked with amusement, but he was sincere. Considering it was Melody's first time receiving a spanking, he could only imagine how she would have reacted if someone had approached them in the middle of it. Although, she hadn't minded being spanked in the club itself.

Perhaps she had an exhibitionist streak.

"Since I saw her leave and Alexander is currently, ah, occupied, I thought I'd introduce myself and see if you wanted an introduction to another submissive?" The offer was made without any judgment. Kawan was sure there were quite a few people who played without commitment, and technically he wasn't committed to Melody but... he already didn't feel like playing with anyone else.

He'd never been very good at dating multiple people at once or 'playing the field'. Once he knew he was interested in someone and thought she might be interested in him as well, he waited to see what happened before seeking out anyone else.

"No, thank you, but I wouldn't say no to a drink." Since he wasn't going to be scening again tonight, he could have one while he waited for Alexander and Sienna.

Chuckling, Jaxson clapped him on the shoulder. "Well then, let me introduce you to Klara and she'll make sure to take care of you in a different way."

That sounded a lot better than standing around feeling out of place because the woman he wanted to scene with had left.

By THE TIME they got to Elliott's car, Peggy was much more her normal self, although Melody kind of wished she wasn't. She wanted to just sit in the back seat and think. Unfortunately, Peggy wasn't really the 'sit quietly' type, especially when she had questions to ask.

"So who was that guy? How do you know him?" Peggy was twisted around in her seat, staring back at Melody. The passing street lights made her look even more intimidating than usual.

"Mr. Park," Melody said. She'd introduced him hadn't she? But Peggy just stared at her blankly. "My lawyer?"

"Oh!" Comprehension dawned. "The hot Asian lawyer. I remember." She blinked. "So he's a Dom. Did you know he was going to be there?"

That sounded almost accusatory, although Melody couldn't understand why.

"Of course not! If I had, I wouldn't have tried to hide when he showed up." She felt herself blushing again at just the memory of it.

"Oh yeah." Peggy snickered. "That was funny. What were you thinking?"

"I wasn't really thinking." If she had been, she wouldn't have done something so ridiculous. Definitely not where Peggy could see. Her bestie was probably going to make fun of her for days about it, and she couldn't really blame her. She'd do the same. That was just how their friendship was. Although she was careful because sometimes Peggy could be sensitive. Melody let most stuff just roll off her back, so she knew she was in for some serious ribbing.

"Did you have a good time?" Elliott asked, his tone almost gentle. She looked up to see him glancing in the rearview mirror with an assessing gaze.

"Yes." And there went the blush again. Her cheeks were starting to feel sunburned.

"What did you two do?"

Peggy's brazen question made Melody glance at Elliott again. He was a nice guy and she was really grateful that he'd taken her to Black Light as a guest, but she didn't really *know* him. While she definitely wanted to break down the evening to Peggy eventually, she didn't really want to do it in front of him. But it would be kind of rude to come out and say that, right? Especially since she'd technically been his guest.

To her relief, he also came to her rescue.

"Maybe the two of you can talk about that in detail after I drop you off," Elliott said. His voice sounded a little deeper than it had a minute ago, a little bit more authoritative. Melody shivered.

"But—" Peggy started to protest, but Elliott shot her a stern look.

To Melody's shock—and gratitude—Peggy subsided, slumping into her seat rather than twisting back around to face her.

Sighing, Melody let her head fall back against the headrest as Elliott turned the music up, effectively ending any further attempts at conversation. So far, he was her favorite of Peggy's boyfriends. Definitely not one she could just run roughshod over the way she did sometimes.

Kawan wasn't the type to be pushed around either. Melody smiled as she stared out into the darkness.

Daddy Kawan.

Yeah. That had a really nice ring to it.

CHAPTER 7

*B*y the time they got back to the apartment, Peggy was practically bursting at the seams with impatience. Melody took the opportunity to slip away to her room while Peggy and Elliott were saying goodbye at the door, hoping that maybe she'd be able to hide out in her own room and Peggy would take the hint, but... no such luck.

Five minutes later, Peggy knocked on her door and came right in without waiting for Melody to answer.

"Tell me everything!" The redhead squealed, practically launching herself onto Melody's bed, bouncing with excitement. "Did he spank you? Did you guys have sex? Was he bossy? Was it good?"

"Slow down," Melody protested, laughing. Even though part of her was craving some quiet time to think and reflect, Peggy's excited energy was contagious. Besides, she needed Peggy's help to loosen the corset. So far she was doing a crap job of it on her own, and she really didn't want to have to sleep in it. "Help me with my corset, and I'll tell you everything."

Peggy immediately bounced up off the bed and came over to begin loosening the strings. Oh man. If taking off a bra felt good, taking off a corset was almost orgasmic. She felt her entire body sag, relaxing, and she sucked in the biggest lungful of sweet, sweet air. That was almost as good as 'I'm not going to jail' air.

Something poked the back of her shoulder.

"Hey, woman, you're killing me! Dish!" Peggy demanded, poking her again before returning to the corset strings and finishing loosening them. Melody pressed her hands over her stomach as the corset drooped, keeping it from falling down completely.

"Okay, well he remembered me, obviously," Melody said, blushing again, although this time it was from pleasure rather than embarrassment. She stepped away, heading over to her dresser so she could get her pajamas. Peggy pranced back over to Melody's bed, bouncing with palpable excitement as she listened. "And we started watching one of the scenes, and he asked me what I knew about, you know, BDSM and stuff."

"Did you tell him about your book addiction?" Peggy teased.

"Yes." Melody replaced the corset with a soft t-shirt, sighing with happiness as the material brushed against her sensitive skin. She felt all tingly where the corset had been. Not surprising since it had left all sorts of red marks on her from where her body had been scrunched together.

"And then what?"

"Then... I kind of lied about something so that he would spank me." She grinned, grabbing a pair of yoga pants. She still couldn't believe she'd had the courage to do that.

"What did you lie about?"

"Reading Daddy Dom books," Melody admitted. She knew Peggy thought those books were stupid.

"Ugh, good for him, you should be spanked for reading those."

Yup, that was about the reaction she'd anticipated, but she found herself bristling anyway. It hadn't bothered her before when Peggy had made her opinion on those books clear, but now it did. Maybe because now it felt like a critique of her and Kawan, rather than just Peggy not liking the books... it was hard not to take the judgment a little more personally.

"He didn't spank me for reading them." She jerked her shirt down and pulled the pants on.

Behind her, Peggy snorted. "It looks like he barely spanked you at all. Did you get off at least?"

"Oh, yes." Melody moved over to her dresser and pulled her pants down, twisting around so she could see her butt. It still felt a little sore, but it wasn't even pink.

Well, that was kind of disappointing. She rubbed the ivory skin and frowned, making Peggy laugh. Hopping up from the bed, Peggy came over and got in almost the same position, mirroring Melody, before pulling up her skirt to show off her own ass. Unlike Melody, she wasn't even wearing a thong, she was completely pantiless. There were some long welts across both cheeks, dark pink lines crossing the pale expanse.

Melody's eyes widened. "Holy shit!"

"Elliott used a cane," Peggy said smugly, running her hand over the marks while watching herself in the mirror. "Want to touch?"

"Uh, yes." She was utterly fascinated. Partly repelled, partly enthralled. The raised welts were a little warm to the touch, the flesh definitely swollen, and she couldn't suppress a little shudder.

The idea of being caned made her want to run screaming, but Peggy seemed proud of the marks, and there was a little part of Melody that wished she had something similar to show off. Not that it was a competition, but she just wanted to know... could she handle it?

"How much did it hurt?" she asked, straightening back up.

"A hell of a lot more than a spanking," Peggy said with a final smirk at herself in the mirror before dropping her skirt. "I guess he went easy on you since it was your first time at the club. Are you going to see him again?"

"Maybe... He said he wants to, but he also wants me to think about whether or not I really want to get involved with him."

"Why wouldn't you want to? He's hot." Peggy fanned herself with her hand, rolling her eyes upwards for emphasis.

Even though she knew Peggy's opinion on Daddy Dom books, Melody didn't have anyone else to talk to about this stuff, so she just decided to go for it. Especially since Peggy thought he was hot, maybe she'd be more open-minded.

"Well, he's a Daddy Dom, and he wants me to think about what I want out of a BDSM relationship before I decide if I want to do anything more with him." She anxiously watched her friend's reaction, feeling a little churning in her stomach. Peggy stuck her tongue out, wrinkling her nose in disgust.

"Ew, wait, he's actually a real live Daddy Dom? Or like a sugar daddy?" Her expression turned contemplative. "A sugar daddy might be okay. We could have fun with that."

"I don't think he's a sugar daddy. He says he wants a baby girl." The nerves in her stomach were actually making her feel a little nauseous, even though she kept her tone normal. She hated it when she and Peggy disagreed, and she was already anticipating that they would about this.

"Gross." Peggy patted her on the shoulder. "Don't worry, we'll go back to the club and find a different Dom. One who's not into little girls. Ugh. Too bad. What a waste of a hottie."

Without waiting for Melody to reply, Peggy was already breezing out of her door, obviously sure that she'd just planned out their next step. Melody pressed her lips together to keep from calling her bestie back into the room. It was really late. She didn't want to start an argument right now.

Heck, she didn't want to argue at all. Fighting with Peggy sucked. It made her feel like she was walking on eggshells until she finally got around to apologizing just to cut the tension.

Peggy was pretty forgiving, but it could be frustrating. Especially when Melody didn't feel like she was doing anything wrong.

This was definitely one of those instances where she didn't think she was doing anything wrong, but she also knew it would start an argument if she tried to convince Peggy of that, and she just didn't have the energy for that right now.

Sighing, Melody moved to the bed and flopped down onto it. She was so tired. It had been a long week. Tonight had been blissful but exhausting. And now she was a little disappointed that her spanking hadn't left her any marks to remember it by. She wasn't going to be forgetting it any time soon, but just a little bit of pink on her skin would have been nice to see.

Because it really had hurt when Daddy Kawan had been spanking her.

She flipped onto her back, pressing her bottom down into the bed. Her body tingled, but only from the memory. It wasn't even that sore anymore. The skin on her stomach and sides was more sore now, just from the corset being off. Staring up at the ceiling, she frowned.

Even though she was tired, she didn't really feel like she could sleep. At Black Light, her brain had turned off for a while, but now it was back on and running non-stop.

Worrying over Peggy and what she would think if Melody said she didn't want a Dom, she wanted Daddy Kawan.

Worrying that maybe Peggy was right and that wanting a Daddy was gross. Sick.

Worrying that maybe a Daddy Dom really was into little girls. But she was an adult. Not to mention a curvy woman. There was no mistaking her for a little girl. And Kawan was seriously hot. If he wanted someone younger, thinner, and more girlish, there were definitely submissives at Black Light who fit that bill. She'd seen them.

Pushing herself up from her bed, Melody grabbed her phone

and walked over to her desk and pulled open the middle drawer. The file she'd put all her court stuff into was right on top and she picked it up. Kawan's card fell out as she lifted it, like it knew she was looking for it.

Picking up the card, Melody chewed on her lower lip, glancing at her phone again. It was after midnight. But he'd still been at the club when she left... maybe he'd still be awake.

Maybe he'd still be at the club and playing with someone else.

Well, at the very least, she could text him.

WALKING INTO HIS FRONT DOOR, earlier than he'd thought he'd be returning home, Kawan hung his keys on the hook he'd installed just last week. He'd bought the house over a month ago, once he'd gotten the official offer letter from Lambert, Urbanski, and Reed. As soon as he'd closed on the house, two weeks ago, he'd gotten to work with personalizing it and slowly moving in his possessions.

This was the first house he'd ever bought. A sign of permanence that he'd never been interested in before, but that he'd wanted when he moved. His mom had taken it as a sign that he was finally ready to meet a nice girl and settle down. Which... she wasn't entirely wrong.

He couldn't help but wonder what she'd think of Melody. His father would definitely approve, but as her only son, his mother could be a bit judgmental about any woman he introduced her to. Which seemed contrary to her stated desire for more grandchildren, specifically from him, but the contradiction didn't seem to bother her. She'd loathed Krissy, although she'd been polite about it. At the time he'd thought it was just her usual snobbery toward any woman he brought home... after the breakup, he'd wondered if maybe he should have listened more closely to his mom.

Although why he was already thinking of Melody in such terms, he didn't know. There wasn't any guarantee she'd want to play with him again, much less do something more. He hoped she would though. The club, which had had such appeal before, was no longer quite as interesting to him.

It hadn't been a bad evening after Melody had left Black Light, although it hadn't been as nice as playing with her either. He'd enjoyed chatting with Jaxson for a bit until Alexander and Sienna had finished their scene. They'd wanted to head home— presumably to finish what they'd started at the club in a more intimate manner—and Kawan had been more than ready as well.

There hadn't really been a reason to stay after Melody had left.

Walking through his house into his kitchen for some water, Kawan pulled his phone out of his pocket. He didn't recognize the number, but the message made him grin because there was absolutely no doubt in his mind who it was from.

Hello, hopefully I'm not waking you up or interrupting anything. You don't have to text me back right away, but I just wanted to know if I can ask you some questions when you're free. You said you wanted me to think about what I want and I'm going to, but I need to ask a few questions to really know what I want, if that's okay.

Melody. She texted without any abbreviations, which somehow seemed very her even though he admittedly didn't know her that well yet. It fit how he saw her. She was also rambling, even in text, and he found it wholly adorable.

He leaned his shoulder against the cabinets next the fridge, quickly swiping a message back.

Any questions, any time, baby girl. I can't promise I'll be able to answer right away, but I will always answer.

Grinning, he put his phone down on the counter while he

got his glass of water. He was a little disappointed when she didn't text back right away, but he didn't let that get him down. Maybe she'd sent the text and then gone to bed. It was definitely late enough.

His phone finally dinged again when he was on his way up the stairs, glass of water in hand and half finished. Grinning, he downed the rest of it so he could focus on the conversation.

Why do you like being a Daddy Dom?

Interesting. Considering how long it had taken her to respond, he'd expected a longer text.

But it was an important question, since it would also encompass what he'd like to do for her... what he hoped she'd do for him.

A lot of reasons. I like knowing that a woman trusts me so completely that she's willing to not only give up so much control to me, but also that she'll let herself be so vulnerable with me. I love being able to give her a safe space where she can just be, where she can indulge the little girl inside of her, and know that she is loved, cared for, and protected.

He studied the response carefully. It was how he felt, but it was something he felt a little vulnerable about sharing too. Submissives weren't the only ones who could be taken advantage of. Still, he was determined not to let the past harden him against trying for what he wanted in the future. He pressed send.

This time her return text came much more quickly.

What do you want from your submissive? How do you want her to behave?

Little Miss Melody might not realize it, but that question bolstered his confidence. Not only was she wondering if she could please him, she was specifically looking for pointers on how to go forward. She probably wasn't going to like his answer though.

I want her to be respectful of me as her Daddy, and obey any rules we agree to, but other than that, it's up to her. We'd set up soft and hard limits together and then go from there.

He could almost hear the frustration in her next text.

But what should she do?

He shot off the reply just as quickly.

Whatever makes her happy as long as she's following the rules.

When she didn't text back immediately, he chuckled and started getting ready for bed. Staring at himself in the mirror while he brushed his teeth, it was all too easy to picture her reading through his texts and trying to pick them apart for clues on what he wanted her to do. But Kawan didn't want a slave. While he liked control, he didn't want to direct his submissive's every movement. Part of what he loved about being a Daddy was that his baby girl would have a lot of freedom to do what she pleased. He enjoyed watching his baby girl enjoy herself.

Of course, if she crossed any lines, then he'd also be there to provide the necessary discipline.

Washing his face, he sighed as he studied himself in the mirror. Even though he was only thirty-four, he was starting to find the occasional gray hair among the many black. His mother had pointed them out the last time he'd visited and claimed that it was because he didn't have a good woman to take care of him.

He thought maybe Melody was done for the night, but she sent him another question just as he was climbing into bed.

What if she doesn't follow the rules?

That made him laugh. There might be a little bit of a brat inside Melody, or maybe she'd just liked the spanking earlier and was hoping for more. Either way, Kawan never minded a little bit of innocent mischief. He enjoyed funishment much more than actual discipline, although he wouldn't hesitate if he felt the latter had been earned.

It depends on what rule she breaks and what her hard and soft limits are. The punishment should fit the crime.

Plugging in his charger, Kawan clicked off the light and lie down. He wasn't going to be able to fall asleep yet, not while he was waiting to see if Melody had any more questions, but resting in the darkness was peaceful.

As he lie there, his mind wandered to the one room in the house he hadn't unpacked yet. The room he'd chosen as his playroom. There hadn't been any rush to set up that room because he hadn't thought he'd use it any time soon. Especially not when he had access to Black Light.

He still planned to make good use of the club, but maybe he'd get the playroom set up sooner rather than later.

Maybe it was too soon... but the idea was tempting. It didn't have to be for her, specifically. They might find they weren't compatible after another few scenes. Kawan needed to find someone who enjoyed weaving the sexual play and the baby girl play together the same way he did.

The way Melody had seemed to tonight.

His phone buzzed again, interrupting his thoughts.

Thank you for answering my questions, I'm going to bed now. Good night =)

Polite little thing. He liked that. And appreciated that she let him know she was done for now.

Sleep tight, sweetheart. Feel free to text me with any more questions that you have in the future.

Setting the phone down on his nightstand, Kawan closed his eyes and tried not to think about how empty his bed suddenly felt.

CHAPTER 8

*K*awan woke up just a little later than he normally did, had a light breakfast, went for a run, and came back to shower. What made it different was that in between doing all of these things, he was also fielding more questions from Melody.

Each text added another little kernel of hope that she was just as interested in him and what he had to offer as he was in her.

What is your favorite punishment?

What do you like to do for aftercare?

Do you always have to be called 'Daddy'?

Have you had a baby girl before?

He answered as best he could, although certain questions—like the one about aftercare—would really be individual to the submissives. Kawan liked to cuddle, but he'd played with subs who weren't interested in being snuggled after a scene. His job as a Dom, as a good Daddy, was to give his submissive what she needed.

Other questions were easier, although confirmation that he'd had a baby girl before brought on such a flurry of questions that he decided he should try to take the next step. Thankfully, she didn't ask why they'd broken up, she seemed more interested in the actual mechanics of the relationship.

Why don't we get together to talk? We could have coffee, or dinner, if you're available, and I can answer all of your questions in person. Or we can keep texting, if you're more comfortable this way.

Since they'd already met, and her questions indicated she was definitely interested, he decided to try and see her in person again rather than suggesting a phone call. It would be much easier to gauge her reactions actually seeing her than just speaking over the phone.

As the seconds ticked by, he started to think that maybe he was pushing too fast, too soon.

He busied his hands with making himself lunch, to keep from rescinding the offer too quickly, and nearly tripped over his feet trying to get to his phone when it dinged again. At least there was no one there to see him acting more like a teenage boy than a grown man, rushing to talk to his crush. That was how he felt right now.

When he saw the message, he grinned, feeling *exactly* like a teenage boy with a crush.

Dinner sounds good. Is tonight okay?

Dinner with Kawan tonight.

The thought seemed to run around in circles in her brain.

Even this morning, when she'd swung by the labs just to check on her petri dishes and make sure nothing had changed, she hadn't been able to think about anything except him. Most of the time she struggled to keep her work from intruding on her brain when she had downtime. She'd never had to struggle to focus on her work before.

"Oo, this is hot!" Peggy's voice sliced through her inner musing, bringing her back to the present. "Melody, look."

She turned to see her bestie holding up a forest green lace bodysuit with an opening in the crotch. It was definitely hot and it would look incredible against Peggy's ivory skin, red hair, and green eyes. Which was exactly what Peggy was going for. She'd been in a bad mood since Elliott had canceled lunch with her earlier today.

Which was why she'd dragged Melody out shopping this afternoon. She wanted to buy something scandalous, so she could go to Elliott's apartment and surprise him with something naughty under her trench coat. Melody wished she had half of Peggy's confidence. She tried to picture herself doing something similar, and immediately felt nauseous with anxiety as all the ways it could go wrong tumbled through her head.

Yup, definitely not a move she'd be able to make. Throwing up from anxiety on a man's shoes was probably not the way to seduce him.

Would Kawan be grossed out and shut her out, or would he go full Daddy Dom and jump right into 'caring' mode? Melody did not hate the idea of being taken care of while she was sick. Sometimes she thought part of the reason she wanted a Daddy Dom so badly was *because* she was so fiercely independent. Even as a kid, she'd felt the need to do everything herself. Her mom had sometimes seemed disappointed that Melody didn't need her more often, but she didn't force the issue, allowing Melody the space she insisted on.

A Daddy Dom wouldn't take 'no' for an answer though; he'd ignore everything but a safe word. And safe wording over being taken care of would be so silly.

"Melody!" Impatience and annoyance were laced through the way Peggy said her name, jolting her.

"It's totally hot," Melody reassured her immediately, making herself focus on the issue at hand. "I was just picturing you in it."

The little white lie was good enough for Peggy, who immediately beamed at her, draping the bodysuit over her arm. "I'm getting it. Are you going to get anything?"

She looked down at the sheer white babydoll she'd stopped in front of. There was lace over the breasts and a little pink bow that tied between them, then a long fall of sheer white that ended in a ruffle which would hit mid-thigh. Melody fingered the soft lace.

"I was thinking about this one." She liked the sexy innocence of it. Plus, it was very baby girl, right? That was kind of the definition of babydoll lingerie. Even though it covered a lot less than what she wore to Black Light last night, she could see herself feeling comfortable wearing this in the club.

Coming between the racks of clothes to see what Melody was looking at, Peggy wrinkled her nose as soon as she saw the garment. "Oh, honey, no, not with your body. We need to emphasize your boobs and cover up your stomach. There's a corset over here I think you'll like."

Turning away, she either didn't see or totally ignored the crestfallen expression on Melody's face. Yeah, she didn't have Peggy's slender waist and flat stomach, but she *liked* her body. Most of the time. Looking down at the sheer fabric again, she bit her lower lip.

Maybe it wasn't the best choice for her body type.

"Melody, here, what about this?"

She blinked back the threatening tears in her eyes, because she knew Peggy hadn't meant to be mean. Sometimes she just didn't realize how harsh she came across. Looking up, she saw her bestie holding up a pink corset with white ruffles along the top and bottom. There was even a white bow right in the middle of the dipping sweetheart neckline. It had the same sexy-innocent flair that the sheer babydoll had, but would cinch in her waist and push up her cleavage. The second she saw it, she fell in love with it, and all the insecurity she'd been feeling vanished in the face of an outfit that both she and Peggy could get behind.

Seeing the expression on her face, Peggy grinned. "Definitely not my style, but you can totally pull it off."

Making her way over to Peggy, Melody took the corset from her. "I love it, thank you."

She still loved the babydoll too, but Peggy was probably right. This would be sexier on her.

"Awesome, now let's find you a garter belt and some thigh highs to go with it." Peggy was already looking around for where those would be located, obviously eager to continue dressing Melody up like a doll.

Melody followed along behind her, kind of amused as she realized that even when it came to her friendship with Peggy, she was kind of subby. That was probably why they got along so well.

It was also why she hadn't dared tell Peggy that she was going out to dinner with Kawan tonight. She'd tried to talk to Peggy about it this morning, but Peggy had just reassured her that they'd find her a better Dom the next time they went to Black Light. Then she'd gotten the text from Elliott, canceling lunch, and Melody hadn't wanted to fight with her when she'd already been upset. Talk about a recipe for disaster.

Besides, Peggy was going to be surprising Elliott while Melody was meeting Kawan for dinner.

If the date turned out to be a bust, Peggy would never know. And if things worked out with her and Kawan, Peggy would get on board. She just wanted Melody to be happy, even if she had strong opinions about how to best make that happen.

~

As FIRST DATES WENT, Kawan couldn't remember the last time he'd had so much fun. Maybe it was because they'd already scened together—or because they'd already been through a stressful situation together—but there was none of the awkwardness that usually accompanied getting to know someone.

They'd met at Sunset Pins, a newer establishment that combined bowling with gourmet cooking. Kawan had asked her for suggestions and immediately jumped on this one.

When he bowled his first turkey, he turned to find Melody scowling adorably at him, rather than jumping up and down in excited awe the way she had the first two times he'd had a strike. She had her arms crossed over her chest, plumping her breasts up under the low cut blouse she was wearing, her eyes narrowed at him. The soft waves of her hair were clipped back away from her face, hiding none of her now suspicious expression.

"Are you on a bowling team or something?" The question was almost more of a demand, and said with enough of a pout to make him chuckle.

"Aren't you glad I didn't take you up on turning this into a competition?" he teased, putting his hands on her waist and pulling her into him, forcing her to tip her head back to keep looking at him. Kawan dropped a kiss on her mouth, feeling her soften slightly under his hands and lips, before he lifted his head again. "And yes, I was on a team in high school. I'm not anymore, but I still enjoy bowling just for fun."

Her eyes sparkled even though she wrinkled her nose at him. "How is it fun if I'm getting creamed?"

"Well, it's fun for me."

Making an exasperated noise in the back of her throat, Melody lightly smacked his chest. Sweet little brat. If they were in the club he'd spank her for that. As it was... chuckling, he turned, guiding her forward and giving her a little swat on her bottom to get her moving. She squeaked, jumping, and then shot him another look over her shoulder as she rubbed where he'd spanked her. Kawan could only laugh at her mock-outraged expression.

Little minx.

After her spanking last night, he knew very well there was no way that little slap had made any real impact on her. But he liked how playful and flirtatious she was being with him. It was a complete turnaround, not only from how she'd been in the courtroom, but also from last night at Black Light. This was Melody when she was comfortable, relaxed. Happy.

Definitely enjoying herself. And so was he.

Being compatible in the club had been one thing, especially once he'd discovered that she had a thing for Daddy Doms, but being compatible outside of it was another. He'd been a little worried that maybe they wouldn't have anything to talk about that wasn't sexual, but that hadn't proved the case.

Before they'd started their game, they'd sat down and ordered their food, talking in between, and sex hadn't come up once. Instead she'd told him a little bit about her research for her dissertation—what he was able to understand of it, anyway. Science had never been one of his strong suits, but he loved to see the passion shining from her face as she attempted to describe her thesis in terms he could understand. Something about studying blood and fecal samples to try and find ways to help diabetics and their mental health. Exactly how they were doing that was where she lost him.

It didn't matter that he only understood about half of what she was saying, as he liked listening to her anyway.

Then they'd started bowling and he'd been completely distracted by the delicious curve of her ass in the jeans she was wearing. So distracted that he hadn't managed a strike until the third frame. Not that he was complaining.

BOWLING HAD NEVER BEEN SO sexy.

Actually, before tonight, Melody had never found anything remotely sexy about bowling. It was part of why Sunset Pins had been one of her suggestions. She'd wanted to meet up with him in a completely different venue than Black Light. Maybe there'd been a small part of her that had wondered if being in the club had influenced how she felt about him.

After all, it would be very easy to be swept away by the big bad Daddy Dom fantasy when they were at a BDSM club, surrounded by sex, leather, and orgasms.

Now they were bowling and she was thinking about how graceful he was when he moved, how nice his jeans looked on his ass when he sent the ball flying down the lane, and how hot his forearms were. Seriously. Was there such a thing as a forearm fetish? Because his were really hot. It didn't hurt that he was wearing a button-down shirt and had rolled up the sleeves in order to get a better range of movement for bowling.

Melody was pretty sure she'd gotten wet just watching him unbutton the cuffs and slowly folding the fabric into place.

I have issues.

At least now she knew for sure that her overwhelming attraction to him hadn't just been because he'd ridden to her rescue in court or that she'd worn BDSM blinders in the club or something. Nope. She was just attracted to him. Period. Whether he was lawyering, Domming, or bowling.

He was smart, funny, charming, incredibly sexy, listened to her talk about her research without his eyes glazing over, and was a Daddy Dom.

So what the hell was wrong with him?

There had to be something, right?

Although, obviously Peggy thought that the fact he was a Daddy Dom was a problem. That was one downside. She'd liked all the answers that he'd given her about why he liked being a Daddy Dom, but once Peggy got an idea stuck in her head, it could be hard to remove it. Which was why Melody was out here tonight, testing the waters while Peggy wasn't home, without telling her bestie about the date.

Just thinking about it made Melody uncomfortable, so she pushed thoughts of Peggy away.

Focus on the hot man's ass instead.

And the way he's kicking your *ass.*

Dammit. Melody felt like pouting again. She could be a little competitive about games. Normally she didn't get competitive about bowling, but that was because she was usually playing with people who scored the same as she did. People who were happy if they managed a three-digit score.

She wasn't used to being totally wiped off the scoreboard.

Watching his fourth strike in a row, Melody sighed. At least she had good forearm porn. His muscles got all flexed and sexy when he was holding the fifteen-pound ball. Made her think about all the things he could probably do with those strong hands and fingers... beyond the things she already knew he could do.

Turning around, he caught her expression and chuckled, walking back to her with a little swing in his step.

"Not quite how you pictured this going, baby girl?" he asked, as he came to a halt in front of her, reaching up to tuck a strand of hair behind her ear.

"Is there anything you're not good at?" she countered. The fact that her voice came out a little higher than usual did not escape her notice. She sounded almost whiny.

But that didn't seem to bother Kawan. If anything, his grin widened, and then his hands were on her hips again, pulling her into him for another kiss. Melody could definitely get used to being kissed in between frames. Especially because this time he didn't just leave the kiss on her lips and then pull away.

This time the kiss lingered, and when she parted her lips, he took immediate advantage and deepened the kiss. His hands slid around her body, making her arch her back as her breasts pressed against his chest, her fingers digging into his biceps, which felt just as muscular as his forearms. Heat and need surged inside of her.

The man kissed like a demon.

A sinful, sexy demon sent to tempt her into all sorts of naughtiness.

And then he'd spank the naughty right out of her.

Yes, please.

"Excuse me." The words were followed by a very loud throat clearing, ending their kiss. Melody turned her head to glare at the man who had interrupted them. The man, who was wearing a polo shirt that said Sunset Pins on the chest, was unimpressed by the dark look she was leveling at him. "This is a family establishment. Please keep your public displays of affection to a minimum."

Her cheeks heated with a hot blush, right on cue, as her glare dissolved under the man's withering look. Somehow, when Kawan had started kissing her, she'd forgotten where they were. Or maybe forgotten wasn't the right word. She just hadn't cared.

"Sorry," Kawan said, sliding his hands to her hips while giving the man an easy smile. The man snorted and walked away. Kawan looked back down at her and her heart jumped a little in her chest. The warmth in his dark eyes filled her all the way up, making her wonder if he was going to suggest they get out of there. "Okay, little girl, let's get back to the game. And let's make it interesting. If you bowl under a hundred twenty-five, I get to take you to Black Light again next weekend."

"What if I bowl over one-twenty-five?" she asked, because now she was torn between wanting to show him that she wasn't a terrible bowler and wanting to just chuck her ball in the gutter.

"Then I'll still take you to Black Light, and I'll give you an orgasm for every fifty points you score tonight." The wicked smile that accompanied that promise made her all wobbly in the knees.

"Every twenty points," she counter-bargained.

Kawan's rich laugh filled the air and Melody beamed up at him.

CHAPTER 9

*T*hey played four games and Melody got her highest score of one hundred twenty-seven on the second game. Since he'd ended up agreeing to every twenty points, that meant six orgasms for the little minx on Saturday. Watching her celebratory dance when she'd scored high enough had him laughing, as had her frustrated pout when she'd actually done worse the next two games.

There were so many different sides to her. The scared defendant hadn't been his favorite, although that had played on all his protective instincts, but he didn't like to see her in trouble. Discovering she was a curious newbie to kink had been a delightful surprise. The serious researcher who was focused on her PhD had his immediate respect.

But he was pretty sure this was her little side, working its way out through an innocent game.

She plopped down on the bench next to him with a sigh, staring morosely at the scoreboard. "I think I peaked early."

"I think your arm is getting sore," he told her, reaching out to take her hand and start massaging it. "But you still managed to break one twenty-five already."

She perked up at the reminder.

"I did, didn't I?" A hot blush immediately followed as she slanted her gaze his way, like she didn't quite dare to look him in the eye. "Does that mean... Are we... Were you serious?"

Oh, how he loved these little hints of shyness, he truly did. Sliding his fingers into her hair, Kawan twisted the soft strands around his fingers, using them to draw her closer to him. He wouldn't embarrass her by doing anything that would bring the manager down on them again, but he couldn't quite manage to keep his hands off of her either.

She sucked in a breath, her eyes flaring, and she blushed even pinker. The noise of the alley seemed to recede to a droning hum as the tension between them grew, his lips hovering over hers.

"Was I serious about taking you to Black Light and giving you six screaming orgasms?" The pink in her cheeks turned red hot in a second. "Absolutely, baby girl. I'm going to show you all the ways a Daddy can reward his good girl."

Her eyes practically glazed over and she squirmed slightly in her seat, immediately and completely aroused. She wasn't the only one. Kawan had gotten his own libido under control for the most part, but it only took two seconds and one little breathy sigh for it to come roaring back to life.

"What if..." Melody's tongue flicked out, nervously wetting her lower lip, and her voice dropped to a whisper. "What if I want to know more about what happens to naughty girls?"

Kawan's grip on her hair tightened and she whimpered.

Fuck, the things she did to him.

"I could show you that right now, if you'd like." He husked out the words. Getting her alone tonight, on their first official date, hadn't been part of his original plan, but he was willing to be flexible.

The expression on her face cleared a little and then fell with disappointment. "I... I have work early tomorrow morning."

"Then we should get out of here now, and you can let me know how much time I have to work with."

Passion flared in her eyes.

DAMN PEGGY.

Damn her, damn her, damn her.

Although, even thinking that made Melody feel like a horrible best friend. Because she was a horrible best friend. Or maybe she was the best best friend ever because she'd given up hot, filthy, naughty sex in order to be there for her best friend when she was needed.

Even if she did feel resentful about it. She was allowed to feel resentful as long as she didn't show it and *did* show up for her bestie, right?

She hoped so because, as much as she wanted to be a perfect, self-sacrificing best friend, she couldn't just make the feeling go away. If Peggy were genuinely heartbroken, she was sure she'd be less resentful... but Peggy seemed more enraged than anything else.

"Can you believe he broke up with me?" Peggy ranted, repeating herself for the third time, pacing back and forth on the living room rug. "While I'm wearing *this?* What the hell is wrong with him?"

She'd been pretty much saying the same thing over and over again, not requiring much more from Melody than a supportive statement of outrage... although, truthfully Melody could see Elliott's side of it. While she was no expert in kink or BDSM just from reading, she knew that Doms didn't always deal well with surprises. Especially since Peggy didn't even try to see that maybe she'd been doing something wrong.

"It is kind of topping from the bottom," Melody pointed out, a little hesitantly.

Peggy immediately stopped pacing and planted her hands on her hips, narrowing her green eyes at Melody. "Whose side are you on here?"

"Yours, of course. He should have jumped on you like a slavering beast because you're too sexy for words." That got a little smile from Peggy, reluctant though it was. "Still though, maybe it's just because he's a Dom. They always like to be in control, right?"

"Ugh, don't be reasonable, I hate it when you're reasonable." Losing some of her bravado, Peggy flung herself dramatically onto the couch beside Melody. "He called me a selfish brat."

"Well, that was definitely mean," Melody said soothingly, scooting over to put her arm around Peggy. It also wasn't entirely untrue, but there were a lot of good parts of Peggy that helped to make up for her occasional self-involvement. "Totally uncalled for."

Leaning her head onto Melody's shoulder, more of the anger leeched out of Peggy's voice, and the resentment she'd felt about being called away from Kawan faded. "I really liked him."

"I know, sweetie." She stroked Peggy's arm, resting her cheek on the top of her friend's head. Peggy had definitely really liked him, but deep down, Melody realized she wasn't surprised it hadn't worked either. Elliott was definitely dominant while Peggy... well, she was also dominant most of the time. Maybe she was different in the bedroom, but apparently that hadn't been enough for Elliott. They'd been doomed to clash eventually.

"Well, fuck him anyway." Peggy jumped back to her feet in one of her lightning fast mood changes. If her anger was half-bravado, Melody wasn't going to call her on it. She knew Peggy preferred action to wallowing. When Melody was dumped, she went for ice cream and *Gilmore Girls*. When Peggy was dumped, she was more likely to be found drinking martinis and watching

Game of Thrones with a scary expression on her face. "I'm going to find a new boyfriend—a better boyfriend—who doesn't expect me to worship at his feet. I'll make *him* kneel for *me.*"

And with that, she was off and running again, leaving Melody to inwardly sigh and settle back into the couch for what was likely to be a long night. Work tomorrow was going to be rough.

At least she had her Saturday Black Light date with Kawan to look forward to. With Peggy on the warpath this week, she was probably going to really be feeling the need for an escape by then.

FOCUSING on work had never been so difficult.

It didn't help that he couldn't stop texting Melody. Especially since she kept texting back.

They weren't even talking about anything important.

She'd sent him an apology this morning for having to leave last night—an unnecessary one, since Kawan understood that her friend had needed her—and then somehow they'd ended up playing the question game with each other. Favorite movie... favorite book... favorite TV show... favorite restaurant... favorite food... Nothing that couldn't have waited for a real conversation, but he couldn't stop.

Every time she sent him a question, along with her answer, he sent her one back... along with his.

In between waiting for her answers, he managed to get work done. And he did turn off the sound on his phone for meetings, but the second the meeting was over, the first thing he did was check it for another message.

The wait for this upcoming weekend was going to be interminable.

Patience was usually one of his virtues, but at the moment, his usual calm eluded him.

When he ran into Sienna exiting Alexander's office, he was distracted enough that he almost didn't notice the slightly dazed expression on her face at first. A second glance and he noted that her lips were slightly swollen and tendrils of her hair had worked their way out of her neat bun. His own lips quirked. It didn't surprise him at all that Alexander took advantage of having his future wife working in the same building.

The second she saw Kawan, a blush bloomed in her cheeks, amusing him even further. Considering he'd watched her scene multiple times at Black Light, he hadn't realized she'd be embarrassed about being caught having some lunchtime fun. Apparently location mattered. His grin widened.

"Hello, Sienna."

"Hello, Sir. Um, Kawan. I mean, Mr. Park." She was adorably flustered and blushing even harder now, wringing her hands in front of her as her gaze lowered and lifted.

"Having a good day?" he asked.

The little sub rallied, although the color in her cheeks remained. Her chin lifted and her eyes sparkled with mischief. "Yes, Mr. Park. *Very* good."

Alexander's deep voice interrupted them as he called out from his office, over Kawan's chuckle. "Stop bothering my fiancée, Kawan. Come in here, I want to talk to you anyway."

Giving him a little wink, Sienna swished her hips as she walked away, regaining her usual sassy confidence with every step. Still chuckling, Kawan moved into Alexander's office, shutting the door behind him. Eyes on his computer, Alexander didn't look at him until he was seated in one of the comfortable chairs in front of Alexander's desk.

With one last tap on his keyboard, Alexander refocused his piercing blue gaze on Kawan. "How's your day going?"

Raising his eyebrow, Kawan settled back into his chair. "Good, as far as I know."

"You seemed a little distracted this morning."

Trust Alexander to have noticed. Kawan huffed out a breath. "I am, but it's nothing dire."

"Is it the lovely Miss Melody from Saturday night?" Alexander asked, cocking his head at Kawan.

"If I'd known you wanted gossip, I would have scheduled a meeting," Kawan joked.

Alexander smiled thinly, but it didn't quite meet his eyes. "Are you seeing her again?"

"This weekend," Kawan said, trying not to sound as defensive as he felt. Something about his friend's demeanor was putting him a little on edge. He gave Alexander a look. "Is there a reason for the interrogation, counselor?"

The other man's gaze sharpened, full of challenge. "Is there a reason you consider a couple of perfectly innocent questions an interrogation?"

Kawan snorted.

"Your questions are never innocent."

The growing tension between them broke as Alexander laughed. "There is that." His expression softened, turning to something more like worry, and Kawan felt his stomach flip over as he saw unwanted pity written there. "I'm just... checking in."

The tension might be gone, but now an awkwardness rose in its place. Kawan knew that Alexander was only asking because he cared, because they were friends, but it still felt invasive. Unwanted. But the questions themselves weren't and he knew it.

"We're seeing each other again this Saturday."

"Is she a baby girl?" Alexander's tone warmed slightly, tinged with just a touch of relief. That disappeared as soon as Kawan hesitated.

"She's interested in Daddy Doms," Kawan said. Of course, Alexander had no problem picking up on what he wasn't saying.

"But she doesn't have any experience with them."

Kawan's fingers drummed on the edge of the armchair. "She doesn't have any experience with BDSM period."

"Oh, like that makes it any better," Alexander muttered, running his hand over his face before returning his gaze to Kawan. "Are you sure you want to do this?"

This.

Get involved with a woman who didn't have any experience in BDSM. One who was interested, but had no practical knowledge. It would be so easy to turn her into exactly what *he* wanted her to be, but that wouldn't be what was best for her in the end. But letting her find her own way meant she might end up deciding she wanted something different than he did. That he wasn't enough for her, or too much for her, or some combination of both.

Like Krissy had. If only that was all she'd done.

The little stab of pain in his chest at the thought of his ex didn't surprise him. What did surprise him was that he also felt a small ache at the idea that Melody might follow in her footsteps.

He couldn't possibly be that emotionally involved with her so quickly, could he?

Kawan leaned back in his chair, fighting the urge to cross his arms over his chest and close himself off. Who knew what Alexander might read into that defensive posture.

"We're just scening," he said, keeping his voice even and completely neglecting to mention the date he'd taken her on last night.

"I'm only asking because I care," Alexander said softly.

"I know. Don't think I don't appreciate it, even if it makes me uncomfortable." Kawan forced a half smile onto his face and batted his eyes. "I'm not used to having to answer to Daddy."

Alexander choked and Kawan's half-smile widened to a full one.

~

DAMMIT. Someone had taken her favorite sharpie.

Melody's lips thinned as she cast a suspicious gaze around the lab. It was just her, Corey, and Richard today and, to be honest, she couldn't really see either of them stealing her purple sharpie. Everyone knew the purple one was her special one. It was a true measure of her distraction this week that she'd left it behind yesterday.

But Kawan had been texting her and she hadn't been paying attention to what she was doing.

Everyone knew not to touch her purple sharpie or she would get medieval on them. At least, she'd thought that message had been made clear. She'd gotten a little spastic the last time it had disappeared. It had rolled off of her work station and thankfully had been found before she'd totally melted down.

What could she say? It was better than all the other sharpies and she wasn't quite sure what she was going to do when it ran out.

Corey's blond head lifted and he blanched a little when he took in her expression and angry stance. Although he could be a total misogynist, he was also a little scared of her and Lisa, the other female grad student on their team. They'd had a serious talk with him the first week they'd all had to work together when he'd tried to send Melody to get him some coffee. Since then, he'd done a one eighty and decided the two of them were 'cool,' but he still didn't like to test either of their tempers.

He cleared his throat, sounding only a little hesitant. "What's wrong, Melody?"

"My sharpie is missing."

The expression on Corey's face almost made her burst out laughing. He so badly wanted to roll his eyes, but he was too afraid to, and he was caught somewhere between his fear of her and his total disdain for her purple sharpie. Of course, he had his favorite sharpie too. They all did. Hers just happened to be purple.

"Sorry, Melody," Katherine said, walking into the room and holding out the marker in front of her like a peace offering. Corey immediately relaxed and went back to his current experiments with the flow cytometer, secure in the knowledge that he wasn't about to blamed for the missing sharpie. "Just borrowing it, I promise."

"Mmmm… I'm watching you," Melody teased, taking her beloved marker back. Well, half-teased. She was mostly joking.

Sharpies were serious business though. Especially in the lab. The good ones had a propensity to go missing. It was better that Katherine had it than someone else though. Her mentor would always return it.

Before she could say anything else, the door opened and McCready popped his head in, his beady gaze sweeping over the room. His eyes lit up when they landed on her and Melody had to suppress a full body shudder.

"Yes, Trevor, did you need something?" Katherine asked politely, hands on her hips. The warm teasing that had just been in her voice was now utterly absent.

"No, no," McCready said, smiling unctuously as he shifted his gaze to her. "Just seeing who is around."

Before anyone could respond, he had already beaten a swift retreat.

Melody glanced at her advisor, but Katherine was still

staring at the door where McCready had just been, her lips pressed in a thin line. Then she finally turned back to Melody.

"If he bothers you, you make sure you tell me." She gave Melody a hard look. Melody nodded immediately. Even though McCready had tenure and Katherine didn't, the man seemed a little afraid of her. Heck, right now, Melody was a little afraid of her. Katherine might make a good Domme.

And now she was picturing her advisor in leather with a crop in hand.

She needed to get her act together.

CHAPTER 10

"**A**re you sure you don't want to come?" The question lacked any edge, so Melody knew that Peggy wasn't going to pressure her. Thankfully. The urge to shove her best friend out of the apartment was strong.

She still hadn't told Peggy that she was going back to Black Light tonight.

After listening to Peggy rant all week about Elliott and his 'perversions' and the way Peggy had talked about Kawan when she'd found out he was a Daddy Dom... Melody just wasn't up for it. Her best friend was already on the warpath and taking no prisoners.

Which, thankfully, was also why she was going out tonight. Not to Black Light, but to Runway. Melody was pretty sure Peggy was hoping to either run into Elliott and be able to flirt with another guy in front of him, or flirt with another guy and hope that it would somehow get back to him. If she could get Elliott to beg to take her back, even better. Not that she would if he asked. But any time Peggy wasn't the one to initiate the breakup, she wanted to make her ex 'pay'.

Melody just had to hope that Peggy wouldn't find her way

into Black Light tonight. She'd lied and said she was staying in. There was a little nugget of guilt in the pit of her stomach about lying, but she pushed it away. Sometimes Peggy wasn't reasonable, and she knew this would be one of those times.

She couldn't even imagine how Peggy would react if she knew Melody was going back to Black Light without her. Especially since she was going back to scene with Kawan again.

They'd talked about it on the phone last night, late, after she'd gotten home. There had been a lot to talk about since he'd sent her a limits list to fill out... all the things they might do during a scene, and she was supposed to fill out her interest level. Then she'd been up late doing research online. Because how could she know what she was interested in when she didn't even know what some of the terms meant?

That had been a pretty serious trip down the rabbit hole, but it had also helped a lot.

Even better, she'd gotten a good idea of what kind of things a baby girl might wear, when she wanted to be sexy. Before that, Melody had had no idea where to even start. When it came right down to it, she was used to letting Peggy pick her outfits when they were going out.

The good news was that last week when they'd been shopping, Peggy had helped her pick exactly the kind of thing that would be good to wear to Black Light tonight. The bad news was that she was going to have to try and get into the corset by herself, but she was pretty sure she could handle that.

She just needed Peggy to *leave* or she was going to be late.

Pulling one of the fluffy blankets she kept stacked in a basket by the couch up over her legs, she settled back against the cushions and held up her e-reader. "I'm good. I just need some time to de-stress."

That part was true. Between Peggy's warpath, her usual job stresses which were exacerbated by how distracted she was by Kawan's texts, and the fact that McCready had been constantly popping his head in when she was working this week, she was feeling on edge. But she was definitely misrepresenting how she intended to get that stress relief.

"Okay, hun, I'll see you later." Peggy turned, fluffed her hair in the mirror next to the door, and then sashayed on her way.

Tense, Melody made herself sit still for a whole minute just to make sure Peggy was really gone before jumping up and rushing back to her bedroom. She couldn't help but giggle madly, already feeling like a naughty little girl sneaking around her mom. Was this what 'Little Space' was?

GETTING to Black Light early had sounded like a good idea at the time. Better to be in the club than just sitting around his house, watching the minutes tick by, right? Except now he was at the club and completely uninterested in the many scenes happening around him. Even if they managed to distract him for a minute, after that minute passed, his eyes would inevitably seek out the door, hoping that maybe Melody had walked through it during the brief time he'd looked away.

He couldn't decide if it was a bad or a good thing.

On the one hand, his tendency to jump into things head first, especially if he felt needed, was what had led to his relationship with Krissy.

On the other hand, it was kind of nice to know that the blow up of that relationship hadn't changed that about him. He was self-aware enough to realize that he'd become more cynical since Krissy. But he truly didn't think Melody was playing him. There had been warning signs with Krissy, red flags that he'd ignored.

Melody, on the other hand, was not only genuinely inter-ested in BDSM, she'd actually tried to downplay her interest in

Daddy Doms. If she was just looking for a sugar daddy, she was going about it in an extremely odd manner.

She's not Krissy.

But she was getting under his skin faster than he thought possible. They'd talked every day this week, whether over text or on the phone. After receiving her list of limits this afternoon, he'd gotten to work on planning a scene for her.

One that he couldn't wait to get started.

Glancing at his watch, he realized she was now three minutes late, and he frowned. Maybe she'd changed her mind.

His eyes flicked back to the entrance of Black Light, and the tension in his chest immediately lightened. She was standing there, looking around the club, uncertainty written clearly across her face and in every line of her body. It had been easy to spot her, because she was wearing all white, making her look like a virgin entering a den of debauchery. His cock immediately thickened as heady lust pounded through him in response to the sight of her. The desire to corrupt all that sweet innocence was strong.

Although, she only appeared innocent by comparison to the others in the club, most of whom tended toward darker colors. The pink corset she was wearing had white ruffles on it and a bow on the center of the neckline where it pushed her breasts up and together, making a deep cleavage that tempted a man to dive right in. Her white skirt was loose but incredibly short, showing off the white tops of her thigh high stockings. No shoes. Kawan made a mental note to buy her some white Mary Janes and then immediately dismissed the thought.

She's not Krissy.

They weren't even in a relationship yet; it was far too early to think about choosing clothing for her to wear, much less buying her any.

He pushed those thoughts away and moved toward her with ground-eating strides. There were several Doms already eyeing her and she looked like she might run at any moment, neither of which he found acceptable. Perhaps he should have waited outside for her, but since he'd been early... It didn't matter.

Next time hopefully she'd agree to letting him pick her up or meeting him somewhere beforehand so they could arrive together.

The second she saw him, her entire face lit up, and her obvious tension disappeared. She stood a little straighter, shoulders relaxing, before blushing and ducking her head slightly. Her hair had been put in two low ponytails and her hands went to one of them, stroking the strands nervously. Though the sharp edge of her anxiety appeared to have evaporated, he wasn't surprised to see a little nervousness remained.

Reaching her, Kawan held out his hand.

"Hello, baby girl," he said, waiting until she put her fingers in his before he tugged her closer. She looked up at him and he took the opportunity to brush his lips over hers, making her blush and squirm.

They'd kissed at the bowling alley, but for some reason she was more wide-eyed, more nervous tonight. Or was she just pretending to be? He shoved the little niggle of suspicion away. It made perfect sense that she'd be more nervous in Black Light than on a regular date.

"Hello um, Sir. Daddy." Another deep blush.

Kawan grinned. "Sir Daddy? I'll take it."

That made her giggle and relax again. She looked down at her outfit. "Did... Do I look okay?"

There was a note of vulnerability in her voice that tugged at him, the needy lilt of a submissive who wanted approval for a decision she'd made. That she wanted *his* approval gave him a sense of satisfaction that he hadn't felt in far too long.

"You look perfect, sweetie. Come on. We should talk before our scene."

WE SHOULD TALK.

Those had to be the most hated words in the English language, and if Kawan hadn't had a tight grip on her hand, she might have run right then and there. As if sensing her reaction, he looked down at her and smiled warmly.

"It's nothing bad, little one, I just want to go over the limits list you sent me."

Oh yeah, that didn't sound embarrassing or anything. "Wasn't the point of sending it so that we *wouldn't* have to talk about all of those things?"

Forward motion ground to an immediate, screeching halt, and Kawan turned to loom over her with a stern look on his face. Whoops.

"There are still details to be discussed," he said, his voice deepening slightly and making her body tingle in reaction. "For instance, how many things you'd like to try tonight." His dark eyes glinted. "Or I could just work my way through the whole list."

The whole list? Melody's breath stuttered at the thought. "Talking sounds good."

He chuckled. "That's what I thought." One eyebrow lifted. "And what do you call me when we're in the club, baby girl?"

Warmth heated her cheeks even as it filled her chest.

"Daddy." She barely recognized her voice, it was so whispery and high, but Kawan—*Daddy*—didn't seem to mind. He just dipped his head down for another kiss. Melody's eyelashes fluttered as his lips pressed against hers, much more firmly than the kiss he'd greeted her with. More like the kiss from their date.

Her free hand pressed against his chest as the fingers of her other hand tightened around his. When his head lifted, she automatically went up on her toes, clinging to the kiss. Reluctantly, she lowered back down to her heels with a sigh once their lips parted and opened her eyes to find him gazing at her with a look she definitely recognized.

It wasn't one she'd seen often, but she knew it when she saw it. And if she had the slightest uncertainty about the lust in his gaze, the thick erection pressing against the lower edge of her corset confirmed that he was highly aroused. So was she.

"Sir Daddy is also acceptable," he said, his eyes twinkling with amusement.

Yeah, she wasn't going to live that one down apparently. She was just going to have to get used to thinking of him as Daddy, or at least Daddy Kawan, in her head while they were at Black Light, so that she got used to actually calling him that.

"Can we talk fast, Daddy?" she asked hopefully, and a little breathlessly.

"Absolutely, baby girl." His fingers gave hers another reassuring squeeze before pulling her along. The way he was dressed gave her no clues about what his plans for the night were. He was wearing a similar outfit from last week, slacks and a dress shirt that was rolled up to his elbows. Sexy as hell, but definitely not themed in any way. She nearly squealed when she realized where he was headed—the medical room.

The room was right next to where she'd come in and set up exactly like a doctor's examining room, complete with a padded table and sterile looking counters. Of course, she'd never seen an examining table with restraints on it. A little shiver went up her spine.

"Are we going to play doctor, Daddy?" she asked nervously. That was something she'd marked as being curious about on the list she'd sent him, but she hadn't expected to jump right in. Should she call him doctor instead of daddy?

"I thought starting off with an exam could be fun," he said, giving her fingers another reassuring squeeze before releasing them and giving her a little push toward the examination table. She squeaked as he added a smack to her bottom when she didn't move fast enough for him. The little slap stung pleasantly, making her feel even hotter and wetter. "Now jump up on the table and I'll get your chart."

The almost salacious way he said it had her running and jumping, already excited to find out what he was going to do next.

SEEING Melody's face light up as she hopped up onto the table facing him, Kawan had to hide his chuckle. She kicked her legs, hands curved over the edge of the padding, watching him with an eager light in her brown eyes. She was a simmering pot of arousal, anxiety, and excitement: exactly how he wanted her.

Picking up the clipboard with her 'chart'—which was really just her limits list—he looked down at it even though he had managed to practically memorize it this afternoon. Thankfully, they had a lot of the same hard limits, but it was clear that she didn't have much experience with BDSM, and there were definitely some things about her soft limits that he would like to clear up.

"Let's start by going over the paperwork you filled out," he said, giving her a wink.

"Okay, um... do I call you Daddy or Doctor?" she asked shyly. Then her smile widened mischievously. "Or Doctor Daddy?" Little minx.

"Just Daddy is fine, baby girl. This is an informal examination." Plus, he wanted her to get used to calling him Daddy, although he didn't object to other sorts of role-play in the future. Melody sat up a little straighter—not that the corset had allowed her to slump—moving her hands to clasp them together on her lap. She looked delightfully squirmy. "Let's start with sex. You marked 'interested,' but does that mean interested tonight? Interested sometime in the future?"

He kept his tone almost clinical, but that didn't stop her from blushing and squirming even more. Kawan definitely knew what answer he was hoping for, but he wasn't going to push her. Tonight could end in a multitude of different satisfying ways, no matter what she chose.

Unable to meet his gaze, she stared somewhere around her feet, her cheeks beet red. "Um, tonight is fine."

Heat surged through him, making his cock jerk. To be honest, that wasn't the answer he'd expected, even though it was the one he'd hoped for. Still, whether or not the scene would actually lead there was up to him. He'd wait to see her responses to everything before making the final decision.

"Oral sex as well?"

The adorable little moan she let out left him grinning, and she covered her face with her hands, peeking through her fingers at him. "Um, yes. Please."

"You marked anal as a soft limit."

Her hands fell back to her lap and she made a little face, not of disgust but of indecision. "I like to read about it, a *lot*, but the one time I tried it I didn't like it very much. I was kind of hoping maybe I could try again, but with someone who knew what they were doing."

The hopeful expression on her face as she looked at him made it clear that she hoped *he* might know what he was doing.

Kawan was very much looking forward to proving that he absolutely did. "I think I can make that happen."

CHAPTER 11

*I*t turned out that answering Daddy Kawan's questions wasn't as embarrassing as she'd feared... and being questioned was way more arousing than she'd thought it would be. Melody was pretty sure the white thong she was wearing was completely soaked. In fact, she wouldn't be surprised if there was a sizable wet spot beneath her on the paper covering the examination table.

Still. Her arousal was tempered with wariness. The first – and only – boyfriend she'd allowed to attempt butt stuff had *not* known what he was doing. Unfortunately, neither had she and it had been a painfully unpleasant experience. Her buttocks clenched tightly at the thought of letting another man back there.

But for some reason, she loved reading about Daddies plugging their baby girls, fingering them, and even fucking them in their bottoms. Especially if the bottom in question had just been punished. It was a fetish she didn't quite understand, but she figured it couldn't always be a bad experience or so many people wouldn't be into it.

There had been quite a few things on the list that she'd never tried before but was interested in. Daddy Kawan asked her about each and every one of them, leaving her a hot squirming mess as her imagination went into overdrive... and he hadn't even touched her yet. When he finally set down the clipboard, she sucked in an excited breath of air, and it wasn't just her bottom cheeks that clenched in anticipation.

"Okay, sweetheart," he said, turning back to her with a warm smile that she felt all the way through her. "Time to start your examination."

Before Melody could ask what to do, he had moved in front of her. Sitting raised up on the table as she was, he was only an inch or so taller than her now—and somehow the man still managed to make her feel like he was looming over her. Not in a bad way though. Just a reminder that he was bigger and stronger. It made her feel like he could protect her, take care of her... just the way a Daddy should.

Daddy Kawan's eyes sparkled as he ran his finger across her collarbone and then down to her cleavage. Behind the stiff fabric of the corset, Melody's nipples itched, aching for some attention as if his mere touch had brought them to life. She gripped the edge of the table harder, her fingers digging into the padding as she pressed her thighs together.

His finger reached the top of her corset and traced just above it, making her skin prickle. The little hairs on the back of her neck were already standing up and she felt like she could barely breathe as he ran his finger over the curves of her breasts and back. The entire time, his gaze never left hers, and the way he held her eye contact made everything feel even more intimate than she'd thought possible.

"Let's take this off so I can start my examination," he said, his voice low and husky. "I want to see you, baby girl."

"Okay." She nodded her head and then saw the expression on his face. "I mean, okay, Daddy."

"Good girl."

Warmth swept through her. While part of her liked being a naughty girl, she couldn't deny the effect the accolade had on her.

"Hands down," he told her, when she started to lift her hands to help him. Melody's breath stuttered as he leaned forward, their upper bodies nearly touching, so he could reach behind her and loosen her corset. Now she had to fight against lifting her hands again; not to help him, but because she wanted to touch him and he was *sooooo* close.

But she wasn't ready to be naughty when they'd just started. She wanted to see what he was going to do.

The corset loosened as he pulled at the ties, allowing her to take a much deeper breath than before. She sighed at the sensation, slumping slightly now that she wasn't being forced into such rigid posture. Daddy Kawan's hands slid around to her front again, flexing the corset to open the clasps.

Her breasts spilled out, her skin tingling. That was when she remembered all the red marks her last corset had left on her, and she looked down to see that it had happened again. They weren't as deep or as dark as last week, since she hadn't been wearing the corset for as long, but she immediately had the urge to cover herself.

Daddy Kawan caught her hands.

"Uh uh, little girl," he said, giving her a stern look. "I can see you're going to have some trouble staying still, aren't you?"

"I... sorry, Daddy," she said, feeling a little miserable, because she hadn't meant to disobey him but at the same time she was feeling incredibly vulnerable with all the rolls and swells of her body fully on display, along with the ugly marks from trying to keep them contained. The sitting position didn't help at all.

"It's okay, baby girl. I'm not going to punish you this time, but I am going to help."

Still holding her wrists in one hand, Daddy Kawan used them to swivel her around so that she was no longer sitting sideways on the table, and then the fingers from his free hand pressed on a spot right between her breasts, pushing her down onto her back. She squeaked as her shoulders hit the examination table and Daddy Kawan moved around to the side so that her arms were stretched above her head.

"Remember, baby girl, yellow to slow down and red to stop."

The reminder settled her. There was no way she was going to call for the scene to stop just over having her corset taken off. She'd known that was coming. Feeling insecure about her body now that the moment was actually here was not a reason to safe word. Besides, all stretched out like this she didn't feel as self-conscious of her stomach. She couldn't do anything about the red marks on her skin—but she didn't have to.

She was in the position Daddy Kawan wanted her in. That he was putting her in.

It made everything so much easier, and as he secured cuffs around her wrists to keep them above her head, Melody felt her entire body relax.

APPARENTLY MELODY WAS one of those submissives who found bondage freeing. Kawan noticed the moment her muscles all went lax, softening under his hands. With her wrists secured and her body laid out for him to play with, he could only grin at how utterly delightful she was.

She might not have any BDSM experience, but she'd been drawn to it for a reason.

"What a pretty little girl," he murmured, loud enough for her to hear, as he ran his hands down her arms until he reached her breasts, cupping the soft mounds and squeezing gently. Melody moaned, squirming and arching her back in response to his touch. Kawan ran his thumbs over her nipples, teasing the sensitive buds into hard little nubs for him to play with.

The red marks on her skin from her corset made him frown inwardly, but he kept his expression smooth. He didn't particularly care to see anything marring her skin that he hadn't put there himself. If she became his baby girl, he'd dress her in soft fabrics and ruffles. Definitely nothing restrictive enough to leave marks behind.

"Very responsive nipples," Kawan murmured, enjoying the blush that immediately heated her face. "They're so pretty and hard, I think they deserve some jewelry."

He pinched the tender buds, making Melody squeak, before releasing them and moving over to the tray he'd set up when he'd first arrived, rolling it over next to the table. Melody's brown eyes widened as she took in the array. Kawan decided to leave it where she could easily see it. Just looking at the toys, knowing they'd soon be used on her, should help build her anticipation nicely.

Picking up the tweezer clamps, which were connected by a long chain, he dropped them on her stomach before returning his hands to her breasts. Her muscles quivered under the cool metal, her eyes wide as she watched him cup her breasts again, rolling her nipples between his thumbs and forefingers while he watched her expressions.

"Oh... oh please..." She writhed when he pinched down, tugging gently on her nipples, her head thrashing back and forth.

"Please what, baby girl?" he asked, pinching even harder and twisting a little, making her gasp. Each small increase of pain was met with a surge of lust in her eyes. She was at least a little bit of a masochist.

"Please... Daddy... I need more..." she begged prettily, panting for breath between her words. Her pleading made his cock throb. She was squirming even more, her legs pressed together as she wriggled, like she was trying to put enough pressure on her pussy to get herself off. Naughty little thing.

"Okay, baby girl, I'll give you more."

Kawan gave her nipples another firm pinch and she squealed before he released them. The pink buds stood out from her breasts, practically begging to be adorned. Quickly, Kawan pinched the base of each nipple with a clamp before sliding the loop up the tweezers to adjust the grip. Tight enough to hold on and keep her nipples hard and sensitive, but not so tight they'd be immediately painful.

"Where else do you need more, sweetheart?" he asked, rubbing his hands over her ribcage and down her sides. The red marks her corset had left on her skin were already fading, but rubbing them helped even more. "Where do you need Daddy's help?"

When Melody answered, her voice was higher than before, somehow both girlish and sultry. Her little side was definitely sexual, and Kawan was thrilled. While he could be perfectly happy indulging a baby girl's little side outside of the bedroom and tending to her needs as an adult inside of the bedroom, he'd always loved it when the two overlapped. It added an illicit taboo feeling to the sex, which he thoroughly enjoyed.

"Um, down... um, between my legs, please, Daddy." She was still pleading.

"Down here?" Kawan asked, giving her a kiss just above the waistband of her skirt on the soft skin of her stomach.

Melody groaned. "No, Daddy, lower, please!"

Playing like this, teasing her like this, was sinful torture. Kawan wanted nothing more than to flip up her skirt and bury himself inside of her, but at the same time he was enjoying himself too much to bring this to a premature conclusion. As good as last week's scene had been, it had been unplanned. He wanted this, the first scene that he'd planned for her, to be utterly unforgettable.

Pulling her skirt up so that it bunched around her hips, Kawan groaned softly when he saw the white thong she was wearing underneath. It was soaked with her arousal, to the point where it had become completely see through over her pussy lips, making it clear that she was completely clean shaven. That or she waxed. Either way, the almost transparent fabric clung to her, hiding nothing.

Kawan cupped her mound, his fingers gently rubbing her pussy through the silky fabric. Her hips lifted, trying to push against his touch, seeking firmer contact. "Here, baby girl?"

"Yes, pleaaaase, Daddy!"

He chuckled to himself then because he knew that as much as this was torture for him, it was so much worse for her... and he had no intention of ending her torment any time soon.

WHEN DADDY MOVED AROUND to the end of the table and grabbed her ankles, pulling them apart, Melody cried out in both surprise and aggravation. He could move very quickly when he wanted to, and before she could even form a protest, he had both of her heels pressed into stirrups and her ankles strapped down to them. Now she couldn't even seek stimulation from pressing her thighs together.

"Daaaaddy!" She sounded so whiny and yet she couldn't make herself stop... and it didn't seem like it bothered her Daddy at all.

If anything, the look he gave her was even more lustful than before. He adjusted something on the table and the section that had been under her legs dropped down, leaving her bottom hanging slightly off the end of the table. She arched upwards.

Ignoring her plea, Daddy made a tutting sound at her.

"What a naughty little girl," he said, sending a rush of heat through Melody's already molten pussy. "Squirming all over the place, wearing inappropriate underwear... I can see I'm going to have to give my little girl some hard lessons in behavior."

The urge to press her legs together intensified. Melody was sure that if she could do so, she'd have orgasmed right then and there. She wouldn't need more than the slightest stimulation to go off like a rocket. Had she ever been so aware of her body?

Her nipples were throbbing, her insides clenching, and her clit was so swollen she'd swear she could feel it rubbing against her pussy lips when she'd been able to squeeze her legs against it.

The smile he gave her promised all sorts of naughty delights and Melody whimpered.

When he picked up a small pair of scissors that she hadn't even noticed among all the other toys on the tray—because who noticed scissors when there were nipple clamps, butt plugs, vibrators, and whips around?—her breath caught in her throat.

"This thong is going to have to go," he said, shaking his head. "Little girls aren't allowed to wear such naughty things."

He was going to cut her thong off! Part of her—the thrifty part—wanted to protest that he couldn't ruin her underwear. But the other part of her, the part that was completely turned on by everything that was happening, that loved how he'd taken control, loved how he was unknowingly fulfilling so many of her fantasies, wanted to cheer. Why was having her panties cut off so hot? She had no idea. But she wanted it.

Moving slowly, to give her time to protest, Daddy glanced at her before he actually began to cut the fabric.

Snip, snip, snip.

Now the cool air of the room was like a huge tease on her heated flesh, doing nothing to actually chill her ardor. She was totally exposed, completely vulnerable, and practically melting into a pile of lust at Daddy's hands. Standing where he was, between her legs, he could see every last millimeter of her pussy, and she'd never felt so exposed.

"What a pretty little pussy my little girl has," Daddy said admiringly, erasing any embarrassment she had about being spread wide like this. Not like she could do anything to cover herself anyway. Oh how she loved not being able to do anything to cover herself. She moaned as he stroked a finger down the center of her wet folds, teasing the sensitive flesh, circling the aching button of her clit.

"Please, Daddy, please touch me more... I want... I need..."

The finger slid inside of her and Melody cried out, her muscles clamping down around the intruder.

"Does my baby girl need to come?" Daddy asked, crooning the question as he gently pumped his finger in and out of her hot pussy, teasing her all the more. Melody felt tears spark in her eyes, he was making her so hot and needy, and she writhed against her restraints.

"Yes, please, Daddy!"

"Mmm, do you think you deserve an orgasm when you've been such a naughty girl?"

Oh no. He couldn't possibly be thinking of denying her, could he? Melody's tears overflowed at the very thought.

"Please, please, please, Daddy, I'll do anything!"

She meant it too. At that moment, Melody didn't care what he wanted from her, because if she didn't get to orgasm soon, she was going to die. A body could only take so much before it exploded. With his finger moving inside of her, teasing her, giving her only the tiniest bit of what she so desperately craved, she was going to go insane if she didn't get some kind of completion.

"Not yet, sweetheart... not until I tell you that you can."

"Please, Daddy, plea—"

She didn't get the second please out before Daddy thrust a second finger inside of her, stretching her around the two digits, as the heel of his palm pressed against her swollen clit. Melody screamed at the sudden onslaught of sensation, the tension coiled inside of her bursting like a snapped wire and sending waves of ecstasy shuddering through her in its wake.

Little sparks of pain heightened her pleasure, something tugging on her nipples making her writhe as the constricted buds stung in response. The fingers inside of her pumped, stroking, her body rocking against the rotation of his hand, the delicious friction against her clit sending her higher and higher.

"Daddy! Oh, god, Daddy!"

The waves of ecstasy rolled through her, rocking her, as she rode his hand through her pleasure. She pulsed around his fingers, all of the suppressed energy being expelled at such a fast rate that she throbbed with the force of it. Every stroke of his fingers drew out her rapture, her cries of pleasure echoing around the room until she couldn't hear anything else.

WATCHING Melody come apart around his fingers was beautiful. Hearing her call him Daddy as she did so fulfilled the needy darkness inside of him, filling it with warmth. Moments like this were why he loved being a Daddy.

She moaned as she came down from her orgasmic high, her body shuddering and relaxing, and Kawan allowed his movements to slow with hers. Letting go of the chain on the tweezer clamps, he pressed his palm over his cock, the pressure relieving some of his own building need. Sometimes he wondered if *he* was also a bit of a masochist, considering how long he'd deny himself during a scene.

Melody sighed, her muscles going lax, and she blinked almost sleepily. Her eyes appeared to be glazed with the aftermath of her orgasm.

Kawan was looking forward to winding her back up again.

CHAPTER 12

*S*liding his fingers from her pussy, Kawan shook his head.

"What a naughty little girl," he said in a low voice. "Did Daddy tell you that you could come?"

Melody blinked, the hazy glow of pleasure in her eyes receding with something like horror as she realized that she had come after he'd told her not to. Of course, he'd known she would. When she met his gaze, he winked at her to let her know that he wasn't really angry. He just wanted a reason for some funishment.

Eventually he'd probably put a moratorium on orgasms without his permission, if they continued on this way, but even then it would only be so he could catch her being 'naughty' and punish her in a manner they'd both enjoy.

As soon as he winked at her, she perked up, the satisfied expression on her face sliding into curiosity mixed with anticipation as she realized they were still playing.

"No, Daddy, I'm sorry." She almost managed to look contrite instead of smug. "I won't do it again."

"I hope not, baby girl, but you're still going to have to be punished," he said, shaking his head. Reaching up, he tugged gently on the chain between her nipple clamps, making her squeak and squirm at the renewed sensation. "We'll get to that in a minute. In the meantime, I'm going to take your temperature. Maybe the reason you're being naughty is because you're not feeling well."

Melody's eyes rounded, picking up on his implication without any difficulty, which made him chuckle. Her reading material must be extremely interesting. "My temperature? No, Daddy, you don't need to do that, I feel fine!"

Even though she was saying the right words, there was no mistaking the excitement in her voice. It was mixed with a bit of apprehension, but she didn't appear to be anywhere near saying either of her safe words. Kawan's own anticipation spiraled higher. This scene was all about finding out more of what Melody liked and what she responded to.

So far a little bit of pain, nipple clamps, role play, and anal play were all definitely on the table. And he already knew from last week that she enjoyed spankings.

Picking up the thick glass thermometer—thicker than a regular thermometer, although much smaller in diameter than all but the smallest of the plugs—Kawan put just a drop of lubricant on the tip of it and then smeared it over the surface. It was small enough not to need much. When he looked at Melody again, she was staring at the implement, appearing to be mesmerized by his preparations.

"That's much too big to go under my tongue, Daddy," she said when she saw him looking at her. She pouted at him, and he almost laughed. "And what did you put on it? I hope it doesn't taste bad."

"Oh, it's not going in your mouth, baby girl," he said, adding a little leer as he moved back between her legs. "I can get a much more accurate reading of your temperature this way."

"Ohhh, Daddy, nooo, please!" she protested, sounding more

gleeful than upset. Kawan could only shake his head, pressing his lips together to keep from smiling. He was definitely going to have to set up some kind of scene where she could work out the non-consensual fantasies she apparently had. He was looking forward to playing the big bad Daddy taking advantage of a sweet little girl.

"This will only hurt if you fight it," he said, managing to sound stern, placing one hand atop her mound to hold her in place so he could begin to insert the thermometer into the little puckered star of her anus.

THE COOL, slick rod pushed inside of Melody easily, making her gasp at the sensation.

It didn't hurt at *all*.

In fact, it felt shockingly good. Different—so different from having something enter her pussy. Fuller. More invasive. There was a bit of a sting as it slid deeper, but in a good way. The same way her nipples stung whenever Daddy tugged on the clamps.

"Oooh, Daddy..." she gasped as he twisted it inside of her, spinning it. Her bottom clenched, trying to stop the movement, which only made the sensation more intense. Tossing her head, Melody shuddered as her back arched.

Pumping it back and forth, Daddy fucked her with the thermometer, letting her feel every inch of it. His hand pressing down on her mound, holding her in position, wasn't enough to give her clit any stimulation, but it still added to the overall mix of pleasurable sensations running through her. The tool was long and rigid, not too thick, but definitely not something she could ever ignore. There was a sense of perversity about it, part of her brain felt like it was so *wrong* to be feeling anything *there* and that made her love it even more.

When he slid the warmed glass back out of her, Melody was

left panting. She wasn't aching for another orgasm again, but she was feeling far needier than she should considering she'd *just* had a major climax five minutes before. The loss of everything inside of her made her want to whimper.

"Normal temperature," Daddy said, barely glancing at it, because checking her temperature wasn't truly the point anyway. Melody wrinkled her nose at him.

"I told you I was fine," she sassed, feeling bolder than before. And maybe a little because she wanted to see what he would do.

Smack!

Daddy's hand slapped against the top of her pussy, making her shriek in surprise and pain. The sting wasn't actually terrible, but it was definitely enough to make her sit up and take notice. Well, if she could have sat up. As it was, she jerked against her restraints at the shock of it.

Her pussy tingled hotly and Melody wasn't sure if it was because the smack had hurt or because some perverse part of her wanted him to do it again.

"DON'T BE SASSY, BABY GIRL," Kawan said sternly, giving Melody a look that made her bite her lower lip. Her cheeks were flushed, with arousal and embarrassment. "You're in enough trouble as it is. I was going to start you off with the small plug, but I think maybe the next size up will make you think twice about mouthing off."

Actually, he was lying about that. He'd never intended to use the smallest of the plugs—it was barely bigger than his finger and about the same diameter as the thermometer, but she didn't know that. Considering the direction she was taking the scene with her pleas and protests, he had a feeling that she'd enjoy feeling like she was being punished with a larger size plug.

Her eyes got even wider as her breathing picked up, making

the chain resting on her stomach rattle slightly with the movement of her breasts. It was a beautiful sight. Her nipples were now a dark, dusky rose and swollen in the confines of the clamps, the pink folds of her pussy were glistening with the juices from her orgasm, and the skirt bunched around her hips and her thigh highs framed her bare pussy perfectly. Between her cheeks, he could see the little star of her anus, glistening sweetly from the thermometer's use.

It was a feast for any dominant's eyes and Kawan did his best to commit it to memory.

"No, Daddy, please, I'm sorry! I didn't mean it!"

"Then this will be a good lesson for you about saying things you don't mean," he said mildly, working lube over the surface of the rubber toy. In fact, he suspected she'd been testing him with her sassy response. Testing her boundaries.

He certainly wasn't going to disappoint her by letting her get away with it.

"Ooooh... Daddy..." She drew out the word, turning it into a moan as he pushed the plug against her rosebud. The first few centimeters sank in easily, stretching the little hole quickly, before he met any resistance. She gasped, pushing upward and away from the plug.

This time, instead of using his hand to hold her in place, Kawan leaned forward and lowered his mouth to her wet pussy. Melody cried out as his tongue slid up the center of her folds, tasting her sweetness. He pulled the plug out slightly before pushing it back in, working it back and forth while he began to delicately explore her pussy with his tongue.

She tasted liked sweet heaven and he groaned against all that decadent softness.

"Daddy... oh god... Daddy... ooooh... please..." Melody's hips moved up and down, trying to get more stimulation from his tongue and simultaneously pushing herself further onto the plug. The only way for her to get what she wanted was to also take the toy deeper into her tight little hole. It wasn't the worst predicament to be in, but it wasn't entirely easy for her either.

Especially since Kawan didn't intend to let her come again anytime soon.

In fact, he was going to make sure that the next time she came, it was on his cock.

$\sim$

THE ASSAULT of sensation was utterly sinful.

The burning stretch of her tightest hole trying to accommodate the plug wasn't enough to deter her movements. She could feel it going deeper every time her hips moved down, trying to get her clit closer to Daddy's tongue. It hurt, but it felt so good too. The urge, the need inside of her made the burn not matter as much.

Her body clenched and pulsed, her pussy quivering emptily even as her bottom was filled.

She was helpless against her Daddy's skilled oral assault, needy for more even as her tight ring of muscle protested against being stretched so fully. Melody writhed, her toes curling as the plug went deeper.

There was a sharp, cramping pain that made her cry out, and then it felt like the toy settled inside of her. Melody gasped for air. She felt much fuller than the thermometer had made her feel, making it seem as though there wasn't quite enough room in her lungs to breathe normally.

Or maybe that was just her growing need stealing her breath away.

Unfortunately, as soon as the toy was securely seated inside of her, Daddy lifted his mouth away from her aching pussy, licking his lips. Melody cried out in protest. It didn't matter that he'd already made her come once tonight, she was already desperate for another orgasm. Being partially, perversely, filled by the plug made her feel even wilder.

She stared at her Daddy in dismay, but he wasn't looking at her. He was undoing the straps on her ankles. Before she could figure out his next move, he had her feet out of the stirrups and she was flipped over so that her upper half was draped across the table, clamped nipples pressed against the surface, and her legs hanging down. Her toes just barely touched the floor.

"Daddy?"

"This is what happens to naughty little girls who come without their Daddy's permission."

SMACK!

The hard slap of his palm against her bottom made Melody squeal and jerk. Her nipples burned as the tortured buds rubbed against the table, the sensation almost too much to bear. The clamps had made them ultra-sensitive. At the same time, her bottom clenched around the plug, so that it felt even larger inside of her.

SMACK!

His hand crashed down on the other cheek and Melody threw her head back, shuddering as she cried out.

Her whole body was a confusing mix of sensations, a chaotic tumble of pleasure and pain and she was starting to mix the two up again.

SMACK!

Her bottom stung.

SMACK!

Her nipples throbbed.

SMACK!

Her pussy clenched.

SMACK!

It felt so good.

She was Alice, tumbling down the rabbit hole, and she never wanted to leave.

~

ALTHOUGH HE'D MEANT to take his time, Kawan found himself turning Melody's bottom a nice, hot pink as quickly as he could, because he was rapidly losing his self-control. Giving himself blue balls was only fun to a point. Now he was beginning to feel quite desperate.

The taste of her was on his tongue, her moans filled his ears, and she was bucking against his hand with every hard swat on her bottom. The base of the plug with its pink crystal was nestled between her quickly reddening cheeks, moving and dancing as he spanked her and she clenched around it.

A man could only take so much.

Quickly pulling off his shirt, he undid the front of his pants before flipping her back onto her back. Melody shuddered as he hooked her legs over his arms, moving his hands up her sides to her breasts. She let out a high cry when he pulled the clamps from her nipples, the head of his cock sliding up and down the wet slit of her pussy. The molten heat of her slick folds nearly unmanned him.

He licked at one swollen nipple, which was now bright red, and Melody arched her back upwards.

"Daddy... oh, Daddy, please," she begged.

"Does my baby girl need to come?" he asked, rocking his hips and running the underside of his cock over her clit. As soon as he asked the question, he sucked her nipple into his mouth, eliciting another desperate cry from her.

"Yes! Daddy, please!"

Kawan let his hips move back, the head of his cock sliding down her body to her entrance, and then he thrust forward. He groaned as she shuddered and gasped at the invasion. Her silken heat enveloped him, muscles clenching and massaging his cock as he sank into her. She was so wet, so slick and ready for him, that he was able to slide fully into her with one long, slow thrust.

"Oh, Daddy... oh, Daddy..." Melody shuddered, her pussy spasming around him as he buried himself inside of her up to the hilt. He could feel her muscles straining, shuddering as they adjusted to their new dimensions, fitting her sheathe around his cock. She panted for breath, arching slightly, and Kawan moved his mouth to her other nipple, distracting himself from how incredibly hot and wet and *good* she felt by concentrating on her breasts.

Then he began to move.

He knew he wasn't going to last long, but it didn't matter. He could tell that his little Melody was already on the brink of another orgasm. With her legs spread wide by his arms, her body completely open to him, Kawan thrust hard and fast, making sure to grind against her clit with every deep stroke.

OH GOD...

Daddy was inside of her, filling her completely. Her muscles strained as she panted for breath, sensations cascading through her as he moved. The hot wet mouth on her nipples soothed the stinging burn that the clamps had left behind, the plug in her bottom jostled and bumped with every thrust, and Melody's pussy was clamping down so hard around her Daddy's cock that she was almost shocked he could still move.

Melody moaned, lifting her hips as much as she was able to meet his thrusts. It wasn't very much. Daddy had complete control over her, keeping her spread wide, pressing her down against the table with every thrust. It made a hot, sloppy, wet sound as he pounded in and out of her; she was so wet that there was no resistance to his hard, fast strokes. She wanted to wrap her legs around his body, but she couldn't.

The power he had over her was everything she'd ever fantasized about.

"Daddy..." Her voice came out in a high-pitched plea. "Daddy, I'm going to come!"

"That's it, baby girl," Daddy said, his voice deep and demanding. He thrust in hard, his body pressing against her pussy lips, and he rotated his hips, rubbing himself against all of her sensitive flesh, grinding against her clit. "Cum all over Daddy's cock."

It was the hottest thing any man had ever said to her and Melody threw back her head as her orgasm exploded. Hot bliss unraveled her, Daddy's cock pumping relentlessly as she screamed with pleasure. Her muscles clenched around them, increasing both of their pleasure, and from what seemed like a great distance she could hear her Daddy's hoarse pants as he thickened and hardened inside of her.

The overwhelming rush of sensation made her feel faint, and she sobbed as he slammed into her, holding himself deep inside. Her muscles pulsed, clasping him tightly, pulling at his cock, and she could actually feel him throbbing against the tight walls of her pussy as he emptied himself into her. Shuddering with small climaxes, she slowly descended into a blissful haze under her Daddy's warm body.

Satiated. Content. And utterly fulfilled.

CHAPTER 13

*I*t didn't take much coaxing to convince Melody to come home with him, although she did beg that he hold off on the rest of the orgasms he owed her. She couldn't take any more.

Kawan was genuinely a bit worried about her state of being after the scene. She was almost like a pliable doll during aftercare, smiling and blinking but barely responding verbally to anything. She didn't even flinch when he removed the plug. She fell asleep while he was holding her, allowing him to cuddle her to his heart's content.

And it was his heart that was involved. Already. It wasn't so much that he was falling in love already, but that he could see the potential there. From their conversations over the past week to how well their kinks were lining up, he was almost shocked at how well they fit together. Thinking about Alexander and Sienna, and Connor and Ella, he couldn't help but think that maybe there was something magical about Black Light, even when it wasn't Roulette night.

When they got back to his place, he carried her inside, stripped her down naked, and got her tucked into his bed.

Watching her roll onto her side and hug one of his pillows, he couldn't help but smile. He'd been a little worried about sub drop after such an intense scene, but if she was having a drop, she was sleeping right through it.

After taking care of his usual nightly routine, and setting out a fresh toothbrush for Melody, pink of course, Kawan slid into bed beside her.

Immediately, she abandoned the pillow for his warmth, snuggling into his side like she belonged there.

He was starting to feel like she did.

～

"MELODY. Baby girl. You need to wake up." The deep voice was soft. Gentle. So was the hand rubbing her shoulder. The combination slowly lifted her up out of sleep, bringing her back to her body.

Her deliciously, delightfully, sore body.

When she shifted, brushing her nipples against the sheet covering her, she could feel how sensitive they still were. Her bottom was also sore, inside and out. And her pussy... still tender, in such a wonderful way. The kind of ache that would remind her of fabulous sex for the rest of the day, every time she moved. Maybe even into tomorrow.

Smiling, she opened her eyes and looked up to see Kawan bending over her. That was definitely a nice sight to wake up to. Melody blinked, her brow furrowing as she realized she wasn't still dreaming.

"Where am I?"

The question received a chuckle. "My house, remember? I was worried about you driving yourself home last night."

"Oh yeah." She stretched and realized she was naked under the sheets. Feeling impish she looked up at him. Unlike her, he was fully dressed, in a fitted t-shirt and jeans. Before she could think of a way to ask if he was into morning sex, he was already speaking again.

"I was going to let you sleep longer, but your phone has been going off like crazy for the past few minutes. I've started breakfast too." He dropped a kiss on her lips and then pointed to the other side of the room. "I put some clothes out on the dresser for you and the bathroom is right through there. The pink toothbrush is yours."

One more kiss to her lips and then he straightened up. Melody already wanted to call him Daddy again. She couldn't think of anything he *hadn't* taken care of. Except...

"Where's my phone?" she asked as he walked to the door.

"Down in the living room in your purse," he said, giving her a wink before closing the door.

Melody wondered if she should be mad that he'd left the phone downstairs instead of bringing it up with him. Of course, he would have had to go through her purse to do so. She decided that she liked him respecting her personal items. Better that he leave the phone alone rather than going through her stuff. As attracted as she was to him, as much as she really liked him, they'd really only known each other for a couple weeks now and had actually been talking for less than that.

Sighing with regret at having to get up, she sat up and stretched, taking the time to look around the room.

Not *the* room, she quickly realized, *his* room.

The furniture was mostly made from light wood and all of the colors were earth tones. Lots of beige and tan, although there was a painting hanging over the headboard that showed an ocean scene. Lots of blue there. The comforter on the bed was a dark brown with stripes of tan across the lower half of it and the sheets she was lying on were cream rather than white.

The room was also cleaner than any room Melody had ever lived in. Getting up, she looked around and saw that everything was neatly in its place. Even the surface of his dresser was clean, other than the clothes he'd folded neatly on top of it for her and a leather catch-all which currently held two quarters and a penny. She tried to remember when was the last time she'd seen the top of her dresser.

It had been a while.

But she had to be so meticulously clean in the lab, she kind of liked having some mess when she came home. She could totally be this clean if she wanted to.

Probably.

Picking up the clothes Kawan had left out for her, she couldn't help but grin. The man was risking a hoodie on her? Immediately she yanked it over her head. Maybe he thought she wouldn't want it because it said Harvard in huge letters across the chest, but if so, he was underestimating the allure of a man's hoodie. She had no problem wearing the name of another university.

It was soft and warm inside, the fleece silky against her skin, and Melody sighed with happiness, snuggling in. The only thing wrong with it was that it didn't smell like him. He must not have worn it since the last time it was washed.

The sweatpants were too long but at least they fit her waist. She rolled up the bottoms before shuffling into the bathroom.

Sure enough, there was a pink toothbrush there waiting for her. She didn't even know why she felt so happy when she picked it up.

NOT KNOWING what Melody actually liked to eat, Kawan decided it was best to have a lot of options rather than making an omelet like he normally did for himself. Bacon, eggs, zucchini, pancakes, and a green smoothie. Which was actually three times the amount of food he normally made, but he found himself almost nervous.

It had been a while since he'd made breakfast for a woman. Even longer since he'd made it for a woman he wanted a relationship with.

Waking up Melody in his bed this morning had been supremely satisfying. He'd enjoyed seeing her burrowed into the sheets, looking soft, sweet, happily content and well-rested. Knowing he'd ensured a good night's sleep for her did something for him.

So did cooking for her.

Her phone went off again, buzzing inside of her purse. The urge to at least pick it up and see who was so insistent on getting in touch with her was hard to push down. Hopefully it wasn't an emergency. Although he couldn't think why else someone would be so insistent on talking to her.

It was a relief when he heard her footsteps on the stairs, making her way to the lower floor. The phone was starting to drive him a little nuts, no matter how amused he was by her *Baby Shark* ringtone, listening to it over and over again was an auditory version of hell.

"Your phone is going off again," he called out, keeping his eyes on the stove. Pancakes could burn quickly. He flipped the one currently in the pan onto the serving platter before pouring more batter onto the surface.

"That's my roommate's ringtone," she said, with a sigh in her voice, coming into the room. He glanced over his shoulder to see her putting her purse down on the counter and digging through it. "She's probably wondering where I am."

Kawan was enjoying the sight of her wearing his clothing so much that it took a moment for him to register exactly what she'd said. He scowled as soon as he did. She hadn't told her roommate that she wasn't coming home last night? Before they'd left Black Light, after she'd agreed to come home with him, she'd been on her phone for a few minutes, texting someone. He'd assumed she was doing the usual safety measure that women took when they were going home with someone new.

He didn't get the chance to ask her though, because she was already picking up the phone and putting it to her ear and crap! The pancake was burning.

"Hey, Pe... Peggy... Peggy... *Peggy! I'm fine!*" Melody went from sounding resigned to somewhat annoyed. Flipping the burned pancake into the trash, Kawan decided they had enough food anyway and started moving everything over to the breakfast bar on his counter where Melody had found a seat on one of the stools. She beamed at him as he moved toward her, and then stared at the platters of food he set down in front of her. Yeah, he might have gone a little overboard. "I'm sorry you were worried... No... I um, ended up going to a friend's house."

Unease shot through Kawan, stiffening his spine. Sometimes roommates weren't that close, but Melody had described Peggy as both her roommate and her best friend. Peggy was also the one who had brought Melody to Black Light with her, as a guest. So why was she lying to her best friend now?

She's not Krissy.

That was true. In fact, she was the opposite. Krissy had been thrilled to tell her friends all about him and all the things he did for her... bought for her... how she manipulated him with her requests. The person she'd lied to had been him.

Still, he couldn't help but feel like it was a red flag. One that got his back up.

Was she ashamed of him?

He couldn't remember a time anyone had ever *hid* him from the people in their life. It was not a comfortable feeling.

Pressing his lips together, he started moving some of the food from the platters to the plate in front of her. While he'd meant to let her choose what she wanted to eat, he needed to be doing something, so that he didn't explode.

"I'll be home soon. No, seriously, Peggy, I'm *fine*. We can talk when I get back." She paused as Peggy said something to her. "I'm about to eat breakfast. I promise I'll come home immediately after." Although he couldn't make out what her friend actually said to her, he could hear the tone. Obviously her friend knew something was up and she didn't like it either. Melody sighed. "See you soon. Bye."

With a groan, she ended the call and put the phone on the counter, face down.

"So you didn't tell your roommate that you weren't coming home last night?" he asked.

Ah, crap on a microscope slide. Not literally, unlike at her day job. Examining fecal matter for bacteria was definitely preferable to the current shit show.

How was everything blowing up in her face so quickly?

Oh, right. Because she'd decided to lie to Peggy, go to Black Light on her own, and then go home with Kawan. She didn't regret any of those decisions, exactly, but every choice came with a consequence and that's what she was facing right now.

"No," she admitted, avoiding his eyes and staring down at her plate. It smelled amazing. And the pancakes looked... well, they looked like a very familiar shape. "Did you make the pancakes into Micky Mouse's head on purpose?"

"Yes. Why didn't you tell your roommate where you were? Did you tell *anyone* where you were?" He did not sound happy at all.

Then again, how would Melody have felt if someone had called him and he'd told them that he had a 'friend' over? Guilt and shame crept up her spine, quelling some of her appetite. She didn't feel guilty about lying to Peggy, but she definitely hadn't meant to hurt Kawan's feelings.

"Do you remember the Dom she was with at Black Light last

week?" she asked, picking up her fork and stirring the scrambled eggs with it before peeking up at him. He was watching her rather than fixing a plate for himself, and the expression on his face was not encouraging. He nodded. "They broke up and... well, she was really upset. And pissed. I didn't want to rub her nose in it that I was going back to Black Light or upset her further."

To her relief, some of the coldness receded from his demeanor. "I see," he said thoughtfully. Then his gaze sharpened. "Did *anyone* know where you were last night?"

"Uh... everyone at the club?" She said it as a hopeful question more than a statement, because she had a pretty good idea where he was going with this.

She was right.

"Melody, that was not safe," he said sternly, giving her such a Daddy Dom look that she practically melted in her chair right then and there. She squeezed her thighs together. Without her panties, she'd really rather not get the inside of his sweatpants all wet. "Anything could have happened to you."

"But I was with you," she pointed out, giving him her widest eyes. It probably wasn't going to work, but it was worth a try. "Are you saying you're not to be trusted?"

"I'm saying we haven't known each other that long and you should always put your safety first." His tone brooked no argument and Melody deflated slightly.

"Sorry..." She almost called him Daddy again, right then, because she felt very much like a scolded little girl. The only reason she didn't was because they weren't in a scene. Were they? The boundary seemed very thin.

"You're going to be," he said, in that same tone, making her shiver. "Not today though, since you have to go home as soon as you've eaten. But we'll deal with this next time." Then his voice changed, becoming less certain. "That is, if you want there to be a next time."

"I do!" She jerked her head up, practically shouting the words. She blushed hotly.

Kawan smiled broadly. "Good girl. Now eat your breakfast."

To her relief, his displeasure seemed to be totally gone. Melody dug in and pushed thoughts of Peggy away. That was a problem for Future-Melody. Yeah, it was the near future, but still not something she wanted to dwell on when she was having a good morning-after meal with the man she was pretty sure she was already falling hard for.

The man she wanted to call Daddy.

Only in the privacy of their bedroom though. She nearly choked on a bite of pancake when she pictured introducing 'Daddy' to her dad.

After breakfast, Kawan took her back to her car. She still wore his clothes because she didn't want to do the walk of shame back up to her apartment. Well, she supposed it was still kind of a walk of shame, but at least in sweats she looked like she *might* have just gone out early without caring what she was wearing. Much better than having to wear her corset and short skirt. The shoes were kind of a giveaway though.

One scorching kiss and a short swat on her bottom later, Melody was in her own car and headed home to Peggy—who had texted her eight more times since their last phone call, all asking when Melody would be home or telling her to hurry it up.

Time to face the music.

CHAPTER 14

The only downside to wearing Kawan's clothing home was that Peggy took one look at her and immediately knew that she'd been over at a man's house, not just a friend's. But she hadn't wanted to put her clothing back on either. Especially because she'd seen the gleam of pleasure in Kawan's eyes when she'd asked if she could wear his clothes home and return them on their next date.

Which would be next Saturday. Something that she felt excited about right up until she walked through the front door of the apartment.

"What the hell?" Peggy burst out as soon as she saw Melody, her eyes widening with shock. She stood in the middle of the living room, hands on her hips. "Why didn't you just tell me you were out getting laid? Who was it? Is that why you didn't want to come to the party? Why would you feel the need to lie about that?" Her gaze dropped to the clothes clutched in Melody's hand and a scowl darkened her face. "Is that the corset we bought? Oh my god, did you go back to Black Light without me? How did you get in? Wait, were you meeting up with that pedophile behind my back!"

"He's not a pedophile!" Melody said, after quickly slamming the door shut behind her. That was all she needed their neighbors hearing. Good grief. She planted her fists on her hips, glaring at Peggy. It took a lot to finally trigger her temper, but that had done it. "Do I *look* like a child to you?"

"Oh yeah, because pedophiles never pretend to have normal relationships." Peggy rolled her eyes. "Seriously, you're so naive sometimes. Why else would he want you to dress and act like a child? *His* child. Incest *and* pedophilia, it's two-for-one."

"That's not what it's like!"

It wasn't.

Last night had been wonderful. She'd felt cared for, protected, and incredibly sexy. Even though she'd called him Daddy, even though he'd spanked her, even though she'd felt almost girlish at times, there had been nothing incestuous or pedophiliac about it. This morning Melody had felt better... well, better than she could ever remember feeling.

Happier.

More centered.

More secure.

And Peggy was ruining it.

Peggy rolled her eyes again. "It's disgusting. It's one thing in those books you read, those are just fiction, but doing it in real life... just ugh. Grow up, Melody. The only people who want to fuck someone pretending to be a child are pedophiles."

"That's not true!" Melody barely managed to keep herself from stomping her foot. She could feel herself getting red in the face as tears started to form at the backs of her eyes. Dammit. Whenever she got really angry, she felt like crying and she hated it. People didn't take weepy women seriously. "You're turning it into something that it's not. You've dressed up like a Catholic school girl tons of times, was that pedophilia?"

"No, that was different, that's *normal.*" Peggy glared at her with disgust, crossing her arms over her chest as she went on the defensive. "Lots of people fantasize about that."

Melody glared right back at her, tightening her fingers around the corset and skirt in her hand. She'd known this was going to happen. This was exactly why she hadn't told Peggy where she was going.

Well, that and because she'd been trying to be sensitive to Peggy's feelings, since she'd just been dumped.

Would be nice if she could get the same in return.

"Well, then I guess I'm not normal," Melody snapped back. She couldn't do this right now. The morning had started off so nicely and now... this. Stomping away, she headed for the hallway and the safety of her bedroom.

"You're definitely doing a good job of acting like a baby right now," Peggy called after her. The pressure inside Melody's chest increased as she held back a frustrated scream.

SOMETIMES KAWAN SWORE his mom was psychic, because she somehow always knew when he had a new woman in his life. He couldn't dredge up even a small amount of surprise when his phone began to ring and her name came up on the screen. Since he'd finished up cleaning the kitchen, had already gone for his run, and showered, he had just been trying to figure out what he was going to do with the rest of his day, and he didn't have a good reason *not* to pick up the phone.

If he didn't answer, without having a good reason not to, he'd end up feeling guilty for the rest of the day.

Sighing, he picked up the phone.

"Hello, *Umma*," he said. Although English was his and his sister's first language, his parents still preferred to be called *Umma* and *Appa*, the Korean versions of mom and dad. "How are you?"

"*Appa* and I are doing well," his mom said, her voice cheerful. "I just wanted to call and find out if you're going to come visit us again soon." Despite the cheer in her voice there was a little hint of warning as well, letting him know that the only acceptable answer would be 'yes'.

Kawan stifled a sigh. His parents lived in North Carolina, just far enough that a day trip would be inconvenient and spending the night would be best. It was a problem he'd anticipated when he'd moved north. Still, he had just visited them the weekend before he'd moved.

"I was just down there, *Umma*," he reminded her. "It might be a few more weeks before I can come stay for the weekend."

She made an unhappy humphing noise. "Very well. I will wait."

The impatience in her voice instantly made him suspicious.

"Is there a reason you're so eager for me to visit already?" he asked, moving into the living room to sit down on the couch. Might as well be comfortable while he found out what his mom *really* wanted.

"Because I miss my *wang-ja-nim*, is not enough?" She did a good job of sounding affronted, but Kawan was used to his mother's tricks, and calling him her 'prince' was not enough to distract him. The endearment had made him feel like royalty when he was a kid; now he was wise to how his mom could use it to her advantage.

"I miss you too, *Umma*. And no, it's not. I can tell that you want something."

"So suspicious," she said. Kawan just leaned back against the couch, waiting. After a moment she sighed with resignation. "You know me too well. Fine. There's a young woman here—"

"*Umma, no,*" Kawan said with a groan. He'd really hoped it wouldn't be something like that. As much as his mom never found any woman he introduced her to quite up to her standards, she was still always looking.

Especially after the Krissy debacle. Although, she'd had some really good points about Krissy.

"She's very nice—"

Kawan cut her off again. "*Umma*, I'm seeing someone up here."

Silence.

He rubbed his hand over his face, waiting to see how she would respond.

"I see." There was another long pause. "What's her name? How long have you been seeing her? Is she why you moved farther away from your family?" There was a definite edge to that last question and Kawan couldn't help but chuckle. That was his mom all over.

"Her name is Melody. I met her after I moved up here, and we just went on our first date last weekend."

"Where did you meet her?" she asked.

"Ah... well..." He stumbled over his words, realizing how woefully unprepared he was to talk to his mother about Melody. Although, it was always possible no amount of preparation would have been enough. His father had always said Kawan took after his mom and that was why he made such a good lawyer. They could both be unrelenting with their pursuit of information. Kawan liked to joke that, as a librarian, his mom used her powers for good. Mostly.

"Kawan." The flat tone of her voice was filled with warning, as if the use of his name wasn't enough.

"She was sort of a client, but not really." He said, the words coming out a little rushed. No matter how self-assured he became, no matter how dominant, somehow his mom always managed to make him feel a little insecure. It was probably good for him, but it was never a comfortable experience. "She's definitely not a client now."

As soon as the words were out of his mouth, he cringed

internally. If a client of his babbled to him this way, he'd assume they were guilty of something.

He forgave himself, because he was a little off-his-game this morning. Realizing that Melody had lied to her friend, which had also been extremely unsafe, followed by a phone call from his mom... Sitting up straight, he gave himself a little shake.

Get a hold of yourself.

"Melody's working toward her PhD in Biomedical Engineering. She's very smart." Although a little naive in some ways.

"Is she Korean?" She sounded thoughtful. His mom was apparently willing to overlook the fact that Melody had needed legal help—at least for now.

"No, she's white."

"Does she want children?"

Kawan pinched the bridge of his nose. "We just went on our first date *last weekend, Umma.* The topic hasn't come up yet."

She tutted at him. "You aren't getting any younger, Kawan, these are important things to know."

"Yes, *Umma.*"

"Don't you make 'dutiful son' noises at me, Kawan, I... Oh. *Appa* wants to talk to you. Hold on." It would only be a temporary reprieve, Kawan knew. Now that she knew about Melody, she needed the time to regroup and adjust how to approach him. Fortunately, he'd also be able to use that time to prepare some answers.

"Bye, *Umma,* love you."

"*Sa-lang-hai, eolin wangja.*" There was a muffled noise as she passed the phone over to his father.

"Hello, little prince." His dad's warm chuckle made Kawan grin.

"If she wants to treat me like royalty, I'm not going to argue with her," Kawan teased.

"Smart boy."

Thankfully his dad just wanted to know how he was settling

in at the new firm and what his new home was like. Melody, grandchildren, and dating never came up at all. It was just a breather, Kawan knew, but next time he talked to his mom, he'd be more prepared.

~

FRESHLY SHOWERED and changed into her own clothes, Melody felt trapped. If she left her room, Peggy was going to want to talk about last night. Melody didn't really see that conversation going any better than the previous one had. As much as she loved her bestie, right now she was being a royal bitch. And Melody didn't understand why Peggy had such an issue, but she wasn't okay with it.

She didn't want to fight. She didn't want to have to defend herself or Kawan or what she wanted.

Why was that so hard for Peggy to understand?

Nibbling on her lower lip, Melody stared at her bedroom door. Maybe she was overthinking things. Maybe, now that Peggy had had time to cool down, she'd realize that she was being unreasonable.

Sure. And pigs were doing cartwheels in the sky right now.

This was kind of her fault, she realized. It was so much easier to just go with the flow when it came to Peggy, but that had turned her into a little bit of a doormat. Melody didn't like thinking of herself that way, but the truth was that she was constantly doing what Peggy wanted her to do. Because it was easier. Because she didn't want to fight.

Or, truthfully, because she hadn't felt like the fight was worth it. Was Kawan, and what he offered, worth fighting with Peggy? She really hoped the answer was yes.

Steeling herself, she made herself walk out of the bedroom and out to the living room where she could hear the television blaring. She made a face when she got there. Peggy was watching one of the trashy reality TV shows that she loved and Melody hated.

It probably wasn't a pointed dig at Melody. At least, that's what she told herself.

Peggy didn't even look up at her. She was sitting on the couch, arms crossed over her chest, glaring at the television. Everything about her posture said 'Fuck off'. The desire to confront all the ugly things she'd said slid away as Melody looked at her.

Whatever. Peggy could think what she wanted. She couldn't tell Melody what to do.

That didn't mean Melody wanted to hang out here either.

"Where are you going?" The question bristled with hostility as Melody picked up her purse.

"Out." Melody could have told Peggy that she was planning on heading over to the university and losing herself in work for a while but... she didn't owe Peggy any explanation. Or maybe this was her way of trying to make Peggy confront *her* again so they could have it out? Ugh. How passive aggressive. But also easier than being the confrontational one.

"Back to the pedo-perv?"

"Stop calling him that." Melody whirled around, glaring at the back of Peggy's head, because she hadn't even turned around to fight with Melody. For a moment she pictured herself slapping Peggy across the back of the head, as if attempting to slap the bitch out of her. Ugh. Not worth it though. Talk about a friendship ender. Right now she was doing her best to salvage the friendship, even if Peggy was being a horrid bitch. "I don't care what you think about my relationship with him, I don't want to hear it. Don't call him that ever again."

"Or what?" Now Peggy did stand up and turn around to face her, challenging Melody with her own glare.

Melody pressed her lips together. Normally she'd say a man wasn't worth ending a friendship over, especially her *best* friendship but... it's not like Kawan was doing anything wrong. Peggy was the one in the wrong.

Breaking the long silence with a snort, Peggy shook her head, sending her red curls flying around her face. "I don't get it, Mel. Your parents are totally normal, you weren't abused, you don't have daddy issues—or at least, I didn't think you did—so what the hell is going on? Are you so desperate for sex that you'll fuck anyone?" Shocked, Melody's mouth dropped open and she stared at Peggy. The other woman's voice softened slightly, her gaze becoming pitying. "Look, we'll work on it. You can lose some weight, I'll dress you up, and we'll find you a guy."

It wasn't all that dissimilar from things Peggy had said to her in the past, but suddenly it was like Melody heard them differently.

Her words didn't sound kind or caring. They didn't sound supportive. They didn't sound like she and Melody were a team. It sounded like Peggy wanting to control Melody's life. Something that Melody had been guilty of letting her do in the past. Because she had wanted to lose weight... because she hadn't felt confident enough to pick out her own sexy outfits... because she had wanted someone to help her find a guy.

But now she'd found a guy that she wanted. And he thought she was sexy. He didn't seem to think she needed to lose weight. When she was around him, she didn't feel like she needed to. Only Peggy made her feel that way.

Melody didn't have daddy issues, but she was starting to wonder if she had friend issues.

"I'm going to the university to get some work done."

She moved so quickly that she was yanking the front door open when Peggy's furious response caught her off guard.

"Don't you dare leave, Melody, we're not done talking about this!"

"I'm done," she snapped back, her temper finally getting the best of her. "I'm done talking about this. It's my life, not yours, and you don't get to choose who I date or where I'm going. I'll see you later."

"If you leave now, don't bother coming back!" Peggy practically screamed it at her.

Melody slammed the door shut behind her and stood in the hallway for a moment, shaking. Only the fear that Peggy would come out after her got her moving again. She could not do this right now. She needed some space. To clear her head. To think about what she was going to do next. About Peggy and about Kawan.

Because she was starting to feel unsure about whether she could have both.

CHAPTER 15

$\mathcal{T}$he monotonous work of staining slides for analysis helped Melody calm down. This was easy. Tedious and requiring focus, but also easy. Which was exactly what she needed right now.

She'd arrived at the lab with her hands still shaking, but now they were perfectly steady. Deep, calming breaths had helped to center her. Joking around with Lisa and Richard, both of whom were also in the lab today, had helped even more. Small talk didn't carry messy emotions with it.

Part of her kept expecting Peggy to call, or text, or even show up in the lab, but as the minutes ticked by, she slowly relaxed.

So when, several hours in, her phone finally beeped with a text, she practically jumped out of her skin. A sick feeling, almost like nausea, curdled in her stomach. She was finally feeling better; she so didn't want to talk to Peggy right now. Unless her friend was texting her an apology, which seemed highly unlikely.

She nearly cried with relief when she the text was from Kawan.

Hey, baby girl, I wanted to check in, since—I'm assuming—you forgot to text me when you got home.

Relief was followed by a rush of guilt and also warmth that he'd reached out to her. She had said she'd text him and then she'd completely forgotten.

I'm so sorry. I completely forgot.

She hesitated and then sent a second text, because she didn't want him to think she was flakey.

Peggy didn't take me being out all night very well and we ended up fighting as soon as I walked in the door.

Rather than getting right back to work, she stared at her phone, anxiously waiting for his response. Thankfully he didn't make her wait very long and her phone lit up again a moment later.

That's okay, sweetheart. I'm sorry you fought with your friend though. Next time please try to remember to message me.

Heat flushed through Melody, warming her from the inside out, from her blushing cheeks all the way down to where her thighs were pressed together. She hesitated... and then tapped out the words that felt so right even though Peggy said they were so wrong.

Yes, Daddy.

KAWAN GROANED when he saw Melody's response, his cock immediately hardening.

Sweetly submissive was definitely how he would describe her. Not that tone could always be conveyed over text, but his instincts told him that she wasn't being bratty or flippant.

Good girl.

It was never as satisfying over text message, but he still smiled as he pictured Melody's cheeks turning pink at the accolade. Hopefully, it would please her. He didn't at all like the idea of her leaving his house all soft and glowing, only to return home and immediately lose the satisfaction he'd given her. Would it make things better or worse if he invited her back over?

Where are you now?

The wait for her answer seemed to drag on, although it was only a couple of minutes at most. The entire time, he stared at his computer screen. Thinking about Melody, and all of the filthy things he wanted to do to her, he'd decided to do some online shopping. While he had a lot of the basics, he wanted some things that were special, just for her. And it never hurt to have plenty of backup for the basics.

Especially for naughty little girls who didn't take enough care with their safety. By not texting Kawan that she'd gotten home, that made twice this weekend that she hadn't taking the measures he would want her to... if she were his. Although she didn't seem averse to the idea of being his either. They hadn't discussed exclusivity yet, but he planned to do so when they saw each other again this upcoming weekend. And he didn't get the impression Melody was the type to date around, if she even had the time to.

Her return text confirmed that.

I went into the lab today to do a few things. I didn't want to hang around the apartment with Peggy when she was all riled up.

Getting a PhD was grueling. Kawan shook his head.

He really didn't like that roommate of hers, even though he knew he didn't have much of an impression to go on. Just the fact that she'd laughed at Melody last weekend and had been pretty pushy for a submissive had put his back up. Now that Melody was hiding out at work, he was feeling even more protective of her. Although, since she was friends with her roommate, she really should have let the other woman know she was going out last night. Even if she had been through a recent breakup.

But he didn't like that Melody had been chased out of her home.

Should he invite her over again tonight?

That was the question.

Part of him was worried about jumping in too deep too quickly. Especially because he knew he had a little bit of White Knight syndrome. But he liked swooping in to the rescue... as long as it was merited, appreciated, and not being used to manipulate him.

He studied Melody's text. It didn't seem like she was fishing for an invitation over.

This morning they'd decided to see each other next week, but...

Do you want to go home after you're done? I don't have plans this evening if you'd like to have dinner with me instead.

Kawan looked at the message for a long moment before hitting send. When he did, he felt almost defiant, although the only person he was defying was himself. He wanted to shield her from her roommate. That was a good impulse to have. It was also the kind of thing that had let his last girlfriend manipulate and take advantage of him.

But if he had never met Krissy, he would have had no problem extending the invitation.

And Melody wasn't Krissy.

Thank you, but I should go home after this. Hopefully she'll have cooled off and we can actually talk.

He hoped for her sake that was true. This was better anyway.

Okay, sweetheart. Please call me if you need anything though.

I will! Thank you.

And that was that.

He ignored the small niggle inside of him that wanted to push for more immediately. They'd talk more this week, and then he'd see her again next weekend, and that would have to be enough for now.

In the meantime, he'd buy some things for their next scene. There were a lot of different ways to be a little and a Daddy, and he wanted to give her more of a taste than he'd been prepared to last night.

~

ALL THE WAY HOME, Melody ran through all the rebuttals she had for Peggy's arguments. A lot of them narrowed down to 'I appreciate your concern, but this is what I want, so you need to accept it,' because Peggy didn't get a say in her sex life or who she dated, damn it.

While yes, she wanted her friends to like her boyfriend... well, the truth was right now Peggy was basically her only close friend and Peggy could be abrasive. Unwelcoming to new people. The one time Melody had tried to bring Lisa home from the lab for dinner, thinking that maybe the three of them could hang out, it had turned into the most awkward, quiet dinner ever. Lisa and Melody had both tried, but afterwards Peggy had told Melody that she didn't like Lisa at all and didn't want her to come over again. And that had been that, because Melody felt like Peggy should feel comfortable in her own home.

She tried to remember the last time she'd been out on a date. It had been a while. Another grad student she'd met at a conference... Chad. They'd gone out to dinner last year. Peggy hadn't seemed to have an opinion one way or another about the guy. But it hadn't lasted past two dates either, so she hadn't had much of a chance to.

There just hadn't been enough of a spark for them to try to make time for each other. They'd planned to go on a third date but they couldn't find a day that worked for both of them and then the texts had fizzled out. Melody didn't consider it ghosting, more like the slow withdrawal and eventual death of a relationship that never was.

But with Kawan, she felt the spark that she and Chad hadn't had. She wanted to *make* time for him.

Right now she really wished she were on her way to his house to have dinner and then see what happened next. She had a feeling that would just make everything worse with Peggy though. Despite the fact that she wasn't a confrontational person, outright avoidance of conflict never solved anything. Especially if she avoided Peggy in favor of a guy.

Chicks before dicks though. Sort of. She wasn't going to end things with Kawan just to make Peggy happy, but she wasn't going to neglect Peggy for Kawan either. That was the compromise she'd decided on while she was in the lab today.

Her hands were shaking a little as she unlocked the door. She really did hate confrontations. Steeling herself, she took a deep breath and walked in. And blinked. There was a pile of clothes in the middle of the main room. *Her* clothes.

"Peggy?" Melody's voice was shriller than usual as confusion and a touch of anger swirled around inside of her. What was Peggy doing dumping all of her clothes in the middle of the room?

Movement out of the corner of her eye made her turn, and she saw Peggy coming out of Melody's room, a box in her arms. There was an odd expression on her face, challenging, but also almost gleeful. Unlike Melody, Peggy seemed to relish confrontations. She didn't say anything though, just walked down the hallway, box in her arms, eyes on Melody's face. Anxiety rippled and Melody's stomach churned.

"What is all this?" Melody finally asked, gesturing at her clothes. She clenched her jaw against her anger, keeping her voice reasonable.

"I'm helping you out," Peggy said. Malice threaded her voice as she reached Melody and dropped the box between them, like a barrier. It hit the ground with a clatter and Melody automatically looked down. Her chest tightened when she saw familiar frames and trinkets piled inside of it. *Her* photo frames and trinkets. "If you're going to date a pedophile, I don't feel safe living with you. You're out."

Melody's head jerked up as she looked at her best friend, the woman she'd *thought* was her best friend, in utter shock. "You can't kick me out!"

"I damn well can." Peggy's face was hard, but it softened just a little as she looked at Melody, her voice turning coaxing. "You don't have to go though… just don't date that creep, and you can stay. It's that easy."

Emotions bubbled inside Melody, a chaotic mix that made all of this feel very surreal. She reached for the arguments she'd prepared, even though this wasn't at all how she'd expected their conversation to go. "You don't get to choose who I date, Peggy."

Immediately, Peggy's expression hardened again.

"But I get to choose who lives in my apartment, and as long as you're dating him, that's not you." Peggy's chin went up stubbornly. She gestured at the pile of clothes. "If you're going to choose some perverted sicko over your best friend, you can't live here." Even though she was staring challengingly at Melody, her green eyes flashed with triumph.

It hit Melody then that Peggy fully expected her to fold. She had brought all of Melody's clothes out to show how serious she was, but she hadn't packed them. Everything about her body language screamed that she thought she'd already won. Because that's what happened every time they disagreed about something. Peggy would make a big scene, and Melody would fold.

And there was no reason for Peggy to change, because she held all the chips. This *was* her apartment. She had invited Melody to live there, but Melody hadn't been put on the lease when she'd moved in. At the time it hadn't seemed to matter.

Melody had come to feel like the apartment was hers as well, but it wasn't really, which was why she'd always let Peggy have the final say.

She hadn't gone on the lease, because it was easier. She didn't fight with Peggy, because it was easier. She didn't upset Peggy, because it was easier. But the reason it was easier, was because Peggy made it so hard. It was her way or the highway.

I can't live like this.

WHEN KAWAN'S PHONE RANG, it was a welcome distraction from the loneliness of eating alone. Normally he didn't feel all that lonely when he was having a meal on his own, but tonight he felt Melody's absence. Her presence had made his house seem cozier, less empty. Warm happiness suffused him when he picked up the phone and saw her name.

"Hey, baby," he said, answering.

A sniffle greeted him in response and Kawan immediately stood up, all of his instincts shouting at him that something was wrong and he needed to fix it. It took a supreme act of will to force his knees to bend and sit back down again. "Melody? Baby girl?"

"Hi. Sorry." Her voice was small, watery, and she sniffled again. "I probably should have waited to call you. I'm a little upset. I should have calmed—"

"No, sweetheart, I'm glad you called me if you're upset." He interrupted her but kept his voice low, soothing, even as anger began to build inside of his chest. It didn't take a genius to know that she must have fought with her roommate again. "What happened? Are you okay?"

"She..." Melody's voice hitched. "She kicked me out."

Kawan froze. He felt like he was at war inside of himself. His Daddy instincts demanded that he run to her rescue immediately, bring her back to his home, pamper her, and claim her for his own. But those instincts were being shouted down by his more cynical side, the one that remembered how often he'd run to Krissy's rescue, how he'd done everything he could to make her feel cherished, special, and loved, and how she'd turned on him when he realized he needed to rein her in because she was draining him dry, emotionally and financially.

Melody kept talking though, not seeming to realize there was anything wrong on his end of the phone.

"I'm on my way to the hotel, or I'm about to be. I'm in my car, but I just thought I should call and let you know, since I forgot to call you this morning, and I said I'd call you after I went home today to let you know how it went and—"

She was babbling, obviously upset, but Kawan's brain finally caught up.

There was no request for rescue, no manipulation to convince him to come help her, she was just... following his orders. Relief swept through him, followed quickly by an inner demand to get off his ass and do something.

"Did you say hotel?"

"Yeah, oh, I guess I should tell you which one, huh?" She was still sniffling, but her voice lifted slightly like, she was trying to make a joke out of it.

"No, baby," he said firmly. "You're not going to a hotel." He stood up again, the urge to get up and do something propelling him forward. "You're coming here."

"Oh, thank you for the offer, but I don't want to impose and—"

"It's not an offer, baby girl, it's an order." Despite the situation, Kawan had to work to keep his amusement out of his voice. It wasn't amusement at her, it was amusement at himself, for thinking—even for a moment—that she might be anything like Krissy. She obviously hadn't even thought that he might help her out, despite the situation.

Then again, their relationship was very new. It was probably a good thing that he'd told her to call him tonight or he might not have found out about this until later.

"Oh... I... thank you?" Her voice held a note of uncertainty. "But you should know, I don't intend to try and fix things with her. I'm going to take off work tomorrow, pack up my stuff and put it in storage until I can find a new place."

"And where are you going to stay until you can find a new place?"

"Um... well, that's why I was going to a hotel."

With the stipend she received from her program, Kawan didn't even want to think about what kind of hotel she would end up at. She'd probably have to find an incredibly cheap one and it was doubtful it would be anywhere near the university.

"No. You'll stay with me until you find a new housing situation." His tone brooked no argument.

"But—"

"No arguing, little girl," he said sternly, letting his Daddy Dom side slide into his voice. "You'll stay with me until we can find you somewhere safe and affordable, and that's final."

There was a long moment of silence and when she finally responded, he could tell that her tears had started again. "Thank you, Daddy."

"You're welcome, sweetheart. Are you okay to drive here? And be honest; if you get here and I don't think you were okay, you're going to be in a lot of trouble."

This time when she sniffled, she also giggled, and some of the worry in Kawan's chest unclenched. "I'm okay to drive. I'll be there soon." The relief and gratitude in her voice was palpable.

"Okay, drive safely, baby girl. I'll see you soon."

Rather than sitting back down to eat the rest of his meal, Kawan sprang into action. He'd need to call out tomorrow as well if he was going to help her pack up. And he needed to put the guest bedroom together in case she didn't want to sleep in his bed. And put a plate together for her in case she hadn't eaten.

Even as he wanted to shake Melody's roommate for upsetting her, he had to admit that right now this felt really, really good. He was a Daddy again.

CHAPTER 16

*B*y the time Melody arrived at Kawan's house, she was feeling a little calmer, and she knew it was because she was *here* instead of the hotel she'd originally planned on finding. The whole sum of her plan, before calling Kawan, had been to drive to the closest, cheap place she could find, and then spend tonight looking for an even cheaper one that she *might* be able to afford for a week or two. She'd thought about calling her parents for help, but she already knew they didn't have extra money to help her out either. They'd try though, if they thought she needed it, but Melody refused to be responsible for them emptying out their retirement funds. She'd figure something out even if she had to sleep in her car.

She was still a little worried that Kawan didn't realize what he was offering. It was probably going to take her a while to find a new place. They'd have to talk about it. But for right now, all she really wanted was a hug.

Peggy had turned into a screaming mess when Melody had finally nodded and said she'd find another living situation. She'd demanded that Melody get out *now*. She'd only taken long enough to dump her clothes back in her room, throw some of them in a bag, and then she'd practically run out of there. The whole time Peggy had been ranting about what a shitty friend she was, how she was throwing their friendship away over a man—a pervert—and how Melody would regret this.

Pointing out that Peggy was the one throwing away their friendship, because she was the one who had laid down the ultimatum, didn't go over well. She'd gotten all red in the face, screamed at Melody that she was a pervert too, that she was sick in the head, and Peggy never wanted to see her again. Then she'd said if Melody wasn't out of there within ten minutes, she was calling the police.

Before leaving, she'd knocked on Peggy's door and said she'd be back for the rest of her stuff tomorrow. Melody had even managed to be a bit of a hard ass and tell Peggy that she'd better not touch any of her stuff since her perverted new man was a lawyer. She didn't like to think that Peggy would do anything crazy to her things, but at the moment she had to admit that she didn't really know.

She wouldn't have expected Peggy to do any of this... and yet, she had to admit that she wasn't shocked either. Somewhere in the back of her head, she thought maybe she'd always known that Peggy could be this controlling. The only reason they hadn't had it out before was because Melody had allowed Peggy to control her pretty much from the moment they'd become roommates.

As soon as she pulled into Kawan's driveway, she saw his front door open and he came hurrying outside. Just the sight of him, and the concerned expression on his face, made her tear up again.

She was so glad she was here and not at a motel.

Before she could open her car door, he was already there, opening it for her to scramble out and straight into his arms.

"Hey, baby girl, come here."

The hug was a balm to her tattered emotions, and the tears

she'd been holding off with varying degrees of success finally broke free. She clutched at the soft fabric of his shirt as a sob ripped through her chest. All the hurt, all the anxiety, all the negative emotions that she'd buried because she hadn't wanted Peggy to see her cry, came bubbling to the surface now.

He held her firmly, stroking her hair and making a gentle shushing noise. Just like a Daddy. Caring. Comforting. Protecting. She could practically feel the tension melting away, knew that she could rely on his shoulders to carry some of the burden. It wasn't that she wanted him to, it was that he was taking it upon himself.

Without a single word, he made her feel like everything was going to be okay.

AFTER CONFIRMING that Melody hadn't eaten, Kawan sat her down at the table and heated up a plate of food for her—reheating his own dinner as well. Thankfully he'd made a big batch of salad, spaghetti, and meatballs, figuring that he'd have leftovers for lunches this week, so there was plenty of food to go around. As she was still upset, he tried not to grin over the fact that she was still wearing his hoodie. He liked the way she looked in it though.

"You know," he said conversationally, somehow managing to keep his temper even after she'd told him everything that had happened when she'd gone home to face Peggy. "She can't actually force you to leave, even though you're not on the lease. You still have rights because of the length of time you've lived there."

"That sounds awful," Melody said, frowning down at her plate. She stabbed a piece of lettuce. "I can't imagine it would make for a pleasant living situation and… honestly, I'm not sure I trust her not to do something completely crazy. I've never seen her act like this before. But I've never really challenged her on anything before either." She looked up and gave him a tight smile, but her eyes were sad. "Don't worry, I won't need to be here too long, I'm sure I can figure something out."

"Melody." He reached out, putting his hand over her free one as she shoved the forkful of salad into her mouth with the air of someone forcing themselves to eat. "That's not what I'm saying. You are welcome to stay here for as long as you need, in fact I'll insist on it. I'd rather have you here than anywhere else while you're looking. I just want to make sure you know your rights, in case you wanted to force the issue with her."

She immediately shook her head, like he'd suspected she would. But he'd wanted to make sure. If she'd had an attachment to the place she'd been living in, he would have fought for her right to stay there. Or even if she'd wanted to make Peggy grant her the rights she was due.

"I don't want to live with her anymore." Tears sprang back into Melody's already red, puffy eyes. Kawan's heart ached for her. "I guess I would if I had no other option, but I think I'd rather live in my car right now."

"That's definitely not going to happen, so put that out of your mind right now," he said firmly. Her car? Hell no. Even if she didn't want to continue exploring a relationship with him, he'd insist she stay with him rather than live out of her car. "You'll stay here and look for a new place. In the meantime, we need to figure out how you're going to live here."

She blinked, startled, and he was reminded of the wide doe eyes she had when he'd met her in court that fateful day.

"How... what do you mean?" she asked in confusion.

"Well, we have a few options," he said, keeping his voice even. He didn't want to influence her decision or pressure her into anything, especially not while she was living with him and might feel beholden to him. "We've started exploring a relationship, but this is obviously an unsettled time for you, so I don't want to push you into anything you're not ready for, especially since we're going to be living together for a bit. So while you're living here we can just be friends and housemates until you find a new place, or we can keep things casual here at the house and play together at Black Light, or we can keep seeing where the romantic side of the relationship leads us."

Melody nibbled on her lower lip while he laid out the options and then smiled when he finished. "You're such a lawyer."

"Guilty as charged." He winked at her and she giggled before ducking her head back down to look at her plate. Swirling the spaghetti around with her fork, she seemed deep in thought, so Kawan concentrated on finishing his own dinner, giving her the time to think.

"You don't have to decide tonight," he told her gently.

When she met his gaze, her face was somewhat somber. "No... I think... I know what I want to do. I just also have some questions. I mean, I've read books and we played in the club a little bit, but how does a relationship like this actually work?"

"However we want it to work." He smiled. "We can figure it out together. What works for one relationship might not work for another."

"That makes sense." She bit her lip again, popping it out from underneath her teeth. "I don't know if I want to do the little girl thing all the time. I don't even know how much of the little girl thing I want to do. I'm feeling very... overwhelmed right now." She looked it too, with tense shoulders and a little crease across her forehead that said she was worried about what his reaction was going to be.

She was a pleaser, he was starting to realize, which was probably why she'd gotten along well with her former room-mate. Unfortunately, rather than appreciating Melody for it, Peggy had used and abused that side of her.

Kawan wouldn't.

"Well, we don't have an official date until this weekend, so why don't we settle in and just be ourselves this week without any pressure, and then this weekend we can explore more of the Daddy Dom stuff," he suggested, and was rewarded when she immediately relaxed, her expression clearing and turning into a bright smile. Well, as bright as she could be when she'd had an extremely upsetting evening.

"That sounds good," she said, almost shyly.

"We can also handle your punishment then."

"P-p-punishment?" she stammered out the word even as her eyes lit up with interest. Kawan had to hide a smile.

"Yes, baby girl. For not taking proper care of your safety, going to Black Light and then my house without telling anyone where you were going, and then forgetting to text or call me when you went home this morning."

Her mouth opened and closed, and a mutinous frown began to form. "I didn't tell anyone I was coming here tonight either."

"Thank you for reminding me," he said calmly. "We'll add that to your tally, and as soon as we're done eating, we'll figure out who you can notify of your whereabouts."

Again she started to say something and then snapped her mouth shut, apparently realizing that she was likely to just get herself into more trouble. This time Kawan didn't bother to hide his grin. She looked very much like a rebellious little girl, and she didn't look like she was thinking about her fight with her roommate anymore.

Kawan started making plans in his head. He hadn't finished putting together his online order yet and there were a few things he wanted to add to it, now that he knew Melody was going to be staying in his house for a while. They might not be used, but he wanted to be prepared. And he had some plans to make for this weekend.

❧

SUNDAY NIGHT, Melody decided she wanted to sleep in the guest bedroom. She just felt weird invading Kawan's room when he'd already opened his home to her. Of course, when she actually went to bed, she wished she'd taken him up on his offer to have her sleep with him.

Not only did he take off of work on Monday, but what should have been an awful experience turned out to be fun. Kawan not only stayed home to help her, but he asked if she wanted some extra assistance as well, and when she asked if he knew of anyone available at short notice, he'd called Alexander. She'd ended up packing up her things with the help of Alexander and Sienna, and two more of Kawan's friends, Connor and Ella. They were all so nice. *Fun.* And none of them asked why she needed to move out of her apartment at such short notice.

The only downside was that she felt even more resentful over Peggy being such a controlling be-otch. If Peggy were more like Sienna and Ella, then she wouldn't be moving out right now. Or... well, who knew. She knew that Alexander and Sienna, at least, went to Black Light and were friends with Kawan, so she assumed they knew. But maybe they didn't and they'd be just as horrified as Peggy had been. Melody seriously doubted it though.

Kawan wouldn't let her put things in storage either, not when he had a perfectly good basement with plenty of space. The men took charge of getting her furniture—her bed and dresser and things—down to the basement along with most of the boxes they'd packed up. It was a little depressing to look at the clock and realize it had only taken them a few hours to completely remove her presence from Peggy's apartment.

But since it *had* been Peggy's apartment first and she'd already been set up to live there, Melody had kept all of her own stuff confined to her room.

"So, how long have you and Kawan known each other?" Ella

asked curiously. She and Sienna had followed Melody into the kitchen to help get lunch together. Afterwards, everyone except Kawan and Melody were planning to return to work. Melody had taken the whole day off, assuming it would take her much longer to pack everything up, and Kawan had told her he'd done the same.

"Um... a couple weeks," Melody said with a blush. She looked at the other two women a little helplessly. "I didn't... he didn't..." She took a deep breath. "I didn't ask him if I could move in here, he pretty much insisted."

"Oh, don't worry, I'm not blaming you if Kawan's moving fast," Ella said. She exchanged a meaningful glance with Sienna. "We both know what it's like with these men. Once they get an idea in their head, it's impossible to get it out."

"Did you and Conner get together really quickly too?" Melody pulled the deli meats and cheeses out of the fridge, along with a head of lettuce and a tomato. Sienna held her hands out for the veggies, taking charge of those.

Laughing, Ella moved over to the cupboard to get out some glasses. "Sort of. We knew each other for a long time before we got together, and we did *not* get along, but once he decided he wanted me..." She shrugged, her eyes sparkling. "Well, it happened really fast."

"Alexander and I happened really fast too, although we took our time about getting engaged," Sienna said, glancing over her shoulder and grinning. Placing the rinsed veggies down on the cutting board Melody had pulled out for them, she grabbed a knife from the block to start cutting. "But once a Daddy knows what he wants, he goes for it, and we're just along for the ride."

Melody froze. "A... a.... Alexander is..."

"My Daddy." Sienna said it matter-of-factly, like it was the most normal thing in the world. Filling up the water glasses, Ella didn't even blink at what Sienna was saying. "Although, really, I was always more of a service sub, but he's a total Daddy

Dom and I have to admit, it's grown on me." She gave Melody a sidelong glance. "You were at Black Light so you know what I'm talking about, right?"

"I hope so, because Kawan is a total Daddy Dom," Ella interjected, grinning. "Conner likes to be my Daddy sometimes, but not all the time. I don't think Kawan ever does anything else."

It felt like the air had been knocked right out of Melody. This whole conversation felt surreal. Especially after yesterday, when Peggy had been so awful, and now these two women were talking about Daddy Doms like they were no big deal. Totally normal. Even though she knew Sienna was kinky, for some reason Melody hadn't quite expected that.

"Yeah, I know what you're talking about," Melody said, blushing furiously.

Sienna laughed. "Just didn't expect us to be so open about it, I guess? You'll get used to it, if you're going to hang around us."

She winked at Melody, as if to say that she was looking forward to having Melody hang around with them.

And that was when Melody started to suspect that breaking up with Peggy—because that's what it felt like right now—might have been the best decision she'd ever made.

THE LAST TIME Kawan had lived with a woman, it hadn't gone well.

Krissy had played at submission, but mostly she'd wanted to take. She rarely gave. There had been times when Kawan had dreaded going home, because he was so tired and all he'd wanted to do was relax. Something she'd made impossible.

A good baby girl should take care of her Daddy too. Caring for her should feed his soul, make him feel replenished, not leave him drained and exhausted.

Living with Melody, even though they hadn't added the

Daddy and baby girl dynamic yet, was already more fulfilling during the first week than living with Krissy had ever been. They woke up at the same time and he made sure she had breakfast, after he realized she was liable to skip food in favor of coffee if he didn't make sure she ate something. In return, she always had his cup of coffee ready, with just the right amount of milk, as soon as he was done putting together something for them to eat.

And she ate whatever he put in front of her. If they were both rushing, she downed cereal as happily as she'd eaten the Mickey Mouse pancakes he'd made her over the weekend. Then she thanked him with gratitude in her eyes. Shivered when he kissed her.

Sent him off to work with a smile on his face.

She worked even later than he did, so he made dinner for them too, and then she insisted on cleaning up so that he could relax. Instead, he helped her so they could both sit on the couch and relax. Rub each other's feet. Talk about their day. Decompress.

It was almost everything he wanted out of a relationship with her, except that the first night she'd chosen to sleep in the guest bedroom and things had remained that way the rest of the week. Other than kisses and a little bit of groping—as well as five hard swats on her bottom after she spanked him while he was bending over and then ran away—they didn't do anything sexual at all.

Kawan didn't want to push her while she was reliant on him for housing and Melody didn't bring it up.

The only time he said anything about it at all was to ask her if she still wanted to go to Black Light on Saturday, or if she'd be interested in exploring some of the different aspects of being a baby girl throughout the whole weekend. Blushing, she said she'd like to stay home and try being a baby girl.

Friday couldn't come soon enough.

CHAPTER 17

*T*he difference between living with Kawan and Peggy was night and day. Melody hadn't even realized how much of the home burden she'd assumed while she was living with Peggy until it was no longer there. The past week had been a revelation, in more ways than one.

She was so much more relaxed. She was no longer the only one keeping the living spaces clean, no longer making all the meals, no longer walking on eggshells to keep someone else happy. Of course, she didn't want Kawan to regret offering a place to stay while she searched for a new apartment, but she didn't feel like she was on edge just because of that. Yes, she wanted him to be happy with her, but she wasn't full of anxiety and worrying that he wasn't.

Peggy had always made it very clear when she was unhappy with something, which she was on a regular basis.

She doubted that Kawan would hesitate to make it clear if he was unhappy, and so far he hadn't done so. It was a whole week without having to listen to any negativity. No daily list of complaints that she had to tune out, no snide gossip about people she didn't know, interspersed with cutting judgments on those people, and not a single statement that she had to brush off or feel bad about.

The difference made her entire day better, from the moment she woke up to the moment she went to sleep.

Without having to expend energy on placating Peggy, on smoothing Peggy's blunt edges, and on taking care of the food at the apartment, Melody felt more alert and energetic than ever. She was getting a ton of work done during the day, getting more sleep at night, and still had plenty of time to daydream about Kawan.

Daydream was about all she was doing, because other than some seriously panty-melting kisses and heavy petting, he wasn't doing much more than that. Something gentlemanly about not taking advantage of her situation, blah blah blah. Even after she indicated that she would really be one hundred percent okay with him taking advantage of the situation.

There was also something kind of hot about being denied though.

Yeah, she was a bit of a headcase.

But she was also happy.

Mostly.

A very small part of her still felt a little guilty about the fallout with Peggy for some reason. Or maybe she was just feeling guilty about how relieved she was to be away from Peggy. It was hard to sort out her feelings toward the other woman.

She'd been there when Melody had needed her. Had been one of Melody's main sources of support for so long and even now there were times when Melody unthinkingly pulled out her phone to text her or would see something and think 'Oh, I need to tell Peggy about that later!'

But at the same time, Melody was happier than she'd been in a long time.

Thankfully, she had Kawan to distract her. Not just him,

either; she was spending more time with other women. Katherine had come into the lab on Wednesday and ended up going out to happy hour at the end of the day with Melody and Lisa—just the ladies of the lab. Ella and Sienna had been texting her all week. She'd told them that she and Kawan wouldn't be coming to Black Light that weekend, but she'd made plans to go out with Sienna next week. Ella would be in California with Connor for a few weeks, but they'd see each other again when she got home.

Melody knew very well that if she was still living with Peggy, she wouldn't have made those plans. She would have had to hurry home to make dinner for Peggy on Wednesday, and she wouldn't have wanted to tell her friend that she'd gone out with other friends. She wouldn't have felt okay making plans with new friends without inviting Peggy along, and she would not have felt comfortable introducing Peggy to Sienna and Ella.

In some ways it felt like she'd gone through a breakup and was on the rebound.

Except that Kawan was definitely *not* a rebound.

And it was *finally* Friday.

Which meant she was a bundle of nerves. Packages had been showing up to his house all week, but he wouldn't tell her what was in them. He just whisked them away to the second guest room, which had also been locked all week, and told her that she'd find out 'soon enough'. Melody had a feeling that 'soon enough' was today and her imagination was running wild.

After all, they were going to be 'exploring' this weekend. She wasn't entirely sure what that would entail, but she knew she was looking forward to it. All week long, in the very little free time she had, she'd been reading all her favorite books and then daydreaming about what 'exploring' they might do.

"Earth to Melody, come in Mel..." Lisa's sing-song voice knocked her out of the daydreaming she was currently doing. The blonde laughed when she saw Melody's expression. Grinning, she pointed at the slide in Melody's hand. "I know the day is almost over, but I thought you might want to do something with that."

"I do," Melody said, giving herself an all body shake. "Thanks. I'm just... super distracted right now."

"Everything okay?" The slight look of concern on Lisa's face touched Melody. While they'd been working together in the lab for a while, this was the first week that Melody had really tried to bond with her outside of it since that first dinner she'd invited Lisa to hadn't really worked out. That Lisa hadn't written her off completely was kind of a miracle, when she thought about it.

"Yeah, just looking forward to the weekend." Even as she said the words, she felt a blush spread across her face.

Lisa laughed and winked at her. "Hot date? I'm jealous."

"Please," Melody said, snorting a little. "Like you couldn't have a hot date if you wanted." Lisa was gorgeous, in the girl-next-door kind of way that drove men nuts. She was also smart, funny, and friendly. There was no doubt in Melody's mind that if she wanted a guy, she merely needed to indicate her interest.

"Well, thank you," Lisa said easily. That was another thing—Lisa was confident. She didn't try to downplay anything about herself or fish for compliments. Melody wished she had half the other woman's self-assurance. "And you're right, I probably could, but I don't just want *a* hot date, I want a hot date with the *right* guy. So far I haven't met him yet." She said it matter-of-factly, not sadly, which made Melody smile.

"Not like it's easy to find time right now either," Melody commiserated.

"Truth. I'm going to be here late tonight. Speaking of, I'm going to go grab a snack from the vending machine, do you want anything?"

"I'm good thanks. Just trying to get out of here."

Lisa flashed her an understanding grin before picking up her purse and leaving the room. Shaking her head at herself, Melody put the slide on the microscope. She was almost done with checking this batch of cultures for the proteins they had isolated and then she could go home.

Home. Kawan. Daddy.

A pleasurable flush of anticipation swept through her.

Focus Melody. Work first.

She was bending over the microscope when she heard the door open behind her. "That was fast."

The vending machine was on a different floor and down several halls. She frowned, turning to look because either Lisa had forgotten something or it wasn't Lisa.

"Fast?" The overly smooth tone of Professor McCready's voice made her wince. Ugh. Of all the people she thought it might be, he was the least welcome.

"Professor McCready," she said politely, a mask of civility falling over her expression. "Sorry, I thought you were someone else."

"Did you?" He stepped into the room, closing the door behind him, and Melody straightened as wariness made her anxiety spike. The guy creeped her out way too much for her to try and ignore him when he was alone in the room with her.

Please hurry back, Lisa.

ALTHOUGH HE WAS FAIRLY certain he was in the correct building, Kawan was otherwise lost. Apparently whoever had designed the building just assumed that everyone would know where to go, with no need for signs. Because it was late in the day, so far he hadn't found anyone he could ask for directions either.

Hearing a strange clunking sound, he moved toward it, hoping that the sound belonged to a person.

He almost felt like cheering when he turned the corner and

saw a blonde standing at a vending machine, bending over to pick up whatever she'd just bought. The sound he'd heard must have been her food dropping into the tray below.

"Excuse me," he said, swiftly walking up behind her.

The blonde screamed and jumped, whirling around with her hand on her chest. Brown eyes glared at him. "Oh my goodness, you nearly made me pee myself!"

Kawan managed not to laugh at the blunt statement, but it was a close thing. "I'm sorry, I didn't mean to."

"Well, I hope not; that would be really mean if you did." She peered up at him, a slight look of suspicion on her face. "What do you need?"

"I'm looking for this lab," he said, holding out the piece of paper he'd copied Melody's information onto. "But I'm not sure I'm even in the right building."

One glance had her frowning. "Why that lab?"

"My girlfriend, Melody Williams, is there. Well, hopefully. She should be finishing up soon. I wanted to surprise her."

Immediately, the blonde's expression cleared, and she gave him a sunny smile. "Ah ha! You're Melody's weekend plans, huh? Well no wonder she's been distracted today. Come on, I'm headed back there right now."

She started walking and Kawan hastily moved to keep up with her.

The blonde hair and her apparent familiarity with Melody gave Kawan the clues he needed. "Are you Lisa?"

She brightened, nodding. "Melody mentioned me? That's awesome. I like her a lot, although we haven't really hung out much until this week." That was said with a sidelong glance as she stopped in front of an elevator and punched the up button. Well, that explained it; he was on the wrong floor. Lisa looked at him curiously. "Melody has no idea you're coming?"

The elevator arrived and they got in. He was only two floors off apparently.

"No, I wanted to surprise her, although I'll wait for her to finish whatever she needs to do."

"That's so sweet." Lisa grinned, putting her hand over her heart again, but for an entirely different reason this time. "I know she's almost done. She keeps getting all day-dreamy for some reason though." She winked at him. "I bet your actual presence will give her the motivation to focus on finishing up."

So Melody was a little distracted today? Good to know. Kawan grinned. He'd been distracted today too, hence the cutting out of his own job early to come and surprise Melody. He'd worked through lunch to get everything done and be able to leave faster.

"That's good to hear," he said.

The elevator doors opened and Lisa moved forward. "Right down here. I'll go in first and then you can follow me. I want to see her face!"

She practically skipped down the hall in front of him with infectious enthusiasm. Kawan had already been looking forward to surprising Melody; now he found himself grinning widely as he watched her friend come to a stop at one of the doors. Then, as she looked through the door's window into the room, her body stilled.

"That bastard," she muttered under her breath, jerking the door open.

Sensing something was wrong, Kawan immediately picked up his pace, coming through the door to see Melody standing stiffly with an older man next to her. The blank expression on her face combined with how closely the man was standing to her, invading her personal space, whipped up a fury inside of him although he didn't let it show. First he needed to know what was going on.

Then, if he needed to, he'd tear the man apart.

"Professor McCready, did you need help with something?" Lisa asked, her tone challenging.

167

"Just stopping by to say hello," McCready said, smiling without any hint of discomfort. Obviously he felt perfectly fine with the situation, even when he looked past Lisa and saw Kawan standing there. "And who is this?"

"Melody's boyfriend," Kawan said. A flicker of relief crossed her expression as he moved further into the room, coming up behind her. The professor stepped back, a small furrow appearing between his eyebrows when Kawan pulled Melody in for a quick kiss. Wrapping his arm around her, he maneuvered them so that she was slightly behind him and he stood between her and the professor. "Hello, sweetheart."

"Hi um, D-dear," she stammered out. From the way she blushed, Kawan was fairly certain she'd almost called him Daddy, right in front of Lisa and the professor, which was a measure of how thrown off she was. By his presence, or by the professor's? Kawan didn't like the way the man was frowning at them. "What are you doing here?"

"I wanted to surprise you." He winked down at her. "And I didn't want to wait to see you."

Melody relaxed against him, snuggling into his side as a smile slowly spread her lips. She still looked a little worried though.

"Are you another student?" The professor asked in an almost aggressively haughty tone. Kawan was certain the other man hoped he was, because he was obviously looking to retain some sort of power in the situation.

Since Melody had never mentioned the man to him, Kawan wasn't entirely sure who the man was or what his problem was, but he could guess. He smiled at the professor, using what Sienna called his 'shark smile'—she'd seen him use it when meeting with the opposition. Lots of teeth and lots of intimidation, and it never reached his eyes.

"No, I'm a lawyer with Lambert, Urbanski, and Reed," he said silkily. "They brought me in to work on their civil cases. You know, suing institutions for things like unsafe work environments, preventable accidents, sexual harassment. That kind of thing."

The professor paled. Out of the corner of his eye he could see Lisa giving Melody a thumbs up and mouthing something to her. He couldn't be sure, but it looked like 'He's hot'. Well, he was happy Lisa approved.

"I ah, good. That's good." The professor stepped back, nodding his head up and down as he continued to back away. "Very good. I... good. It was nice speaking with you, Miss Williams. You're doing good work here."

Apparently realizing that he sounded like an idiot, the man managed a sickly smile before fleeing from Kawan's hard gaze.

"So hot!" Lisa mouthed at Melody, putting the back of one hand to her forehead and acting like she was swooning. Melody's lips twitched, but she couldn't disagree.

Kawan had made Professor McCreepy run away with nothing more than a few words. Not that Melody had any proof of wrongdoing. He'd been standing way too closely to her but that wasn't something she could take to the school board. Close standing was creepy, but not actionable. Especially against a tenured professor.

Still, after the way he'd just run away, she had to hope that he'd be less of a creeper from now on. He'd definitely been intimidated by Kawan.

And it *had* been really hot to watch Kawan go all lawyer on him.

Although, when Kawan turned his gaze on her, she winced a little as he frowned sternly. There was definitely some Daddy shining through there.

"Was that man harassing you?" he asked, his voice steely.

"Not exactly," Melody said with a sigh. "He's very careful to not cross the line into actual harassment. Well, at least with me." She looked over at Lisa, who shrugged in agreement.

"He's a total perv, but he's good at toeing the line and talking around things," Lisa agreed. "The fucker."

Melody snorted and even Kawan chuckled, relaxing slightly. "Well, tell me if he bothers either of you again. Or if you hear of him bothering someone else. I'd be perfectly happy to have a talk with him about appropriate behavior."

Leaning into him, Melody felt her pussy quiver. Yup. So hot.

He looked down at her and his gaze softened. "Go finish up your work so we can go home, baby girl."

"Yes... yes, okay," she said, barely managing to keep from saying 'yes, Daddy' to him. While Lisa was definitely becoming a friend, Melody was so not ready to out herself like that in front of the other woman. Who knew how she would react.

She just wanted to finish up her work and go home so that Kawan could be her Daddy all weekend. Melody was ready to explore.

CHAPTER 18

$\mathcal{W}$hile Kawan was driving them back home, he put on Disney songs in the car. Melody sang along and was feeling very in touch with her little girl side by the time they got to the house, which she was pretty sure was the point. It made her giggle every time Kawan sang along with the men's parts, because he did all the voices too—including during *Be A Man*. He had a really nice voice.

When he parked, Melody started to undo her seat belt, only to be stopped by Kawan's hand covering hers.

"No, little girl," he said gently but firmly. "You sit there and wait for me to come let you out."

Oh. Melody's thighs clenched and her pussy pulsed in response. There was a small part of her that wanted to protest at not being able to do such a simple thing but... that was the point, wasn't it? To give him complete control, to let him take care of her.

He sat there, watching her, dark eyes full of patience as he waited for her response.

"Okay, Daddy," she whispered, and she swore she felt a little mental shift inside her head. He was her Daddy, which meant he was going to take charge of her.

She tried not to fidget with anticipation as he walked around the car to open the door. Leaning over her, he unbuckled her seatbelt and helped her out of the car. Was such a small thing supposed to leave her feeling breathless? Or maybe it was just the excitement at this clear and distinct sign that the weekend she'd been fantasizing about all week was finally beginning.

As soon as she got out of the car, she bounced up and down with excitement, making Kawan chuckle.

"Okay, baby girl," he said, taking her hand firmly in his. Despite how calm he appeared, Melody could hear the anticipation in his voice as well. "Let's get this weekend started."

Leading her into the house, he took her straight to the room she hadn't been allowed in all week, and Melody could barely contain her glee at finally getting to see what was inside. She truly felt like a little girl as she hopped up and down impatiently while he unlocked the door. Normally she would have tried to contain her reaction, but Daddy's obvious enjoyment of her enthusiasm encouraged her to do *more*, not less.

With a smile, he opened the door and she practically vaulted inside.

She gasped, her hands going over her mouth as she took in the room.

It was more than a little girl's room; it was a room fit for a princess. The walls were lavender, the canopy bed was white with violets, and white lacy curtains were drawn back from the windows. There were half full shelves of stuffed animals and toys, a bookshelf with everything from children's picture books to small chapter books, and a large white armoire took up one full corner of the room.

"What do you think, baby girl?"

"It's *perfect*." She especially loved all the purple, since it was her favorite color. Something he'd obviously kept in mind when he'd been setting the room up.

She ran over to the bed, putting one hand around the post and looking up at the canopy. When she was a little girl, she'd had a similar bed and she'd loved it. She couldn't believe that he remembered her mentioning that in passing. Tears sparkled in her eyes as she looked back over her shoulder at him. "I can't believe you did all of this."

It was an incredible amount of effort and thoughtfulness, all of which he'd kept hidden from her.

Leaning against the doorframe, hands in his pockets, he was watching her with a combination of pleasure and lust, and Melody felt her own body heat in response. Her fantasies were coming to life. What was he going to do next?

SEEING Melody's joy in her little room was everything Kawan could have hoped for. He'd left plenty open for her own touches, but he'd wanted to have the basics put together. It might be a little presumptuous, designing the room especially for her when their relationship was still so new and they had barely started exploring what kind of little she was, but he hadn't been able to help himself.

Something in her expression changed, a furrow creasing her brow, and Kawan raised his eyebrows at her. "Something wrong, little girl?"

"Um..." She looked down at the bed, nervously running her hand up and down the metal post. Kawan wondered if she'd seen the special design that would allow him to easily attach cuffs or anything else he'd like to the bed. "Am I going to be sleeping in here from now on?"

Her voice was a little higher and softer than usual, and definitely not as happy as it had been a minute ago.

"Not if you don't want to," he said easily. "If you'd prefer to sleep in Daddy's bed at night, then we'll only use this one for naps."

She'd brightened up as soon as he'd told her that she didn't have to use it at night, which pleased him because honestly he didn't want to be separated from her either, but then she frowned.

"Naps?"

"Oh, yes." Kawan pushed himself off of the doorframe, stalking into the room and over to her. Her eyes widened as he moved closer, making her look a little bit like a deer-in-head-lights as she froze. "Sometimes little girls require naptime."

"Hmm." Melody bit her lower lip, but she didn't argue with him.

"Just try it," he said, cupping his hand under her chin to lift her face up to him. Her expression immediately softened, her tension easing. "This weekend is about finding out what kind of little you are. I'm going to want you to try some things that may not appeal to you at first, and we may never do them again after this weekend, but at least this way you'll know. Can you do that for me?"

Her breathing had changed while he spoke, her pupils dilating. Melody was turned on by even that small show of dominance. Probably also because she was wondering exactly what he would have her do this weekend. She nodded.

"I need the words, baby girl. What do you say?"

"Yes, Daddy, I'll try." The words came out breathless with excitement and she blushed as she realized how eager she sounded. Kawan grinned, lowering his mouth to hers for a deep kiss, a reward for being a good girl. There'd been other kisses during the past week, but not like this one.

Deep. Possessive. Demanding.

Melody mewled against his lips as his tongue delved

between hers, claiming her mouth. His cock filled, hardening so fast he could almost feel the blood rushing to the organ.

Which was why he had to end the kiss before he was ready to. Otherwise he was going to become distracted. He hadn't controlled himself all week just to lose it now. He had plans.

"Okay, baby girl, let's get you ready for tonight." Her eyes lit up with anticipation and Kawan chuckled, wondering exactly what she was going to think when she found out what he wanted. "Sit down on the bed."

While she was following his order, Kawan went over to the armoire where he had some of what he needed. When he turned around, a lavender colored frilly dress in one hand and a diaper in the other, Melody's mouth popped open.

"A diaper?" Her voice went so high and shrill that it broke on the word and he almost had to laugh.

"I thought we'd start the weekend off with the youngest you can go and let you grow up a little each day." Kawan gave her a look. "Remember what I said about trying?"

"But..." She bit her lip and then looked at him pleadingly. "A diaper isn't sexy. I mean, I've read about them being used but..."

Interesting.

"Some baby girls prefer to separate their little side from sex completely," Kawan told her, noting the disappointed slump to her shoulders. "But it sounds like you are more interested in having a sexual component even when you're little."

Her shoulders hunched inward, a shamed blush reddening her cheeks. "I mean..."

"That's not a bad thing, sweetheart," he said soothingly, moving over to the bed. He sat down next to her, putting down the diaper and dress so that he could rub her shoulders, soothing away the tension. "It's just two different ways we can do this. Do you want your little play to be sexual?"

Despite her blush, she nodded, looking down at her hands.

Then she peeked at him, head tilting to the side. "Does that mean I don't have to wear the diaper?"

Kawan chuckled. "Oh no, baby girl. You're still going to wear the diaper. You're just going to wear it a little differently."

~

DAMMIT. Melody wasn't sure how she felt about actually being diapered.

But he'd told her that he wanted her to try things, so she didn't want to wuss out on the very first thing he wanted her to try. And it wasn't like a diaper was painful or anything. Just embarrassing. Definitely not something she felt like she could safe word over.

But maybe, just maybe, she could talk him out of doing it since she wasn't interested. She turned to face him more fully, widening her eyes pleadingly.

"Shouldn't we focus on things that I want to try though? Since I'm exploring?" There was the tiniest hint of begging in her voice.

Daddy smiled, and something about his expression made her feel like he could see right through her attempt at manipulation. Letting go of her shoulders, he bopped her on the nose with his finger.

"Actually, since I owe you some discipline, this seems like an appropriate time to explore nontraditional punishments."

"Nontraditional punishments?" She wasn't sure she liked the sound of that. But at the same time, a little shiver went down her spine, as if some part of her *did* like it.

"Oh, yes. I think being treated like a baby might be a very a good punishment for behaving irresponsibly. If you're not interested in being diapered, then I'm sure you'll remember this the next time you're forgetful about taking proper safety measures." He gave her such a stern look that Melody felt her insides churning a little.

Right. The whole not telling anyone about going to Black Light last weekend. And forgetting to let him know when she got home on Sunday. All things considered, wearing a diaper didn't sound like too bad a punishment for that. It was just a little embarrassing, but as long as they didn't go anywhere then she thought she could handle it. It wasn't sexy, but punishments weren't really supposed to be, were they?

Plus, she was kind of curious about what he meant by wearing the diaper differently.

Before she could say anything, Daddy stood up in front of her. "Now, let's get you undressed, baby girl."

Melody blushed as she realized that he wasn't going to wait for her to agree. Of course he wasn't going to wait. He was the Daddy, so he decided what they were doing.

And even though she wasn't super interested in being diapered, him taking control like this turned her on. She held up her hands, feeling strange as he began to take her clothes off. Shirt, then bra, then pants and undies, all while he remained fully clothed.

It made her feel vulnerable. Small. Incredibly turned on. As he knelt in front of her, tugging her panties down, Daddy's fingers trailed over her smooth mound. She'd just shaved that morning and her skin tingled with pleasure in the wake of his touch. If this was the prelude to being punished by diapering, this wasn't going to be so bad at all.

"Very nice, baby girl," he said approvingly. Melody nearly fell over when he gave her a kiss there, right at the front of her slit, over her clit. It was a chaste kiss but it made her ache for more. "Now lie back and put your feet flat on the mattress, hands above your head."

Why was being bossed around so sexy? She didn't know, but there was no denying the effect it had on her. Her nipples were already hardening into little buds, and it was all she could do not to wriggle around once she was lying down horizontally across the bed.

Legs bent and spread, feet firmly planted, fingers laced together above her head, she didn't know that she'd ever felt so completely vulnerable before. Daddy stood above the bed, watching her, his eyes gleaming as he looked over her naked body. Melody's breath hitched under his penetrating gaze. Even though she knew he was about to put a diaper on her, in this position, with him looking at her like that, she felt strangely sexy.

"Good girl," he said, giving her pussy a little pat before moving over to the nightstand.

Melody craned her head, trying to see what was in the drawer he opened, curiosity creeping through her. "What are you doing, Daddy?"

"Just getting a few things to make this punishment more interesting for you," he said, straightening back up. She couldn't quite see what he had in his hand, but it looked like a tube of something.

The expression on his face when he moved back to stand right in front of her pussy, was not reassuring.

"Now, Melody, you were a very naughty girl last weekend, weren't you?" he asked, looking down at her. Heat spread through her at being called a naughty girl. It was just as good as being told she was a good girl, just in a slightly different way, although her body reacted the same. "You didn't let anyone know you were going to Black Light and you didn't check in after I asked you to."

"I'm sorry, Daddy," she said immediately, although she had to admit she didn't feel particularly sincere. It felt more like she was playing a game.

"Oh, I'm not sure you are yet, baby girl," he said. "But you're about to be."

The way he said it made apprehension shoot through her and Melody squealed a little as he picked up an ankle in each hand, swiftly bringing them together so he could hold them in one hand. The position was humiliatingly vulnerable, especially with her hands above her head. She barely resisted the immediate urge to reach down and cover her bottom—which was good because Daddy immediately started spanking her.

SMACK! SMACK! SMACK!

Three hard swats on each cheek, laid down in the exact center, one atop of the other, so quickly and harshly that she barely had time to cry out before it was over. Being on her back and seeing the look on Daddy's face as he spanked her actually made everything a little bit harder. He didn't look turned on at all, he looked like a disciplinarian meting out the necessary punishment to a naughty little girl.

The stinging centers of her cheeks throbbed with heat as he lowered her legs back down, and Melody felt just as chastened as he'd obviously intended. It didn't matter that the spanking was over quickly, Daddy's stern demeanor in addition to the hard swats had driven the message home.

"I really am sorry, Daddy," she said in a smaller voice.

A little trickle of warmth went through her when he smiled at her. It wasn't a very big smile, but just enough of one to let her know that she was forgiven.

"I'm glad to hear that, baby girl," he said, giving her hot bottom a squeeze before lowering her legs back down. "Now put your legs back in position, we're not quite done yet."

Right. The diaper. Melody spread her feet back open, trying not to wriggle too much as her sensitized cheeks touched the comforter. What had been soft and cushiony a few moments ago now felt a little scratchy on the two red spots. At least, she assumed she was red where he'd spanked her, it certainly felt like she should be.

Being diapered might not turn her on, but being spanked

definitely did, even though this spanking had been sharp, quick, and surprisingly painful. Now that it was over, the afterburn combined with being naked in front of Daddy while he was fully clothed and controlling her every movement, was highly arousing.

As she watched, Daddy unscrewed the top of the tube he'd gotten out of the drawer, squeezing a little bit of something clear onto his finger.

"What's that, Daddy?" she asked, her curiosity spiking again and almost making her forget about the discomfort of her bottom.

Rather than answering her, Daddy put down the tube and used two fingers on his other hand to spread her labia apart. Melody immediately felt a little uncomfortable with how intimately he was able to view her right now, but she was also unbearably aroused by his casual handling of her most private areas. Daddy's finger ran over the sensitive nub of her clit, making her hips jerk as she gasped in reaction.

He rubbed for a moment, making her writhe as the sensitive nub responded to his touch. Melody moaned, her hips lifting eagerly against the stimulation. When he stopped, she cried out, but even when he moved his finger away, her clit kept tingling.

Daddy picked up the diaper with his other hand and slid it under her bottom. Melody wasn't really paying attention to that though, because the tingling in her clit was starting to feel warmer—actually it was starting to feel hot, like a slow-building burn on her most sensitive spot.

"Daddy, what did you do? My... I'm burning!" She started to reach down toward the diaper he was finishing securing to her hips, and Daddy immediately grabbed her hands, pushing them back up above her head. Now she was burning in two places, on her clit and her bottom cheeks. The lingering sting from her spanking was already fading in comparison to the growing heat prickling her sensitive nub.

"It's just a little bit of ginger oil, baby girl," he said calmly. "You didn't think the diaper was the only part of your punishment, did you?"

Actually, she kind of had. The burning was intensifying, and Melody cried out as she squirmed. The mix of unfamiliar and erotically painful sensations was starting to drive her a little wild.

"Now stay right here, just like this," Daddy said, pressing her wrists into the mattress slightly before he let them go and straightened back up. "I'm going to go wash the oil off my hand, and then I'll come back to help you finish getting dressed. If you move, I'm going to have to add to your punishment."

"Yes, Daddy." Her voice came out in a high whine, back arching slightly because already she was dying to move her hands down to try and soothe her clit. This might be punishment, and maybe she hadn't thought being diapered would be sexy, but she was so turned on she could barely stand it.

She bit her lip, wondering if she'd be able to stand the burning on her clit. It hurt, but at the same time, all she wanted to do was rub it until she came. Her Daddy was devious at punishments. Melody didn't think she'd forget to take care of her basic safety checks ever again!

FULLY DRESSED in the ruffled lavender dress, hair in two pigtails hanging down on either side of her face, diaper making it hard for her to stand with her legs together, Melody looked adorably pouty. At least half of that pout was from sexual frustration; she'd turned delightfully squirmy under the effects of the ginger. It should help keep her at a nice, low simmer all evening, until Kawan decided she'd been good enough to earn her orgasm.

Kawan had put her on the couch and turned on *Frozen* for

her to watch while he made dinner. Every time he looked over at her, she was squirming again, making him grin. Even the movie could only distract her to a point.

As soon as dinner was ready, he stopped the movie, and she immediately protested.

"Hey! It's not done!" The childish outburst was completely natural, not at all fabricated. Kawan had a feeling her little age was going to end up being several years older than a baby, but probably not too many.

"No, but dinner is. Come and eat and then we can finish the movie together after dinner."

Melody got a slightly mulish expression on her face, but she sighed and stood up. The short dress swirled around her thighs as she whirled around and flounced over to the dining room table, giving Kawan delightful little glimpses of her upper legs and the diaper she was wearing.

As soon as she got there, she brightened up. "Chicken nuggets? And smiley fries?"

"And broccoli," Kawan said firmly, but that didn't dampen her spirits at all, since he knew that broccoli was one of her favorite vegetables. Happily, she sat down at her placemat, with just a slight wince and a wriggle. The spanking he'd given her had probably mostly faded, but she was still getting used to the diaper. She only paused for a moment when she realized there were no utensils for her, before picking up a broccoli floret with her fingers. The purple sippy cup made her giggle, and she beamed at him as she picked it up to inspect it.

Smiling, Kawan sat down at his place, enjoying watching her discover the small joys of being his baby.

CHAPTER 19

$\mathcal{T}$he next real test for Melody came while they were watching *Frozen*, after dinner. She was cuddled up on his lap, head resting on his shoulder, his hand caressing her thigh while they watched the movie. The crinkling sound of the diaper when she occasionally shifted made him grin every time. He was hard as a rock, but content just to hold her and watch the movie for now. She was shifting more and more often as the movie played, until she finally tugged on his shirt.

"Daddy, can you pause the movie? I have to potty." From the way she shifted, Kawan could tell she was about to stand up.

He tightened his grip on her, keeping her on his lap. "No, sweetie, you don't need to use the bathroom. What do you think the diaper is for?"

The utter look of horror on her face almost made him laugh, but he managed to hold it back. He'd expected this reaction, after all, it wasn't an uncommon one, even from baby girls who liked the idea of being diapered.

"I didn't... I can't..." she sputtered. She turned bright red with embarrassment over the very idea.

Keeping a tight grip on her with one hand, Kawan grabbed

the remote with the other to pause the movie. Not so that she could go use the bathroom, but so that they could talk—and also because he was going to need to change her as soon as she finished.

"You can safe word," he offered. "But unless it causes you real distress, I want you to use your diaper like a good baby girl."

She squirmed slightly, obviously uncomfortable, torn between wanting to please him and wanting to maintain her dignity. Kawan shifted his hand, moving it fully over her lower belly and pressing his fingers into her, right over her bladder. Melody gasped.

"No.... I can't..." She grabbed at his hand trying to pull it away.

"No isn't your safe word, Melody."

She whined in response.

Satisfaction washed over him. He was already sure that she wasn't going to say her safe word. She was going to submit. Kawan wasn't turned on by her need to use the bathroom, exactly, but by the complete control she was giving him over her body.

Oh no...

She couldn't actually do it, could she?

But he wanted her to.

Despite the thick cushion of the diaper, Melody had been very aware of her Daddy's erection from the moment he'd settled her onto his lap. Especially because her clit was still tingling from the ginger oil even though it didn't burn anymore. She'd been aroused the whole time but tried to concentrate on the movie.

But he was still hard now, even though he'd basically just ordered her to wet herself while she was sitting on top of him.

She didn't find that part sexy, but being held in place and told to do something she didn't want to?

Yeah. That got her going.

Perverted.

Peggy's voice whispered in her head.

Strangely enough, that was what helped her decide. Because she wasn't going to let Peggy determine what she was willing to try.

Well, that and the fact that unless she safe worded, Daddy wasn't going to let her up and she *really* needed to go. Had needed to go for a while but had been trying to hold out until the movie ended.

His fingers pressed against her tummy and Melody whimpered again, closing her eyes because she could feel it starting.

Oh god...

It was too embarrassing. She turned, burrowing her head into Daddy's shoulder as her bladder released. It felt so strange to be peeing while she was sitting on top of him, being held by him.

Daddy's hand moved to stroke her back. "Good girl, sweetheart, I knew you could do it."

There was a kind of possessiveness in his voice that soothed her embarrassment, like he knew she would do this humiliating thing for him and only for him. She felt a strange kind of pride in that, like she'd passed some kind of test, even though she knew he wouldn't have been mad if she'd safe worded.

She squeaked as he slid one arm under her knees and pushed up to stand, holding her in his arms. Lips pressed against the top of her head, a sweet kiss as a reward.

"Let's go get you changed and then we can finish the movie."

Being a baby wasn't that bad. That had been the worst of it. She blushed all the way through having her diaper changed, but she was happy to be snuggled back in his arms while they finished watching the movie.

185

As soon as it ended, Daddy shifted her in his arms so that he could see her face.

"Well, baby girl, it's time for bed. How do you feel about your first night as a baby?"

Melody wrinkled her nose. "The diaper wasn't as bad as I thought it would be, but I still don't like it much. I wouldn't want to wear one all the time. And... I really don't want to do a number two in one. I think that's a hard limit for me."

Daddy chuckled. "Noted. You've been a very good girl all evening. Do you know what good girls get?"

"Is it cock?" she asked, brightening up with excitement. Daddy choked on a laugh, coughing to try and cover it while Melody giggled. She hadn't been joking, she really was hoping it was cock, but his deep laugh was infectious.

Still laughing, he pressed his forehead against her shoulder, shaking his head. "Oh, you are going to be handful, I can tell."

"A handful of cock?"

Daddy straightened up, his expression becoming more stern, although his eyes were still dancing with amusement. "Little girl, if you keep using naughty words, Daddy's going to have to wash your mouth out with soap. Those kinds of words are for the bedroom only."

Ugh. Melody had had her mouth washed out with soap when she was a kid and it was not a fond memory. Pressing her lips together, she ran two fingers along them, miming a zipping motion. Daddy laughed again and she grinned. This was fun.

"Let's go to the bedroom, baby girl, and then you can use those naughty words all you want." Daddy stood, picking her up with him, and she wrapped her arms around his neck as he carried her to his bedroom.

STRIPPING Melody out of her dress, leaving her only in the

diaper, Kawan had to grin as he lay her back on the bed. As far as he was concerned, she looked adorable, and he enjoyed the view since he had a feeling she wouldn't be wearing a diaper very often after tonight. Well, not unless she was a lot naughtier than he expected she would be.

While she was a mischievous little imp, she also had an innate desire to be a good girl. He thoroughly enjoyed both impulses.

"Hands above your head, baby girl," he ordered as he began to take off his own clothes.

Melody's eyes gleamed as he undressed, her arms stretched above her head, thrusting her breasts up. The diaper didn't allow her to press her thighs together the way she needed to in order to get the right pressure on her clit. She still tried though, and Kawan enjoyed watching her squirming as she made the attempt.

He turned his back on her just long enough to set his clothes down on the top of his dresser, and when he turned around, she had one hand pressing down over her diaper. Seeing his movement, she immediately whipped it back up above her head, but it was already too late.

"Very naughty, baby girl, where are your hands supposed to be?" he asked, shaking his head as he moved back toward the bed.

"Above my head," she said, looking a little shamefaced. Then her eyes opened wider, full of pleading. "But I wasn't rubbing! I just need to press down, just for a second..."

"If you really *needed* to, what should you have done?" he asked, stopping next to the bed and putting his hands on his hips. His erection jutted out in front of him, like it was trying to reach for her, but both of them were going to have to wait a little longer.

Some indiscretions, a daddy couldn't ignore.

Melody's gaze guiltily slid away from his.

"Asked you?" she mumbled, making it into a question.

"Exactly right, little girl."

Crouching down, he pulled open one of the under-bed drawers. He couldn't help but wonder what Melody would think if she knew everything that was neatly tucked away under his bed. For now though, he only needed the soft-lined cuffs.

"When little girls can't be trusted, they have to be restrained," he said as he stood, holding them up for her to see.

Her face fell. "But I wanted to touch you!"

"Then you should have stayed in position." The stern look he gave her made her wilt, and his cock throbbed in response. He loved seeing the chastened expression on her face.

Another time, perhaps, he would make even more of an example out of her indiscretion, but it *was* her first weekend, and he was inclined to be lenient. Plus, he was only willing to torment *himself* so far in the name of disciplining her.

It was quick work to wrap the cuffs around her wrists and secure them to his headboard. Then he took each of her ankles in turn, spreading her legs far apart and cuffed them as well, attaching them to the bedposts and leaving her completely open and vulnerable. Her eyes were wide with both apprehension and excitement, her body quivering under his touch.

"Beautiful, baby girl," he murmured, getting onto the bed between her thighs, running his hands up her legs to the diaper. She shuddered, and then blushed furiously when his hands reached the diaper, as if she'd forgotten it was there. Then she moaned a little in disappointment when his hands kept sliding, over the diaper, up her torso to her breasts.

The soft mounds were heavy in his hands and Kawan squeezed them together, running his thumbs over her nipples. The little buds hardened further, tightening into tempting little points. He wasn't particularly interested in fighting temptation at this point, so he leaned over to suck one into his mouth.

MOANING, Melody arched as Daddy played with her breasts, pleasure surging in a direct line from her nipples to her pussy. His touch was gentle, arousing, until he bit down, and then she keened at the hot wash of painful pleasure, twisting in the restraints. Just that little touch of pain was enough to kick up her need from 'overwhelming' to 'desperate'.

Her clit was throbbing against the diaper and she was sure this one was wet too, although not for the same reason as her previous diaper. She was so turned on she wasn't sure she could bear much more stimulation. Being bound to Daddy's bed was the hottest thing that had ever happened to her.

It didn't matter how she jerked her hands or legs—*she couldn't move.* And every attempted movement confirming that fact only made her hotter and wetter.

"Daddy, please," she begged as he switched breasts. The cool air against her wet nipple just made her even more aware of the little bud, contrasting with the way his hot mouth suckled at her other nipple. His fingers moved to the wet nipple, pinching and pulling, tormenting her by playing with her breasts while completely ignoring her pulsing pussy.

She tried to twist again, writhing, moving her hips up in a desperate attempt for contact. The diaper brushed against what she was sure was his cock and she moaned because she still couldn't *feel* anything.

When he finally pulled back from her nipples, leaving them dark pink and throbbing, she almost cried with relief as his hands went to her diaper. Chuckling, he pulled it off of her, tossing it to the side. The cool air of the bedroom on her heated pussy did nothing to cool her fervor.

"Daddy, pleaaaase, I need you." She moved her hips upwards, showing him where she needed him.

Rather than answering her, Daddy lowered his head between

her legs. It wasn't quite what she'd wanted, but she wasn't going to argue either. She moaned, shuddering as his tongue pressed against her sensitive pussy, sliding between her lips and licking straight up the center to her swollen clit.

"Oh, Daddy!" It felt so good. She moved her hips, desperate for more stimulation, desperate to come. "Oh!" She cried out again as she felt his fingers dipping into her pussy, sliding easily through her wetness and stretching her open. Immediately she clamped down around his fingers, shuddering as he moved them back and forth inside of her, mimicking sex but not giving her the satisfaction she yearned for.

When he slid them out of her completely, she whined—and then whimpered as he pressed the slick digits to her anus.

"Daddy!"

But his mouth was too busy to answer her, suckling on the sensitive lips of her pussy, teasing at her clit, and his fingers began to burrow into her bottom, unchecked. He hadn't touched that particular hole since last weekend at Black Light, and it felt particularly sensitive right now. The little nerve endings ignited, sending a flush of pleasure through her as he stretched the tight ring, twisting and pumping with his fingers so that she could feel every centimeter of the invasion.

Melody panted for air, flushed with the long build-up. Even though her pussy was empty, even though his tongue would only tease her clit, she could feel her orgasm building. The drag and push of his fingers rubbing in and out of her was so close to what she needed, but not quite. She wriggled and squirmed, the rising passion inside of her building and building, like she'd been running a marathon and the finish line was finally in sight. His tongue flicked over her clit again.

"Daddy, please…"

Her body tightened—and Daddy pulled away, leaving her pussy pink and needy and untouched.

"*No!*" The orgasm, which had seemed so imminent, was

stymied from lack of stimulation. Melody felt tears pricking her eyes at her need and she practically sobbed as Daddy's fingers twisted in her bottom, keeping her on edge without allowing her to tip over. "Daddy, *please*, I'm so close!"

"Are you going to remember to leave your hands where Daddy tells you to next time?" His voice was deep, dark with emotion and need, and Melody felt her insides twist in response.

"Yes, Daddy, I promise!" In that moment, she would have promised anything, if he'd just let her come.

The fingers inside of her pulled out and Melody cried out at the loss as their withdrawal left her completely empty.

Then Daddy's weight was on top of her, pinning her down to the bed, his lips descending to hers as his cock pressed against her pussy. She could taste herself on his mouth as she kissed him back desperately, finally able to touch him in some way. She sucked on his tongue, trying to pull it further between her lips, in a way that she couldn't with his cock.

Then she screamed, because he was thrusting into her, so hard and fast that it was almost painful, but her brain didn't register it that way. She was finally full where she'd been empty, Daddy's body pressing against her clit where she'd had no stimulation, and it was exactly what she needed to cross the finish line. The tightness inside of her exploded, curling her toes as bursts of ecstasy went off like fireworks throughout her entire body. She clenched and pulsed as he began to thrust atop of her, filling her so perfectly as wave after wave of pleasure rolled through her.

The hard unrelenting thrusts were almost overstimulation and her legs struggled to try and close. Jerking on her restraints only served to turn her on even more, adding another layer to her climax, and Melody felt tears run down the sides of her face as the intense sensations swamped her body. Her cries were muffled by his lips until he began to move so fast that they couldn't continue the kiss any longer. Then they rang out in the room as he pounded between her thighs, making her scream with ecstasy.

~

Melody quivered helplessly beneath his thrusts, her hips tipping upwards to meet him, her pussy clenching around him as she came. Every time she started to come down from the high, he would change his thrusts slightly, press against her clit from a different direction, sending her into a new wave of rapture.

He wallowed in her body, sinking into her over and over again, filling his senses with her, taking his fill of pleasure from her. All the while, she writhed in her own erotic bliss squeezing his cock with every throb of her body. As her cries slowly began to turn to whimpers, he began to thrust harder and faster again, now for his own pleasure rather than hers.

The rough stimulation made her spasm and she let out a sobbing wail as his balls tightened in readiness. The tension broke and he groaned, burying himself inside of her so that her clenching walls massaged his cock while he emptied himself into her. Beneath him, he could feel her breasts heaving as she panted, and he rested his forehead against hers. Her eyes were closed, lashes dewy with tears from the intense sensations, lips open as if waiting for a kiss.

Kawan obliged, dropped a gentle, undemanding kiss on her mouth as his cock pulsed for the last time. After a moment, she returned the kiss, tipping her head back to give him better access to her lips. It was sweet intimacy to cap the riotous passion they'd just shared, leaving him satisfied in every possible way.

CHAPTER 20

The morning with Melody went well. Kawan woke up before her, his body curled around hers in a spooning position, which he decided to take advantage of. Perfectly vanilla but highly enjoyable, especially because she was so soft and sleepy at the beginning. By the end, she was bucking back against him, her hand over his as he played with her clit, giving her a very good morning wake-up call.

Then he got her dressed in a ruffled dress with ruffled panties, although the style was enough to make her 'older' than she'd been last night. She had fun twirling in front of the mirror and then coloring while he got breakfast ready. After they ate, he did her hair in two curly ponytails and then they played games until he needed to get lunch ready. He smiled to see her going right back to the princess coloring book he'd gotten for her—it was obviously one of her favorite activities already.

Following lunch time, she was agreeable to changing and 'growing' a little bit more. The dress he put her in didn't have any ruffles and it wasn't quite as childish. The dress was lavender with a white collar and had a dark purple belt around the waist that tied with a bow in the front. The skirt fell to just above her knees and he put her in little Mary Jane flats, but left off the socks this time. He'd chosen it deliberately because the style wouldn't stand out in a crowd. Unfortunately, Melody disagreed and that's where they ran into the difficulty.

"I can't wear this out in public!" Her voice had changed from the higher, little girl's voice she'd been using to a woman's. She whirled around, away from the mirror, two bright pink spots on her cheeks. Kawan raised his eyebrows at her change in tone, giving her a Daddy look.

"Why not? You look adorable." He kept his voice mostly neutral with just a slight warning.

"I look like I'm ten." She jutted her chin up as if daring him to contradict the exaggeration. And it *was* an exaggeration. She didn't actually look like a ten-year-old, even if the dress was something that could pass as part of a ten-year-old's wardrobe. It also was something that could pass in an adult's wardrobe— although, from what he'd seen of her clothing, it wasn't something she would wear as an adult.

Kawan tilted his head at her. "You were perfectly fine with the dress a few minutes ago."

"That was before you told me you wanted to go somewhere!" Her lips were mulish, pouty. Interestingly, the more she argued with him, the more she regressed again. Her voice was becoming higher and her foot jerked a little, like she'd been about to stomp it.

"Do you want to spend all weekend inside with just each other?" he asked, trying not to feel upset about the idea. Just because he'd planned some enjoyable outings didn't mean she'd be ready for it, and he did want to be sensitive to how new she was to all of this. Although eventually she'd have to get used to the idea. They'd have adult dates too, but he enjoyed doing little dates just as much if not more sometimes. "I wanted to take you somewhere fun, but—"

"This is stupid!" she interrupted him, clenching her fists.

"You're stupid!" With that shocking reaction, she ran out of the door of her bedroom, and he could hear her footsteps pounding down the hall and down the stairs.

Flummoxed, Kawan went very still, listening.

The front door never opened. Which meant she was downstairs somewhere. Possibly hiding.

Ah. So she wasn't going to call her safe word, this was just another testing of boundaries.

Well, he had just the medicine for that.

Why did I do that? Why did I call him stupid? Oh my god, I'm in so much trouble!

Melody's heart was pounding as she tiptoed through the living room, her eyes frantically scanning for a good place to hide. She didn't know what had come over her. He'd put on her shoes and then had said she was ready to go out... and then she'd asked where and he'd said it was a surprise, and she'd panicked.

Out? Where people could see her? Where *anyone* could see her? She'd had a sudden flash of running into people she knew, like Lisa or Katherine, or, even worse, McCready... worst of all would be Peggy. She might sink into the ground and die of shame if Peggy saw her dressed like this.

Peggy would know Melody had never worn anything like this since they'd met. It wasn't her style at all.

That she actually really liked the dress didn't make a difference, *adult* Melody would never have bought it.

Maybe adult Melody is the stoo-pid one.

That was entirely possible. All she could think about now was that Daddy was probably really mad at her. Maybe he wouldn't even want to be her Daddy anymore. She'd simultaneously rejected and insulted him at the same time.

See? Stoo-pid.

Was he even going to come after her?

Melody froze. She might not need to hide. Why would Daddy look for someone who acted like she didn't want to be his little girl?

But I do!

Biting her lower lip, she glanced over her shoulder, back toward the hall where the stairway was. No sign of Daddy. Maybe if she begged his forgiveness, he wouldn't be mad? He would understand that she was nervous. She was pretty sure that he'd even started to offer staying home. But that made her feel bad because he obviously had planned to take her out and she didn't want to disappoint him.

Dragging her feet slightly, she tiptoed back to the stairway. Because of the wall there, she couldn't see up the stairs until she was right in front of it, and the moment she turned the corner, Daddy swooped in. Melody shrieked as she found herself upended over his shoulder and being carried up the stairs—and not in the romantic way he'd done last night.

"Little girl, you are in so much trouble."

She bounced on his shoulder, half anxious and half elated. Elated, because obviously Daddy wasn't going to kick her out. Anxious, because she was in soooo much trouble. But the relief coursing through her made the anxiety worth it. She'd much rather be in trouble than have the weekend end.

Why had she balked anyway?

To see what he'd do, the little voice in her head whispered.

Ugh, how very... childish. Melody almost smiled as the thought hit her. That was kind of the point, but she had a feeling she was going to regret the impulse. A preemptive apology couldn't hurt her cause, right?

"I'm really sorry, Daddy," she said, sincerely and contritely. "I was just scared about what other people would think when we go out."

Daddy's hand patted her bottom, which, given her current position, was not as reassuring as it might have been under other circumstances.

"I understand, baby girl," he said, and his voice was kind. Melody slumped with relief, only to tense again at his next words. "You were very naughty though. We're still going to go out, but you need to be punished first."

Melody let out a little moan even as her pussy clenched with excitement.

KAWAN WAS PLEASED that Melody had come around on her own, although he wasn't going to go any easier on her punishment. This weekend was about exploring her little side, but it was also about setting her boundaries when he was being her Daddy. Calling him stupid was several steps over the line and he was going to make sure she knew it and remembered it.

With that in mind, he headed for the bathroom instead of the bedroom.

"No, wait... what are you doing?" she asked, a slight hint of panic in her voice. The change in venue had unnerved her, as it was meant to.

"You were a very naughty little girl calling your Daddy stupid," he said, bending to set her down on her feet in front of him. His body blocked her exit and her eyes darted around the small room, looking for a means of escape. Rather than looking him in the eyes, she stared at the ground, hands wringing in front of her, looking like a rather sorry little girl. She was going to be a lot sorrier in a minute. "We'll start off with a mouth soaping for insulting your Daddy."

Now her head swung up, eyes wide with horror. "A mouth soaping?"

Kawan already had the bar of soap in hand and Melody

swayed slightly on her feet, like she was about to retreat. He froze her with a look, his cock hardening when she went still. He loved how she responded to him, even when she was in trouble. Maybe especially when she was in trouble.

"To begin with," he said, holding up the bar of soap and waiting to see if she'd protest. She gulped audibly but didn't say anything. "Good girl. Now open wide."

A little whimper escaped her throat, but she opened her lips. His cock throbbed. He ran the bar under the tap quickly and then pushed it between her lips, moving it back and forth over her tongue to make sure it got sudsy. Melody's nose wrinkled and she gagged slightly at the taste, but she didn't try to reach up and stop him. Her hands were tightly gripping each other, her knuckles white as she kept from reaching up.

"Good girl," he repeated. Her pupils dilated. "After your mouth soaping is done, I'm going to give you an enema, and then I'm going to plug your naughty bottom. Having a plug in should help remind you to behave for the rest of the day." The enema might be pushing her limits a little, but she hadn't made it a hard limit, and since he wanted her to wear the plug all afternoon, it was the best course of action. She made another little whimpering sound, squirming slightly, and he could tell she was pressing her thighs together, aroused despite her soapy mouth.

He almost smiled, but he managed to push it down. After all, he was disciplining her right now; he didn't want to ruin his stern Daddy facade.

Pulling the soap from her mouth, he saw with satisfaction that there was a nice white sheen to her tongue and lips. She immediately started to turn toward the sink, but his hand on her shoulder stopped her.

"Oh no, little girl. We'll rinse your mouth out after your bottom is cleaned out and you're plugged."

"Pleaaaathe, Daddy," she begged, her words sounding a little strange, because she was trying to move her tongue as little as possible. Her eyes pleaded with him. "It'th tho groth!"

"I hope you remember that the next time you're about to insult me," he said, giving her a stern look. "Now unless you want a spanking to go with your punishment, you need to turn around and bend over the side of the tub. I want your skirt up and panties down."

She whined and hung her head, looking like a very sorry little girl now, huffing a little as she moved to do what he said. Kawan got the enema kit out from the cabinet under the sink. Today he'd use the syringe rather than the hose and bladder; although that was his favorite, they were on a bit of a time crunch. Keeping one eye on her as she knelt in front of the tub, he began to prep the enema. Warm water would be enough for today, since it was her first one ever and because she'd apologized without being asked.

Any fight seemed to have gone out of her though, and she obediently draped herself over the tub, pulling up her skirt and pushing down her panties. The position revealed that she was very wet, her pussy glistening under the bathroom light. Between her rounded cheeks, her anus winked at him as her cheeks clenched, as if in anticipation of what was about to happen. Kawan's cock was hard as a rock when he finally stepped up behind her to administer her 'medicine'.

SOAP TASTED AWFUL. Melody could feel her stomach churning, wanting to gag at the flavor that lay thick on her tongue. How she could be so aroused when her mouth felt so terrible was beyond her, but she was.

Bent over, butt up in the air for her Daddy, about to get her first enema, and she was both very uncomfortable and very turned on.

I can't believe I'm about to do this.

I can't believe I'm letting him do this.

I can't believe I'm turned on by this.

She bit back a moan as she heard him moving behind her, felt his presence looming over her. It made her want to whimper again. Her bottom clenched, as if a mere muscle spasm could stop him.

"Just relax, baby girl, this will only be as uncomfortable as you make it." His deep voice was soothing, the words were not. How was she supposed to make an enema more comfortable? Something slick and hard pressed against her little hole and Melody tensed. "I said, relax, sweetheart."

A warm hand rubbed her lower back and Melody squeezed her eyes shut, forcing her muscles to release their tension. It slid inside of her, shorter but harder than his finger.

Warm liquid began to stream into her, steady and inexorable, and Melody gasped. Her bottom clenched again, but this time the nozzle was already inside of her and it was too late. Daddy easily held it in place, keeping her impaled on the implement as water continued to rush into her bowels. She hadn't thought anything could distract her from the distasteful soap still lingering in her mouth, but the enema managed it.

It felt strange, uncomfortable, and oddly pleasant. Melody moaned, her thighs quivering as she pressed herself more firmly against the tub, caught between its porcelain edge and the hard nozzle. As her stomach filled, it cramped again.

"Daddy, too much!" She wriggled, trying to get away but there was nowhere to go and more water gushed in. It was getting hard to breathe.

And then it stopped.

Melody shuddered. Her insides sloshed. Daddy's hand rubbed her lower back again and her pussy clenched.

"I'm so proud of you, baby girl."

Somehow that made the embarrassment over what came next better.

She'd thought he'd leave the room. He didn't.

Shame, humiliation, and arousal all licked at her in equal measure. The last was the most confusing. At some point, shouldn't her pride rear up? Although, pride was what had gotten her into this position in the first place, so maybe it was for the best that it took a back seat right now.

Once she was empty, Daddy bent her over the counter facing the mirror. Now she could see her flushed face, her wide eyes, and Daddy's expression as he held up a long black plug with a fat bulb.

"This is a punishment bulb, baby girl. You're going to wear it all afternoon and it will help you remember to behave."

"I'll remember without it, I promithe." The last plea of a desperate little girl. Her insides felt sore and sensitive already, she doubted she'd be able to forget her first enema so quickly. But that was about as far as she was willing to argue. The sooner the plug went in, the sooner she could wash the soap out of her mouth.

Meeting her eyes in the mirror, Daddy didn't respond as he pressed the tip of the plug against her bottom. It was slick with lube and the first few centimeters went in easily before her muscles began to strain.

"Open your eyes, baby girl," he said, pinching her clit and making her squeal as her eyes flew open. She hadn't even realized she'd closed them.

Her clit throbbed between her legs as Daddy pushed harder on the plug. The tight ring of her sphincter resisted and she watched herself grimace in the mirror. He pulled it slightly out of her and began to move it back and forth, fucking her ass with it and stretching her wider with each tiny thrust. Melody panted as she was stretched, the burning discomfort making her want to wriggle and squirm.

It was definitely bigger than the one he'd used last week, pushing deeper inside of her and stretching her wider.

"Good girl, almost there," Daddy murmured encouragingly. His eyes were flicking back and forth between watching what he was doing and looking at her expression in the mirror. Melody almost wished she could see both views as well, so she could watch the large piece of rubber slowly disappearing into her backside, the thick black base nestling between her cheeks once it was inserted.

She cried out as her muscles screamed in protest, the thickest part of the plug finally pushing inside of her. There was a sharp burst of pain and then it was over, leaving her even more full than the enema had felt. Now she understood what Daddy meant by saying she wouldn't be able to forget to behave this afternoon. There was going to be no way to ignore this plug.

Pressing her cheek against the cool counter, she breathed in and out as her body finished adjusting. Daddy's hands gently stroked her bottom, teasing the outside of her pussy, making the invasion easier to bear. After a few moments, he patted her backside.

"Okay, baby, all done. Now let's rinse out your mouth, and then you're going to show me how sorry you are."

ON HER KNEES in front of him, hands bunched in the skirt of her dress, Melody's eyes were full of needy arousal. Her freshly rinsed out mouth was open, and he slid his cock between her full lips, groaning with pleasure at the sight and sinking his fingers into her hair to pull her more fully onto him. Automatically, she sucked, her tongue pressing against the underside of his cock.

Caressing her head, he knew he was going to have to redo

her pigtails and it didn't bother him at all. He watched her through half-lidded eyes as she bobbed her head up and down along the length of his cock, leaving it shiny and wet from her attentions. She hummed, low in the back of her throat, and the vibrations went straight up the back of his spine.

Groaning, he thrust, mostly gently... mostly allowing her to control the movements for now.

"That's it, baby girl, use your tongue," he urged. He shuddered with pleasure when she obeyed, her tongue dancing along the length of him every time she slid her lips down. Moving her hands to his thighs to help her to balance, she pushed forward, trying to get him deeper, to take more of him between her lips.

Suckling, swirling her tongue, she laved pleasure over his cock. The dichotomy between her modestly innocent outfit and the way she was eagerly sucking his cock was straight out of one of his fantasies. She squirmed, rubbing her thighs together, and he didn't stop her. It wouldn't be enough to make her cum, only enough to frustrate herself, and that served his purposes nicely.

"Good girl..." He said throatily, beginning to move his hips faster, pushing his cock in deeper. Her fingers gripped his thighs more tightly. "Swallow for Daddy."

The head of his cock pressed into her throat and he felt the delicate muscles convulse, which was all it took. He dug his fingers into her scalp as jet after jet of cum spurted down her throat, straight into her belly. Melody's mouth worked, enhancing his pleasure, as she sucked him dry.

"Such a good girl."

CHAPTER 21

The surprise outing was to the zoo, which was both wonderful and awful.

Wonderful because Melody loved the zoo. She loved seeing the animals, watching the shows, and the ice cream carts.

Awful, because it was a *lot* of walking and the plug jostled inside of her with every step. She couldn't help but be aware of it, no matter what she was doing. Even more awful was that it turned out the plug was also a vibrator, with a remote, and Daddy enjoyed turning it on and off at odd intervals. She almost wished she was wearing a diaper again because she was pretty sure she was soaking through her panties.

All her fears about people staring or judging her had totally disappeared. No one even looked at her twice. They were just two people out on a date. The Daddy thing was as hidden from the public as the plug. Actually, it almost would have been kind of nice if someone would stare or show that they cared about the childishly styled dress, because then she wouldn't feel like she'd freaked out for nothing.

Wouldn't have had her mouth soaped, her bottom cleaned out, and be wearing a plug for no reason.

Wouldn't be walking around horny as hell with no orgasm in sight for nothing.

The fact that Daddy had used her mouth to get off but not done anything for her just made her even hotter.

There's something wrong with me.

Kind of a wonderful something though. Because no matter how itchy she felt between her legs, no matter how her insides clenched and throbbed, no matter how uncomfortable she was, she couldn't remember ever feeling this satisfied. Couldn't remember ever having this much fun on a date.

She practically felt like skipping between the animal pens. Might have tried if it weren't for the plug. At least she had panties to help keep it inside of her, but if she accidentally pushed it out entirely, she was pretty sure the panties wouldn't hold it. Then she really *would* be publicly humiliated. So she had to clench constantly to keep it in.

So no skipping or running or jumping of any kind.

"Where to next?" Daddy asked, as they walked away from the sleepy tigers. The indulgent look in his dark eyes made her feel warm and happy all over. His fingers were wound around hers, and he was just as relaxed and enjoying himself just as much as she was.

She looked up at the signs denoting what was on each path at the crossroads.

"Seals!" She did a little dance in place. A very small dance. Because the plug shifted and she had to clench around it.

Chuckling, Daddy led her down the path toward the seals.

Then, while she was watching them swim, the big meanie set off the plug again and Melody nearly moaned out loud as she gripped his hand more tightly. If he wasn't careful, she was going to end up climbing him like a monkey in a tree.

But she couldn't forget to behave, even if she wanted to.

～

KEEPING Melody on edge all day meant that she was a little cranky by the time they returned to the house. Baby girl needed an orgasm... but she was going to have to wait. They needed to eat first. And, he admitted to himself, he was going to enjoy watching her squirm.

When he took the plug out, he let her have the bathroom to herself but warned her that she'd better not play with herself or she'd regret it. When she joined him in the kitchen to help make dinner, she was as flushed and tense as before so he knew she'd followed his orders. Kawan gave her a deep kiss as a reward before setting her to wash the vegetables.

She squirmed her way through dinner even without the plug teasing her. After having it inside of her for such an extended time, he was sure her little hole was a bit sore and would be for a while. It made for uncomfortable sitting. Kawan enjoyed watching her wriggle while they talked about the zoo and her favorite animals.

"Ice cream for dessert," he announced when she'd cleared her plate.

Melody pouted for a moment before her eyes turned pleading and a little sultry. "What if I want something else for dessert?"

It didn't matter that she was using the same high, girlish voice that said she was firmly in her 'little' head space, the implication was clear. She wanted 'big girl' time with him.

He kept his expression inscrutable.

"Ice cream for dessert," he repeated in measured tones. It was more fun to keep her guessing about whether or not she'd get her orgasm.

Since she'd been a very good girl this afternoon and evening, he intended to reward her, but she didn't need to know that yet. She sighed dramatically, and he just barely managed to keep the smile from his face.

"Fine, ice cream," she grumbled, looking wholly adorable as she did so.

Despite the grumbling, she perked up quite a bit when he pulled the pint of Cherry Garcia and a bottle of chocolate syrup out of the fridge.

"My favorite!"

"I know." Smug satisfaction threaded through him seeing her happiness. This was one of his favorite parts about being a Daddy; little moments like this when she beamed up at him like he'd hung the moon just because he'd remembered one small detail.

Another good part about being a Daddy was telling her that it was time to get ready for bed as soon as he was done with the dishes and watching her balk before submitting.

"It's too early!"

"Little girls don't get to decide their bedtimes." He arched a brow as she fumed. "And naughty little girls don't get their reward for being good all afternoon. Now go on upstairs and pick out your nightie from the wardrobe. I'll be up in a minute." She started to stomp her way up the stairs and he called out after her. "No stomping!"

An aggrieved sigh floated down the stairwell, but she stopped stomping, and Kawan chuckled under his breath. She was going to be an interesting 'teenager' tomorrow, he was sure of it.

Once he was done with the dishes, he followed her upstairs, took her into his bedroom and helped her out of the nightie she'd put on, before setting her atop his cock so she could ride him to her heart's content while he fingered her sore bottom. After two orgasms, she was practically falling over, so he flipped her onto her back and pounded between her thighs until she was crying out in ecstasy again and he followed suit.

They fell asleep not long afterward with her snuggled in his arms.

~

A HAND firmly gripped her bicep as Daddy finally caught up with her.

"Young lady, you are in so much trouble," he growled in her ear.

Well shit.

Today she was being a teenager and Daddy had taken her to the county fair. So far it wasn't going very well. It wasn't a hard role to slip into, but Melody wasn't sure she liked herself as a teen.

What had been fun and bratty when she was 'younger' now felt kind of mean. She also didn't like the way Daddy's stern look made her want to melt down. It made her feel even younger, but not in a good way. She felt almost resentful, because she was pretty sure that if they'd come here yesterday, she would have been having a blast. Instead, she kept looking around at the animals and the rides, but she didn't really feel like she could indulge in them the way she wanted to.

Teenagers didn't squeal and jump up and down like little girls just because they saw a fluffy bunny. They didn't try to go running to the funnel cake truck. They definitely didn't try to milk a goat. She was standing next to an actual teenager when the girl's mom suggested she try. Going by the teenager's reaction, Melody's desire to try did not fit the age.

Which made her feel pouty and sulky. Although, at least that fit. She just wasn't enjoying herself though.

She'd gotten distracted by the giant stuffed tiger while she was waiting for him to finish up in the bathroom. The ring-toss stall was only a *little* ways away from the restroom building, and she'd thought she could check out the game and get back before Daddy was done. For once, the line had been longer for the men's room than the women's, and... well, she'd just had to run over.

Rather than apologizing, she let out an aggrieved sigh, letting her resentment show through. She hadn't wanted to wait; she'd wanted to go see the tiger. Not that she could show how much she liked the tiger. Right? She couldn't remember ever buying a new stuffed animal when she was a teen. That just frustrated her even more. "I didn't go very far; obviously you could still see me."

If she could make herself stop, she would, but somehow the words just kept coming out. Even when he was doing something nice for her, she'd been nothing but snarky since they'd arrived, and it was making her miserable.

The hard look he gave her now made her shrink into herself, and she stared down at the ground, feeling tears prick her eyes. She didn't like today at all.

"Melody, baby girl, what's wrong?" The unexpected warmth in Daddy's voice made her wince. She didn't deserve it.

She sniffled. "I don't like being a teenager," she said in a small voice. A voice that was nothing like how she'd sounded a minute ago.

"That's okay, sweetheart, you don't have to be a teenager." Daddy's arms wrapped around her, pulling her into his chest. Melody rested her head against the little nook of his shoulder, sighing as she burrowed in.

Even though he said it was okay, she felt like she'd failed at something.

"I'm supposed to be a teenager today, though."

A deep rumble went through Daddy's chest, right under her ear; he was chuckling. "Sweetheart, the point of this weekend was to find out what feels right for *you*. If something doesn't feel right, you don't have to do it."

"You aren't disappointed?" Relief swept through her.

Daddy's fingers slid through hair, untangling the long strands with his fingers, soothing her. "Not at all. Although I was having fun thinking up good punishments for when we get home."

Crap. Her bottom tingled as if already preparing for a spanking. Melody's thighs pressed together. The surface of her bottom wasn't the only thing tingling.

I'm a dirty girl.

The thought held only amusement, no shame or embarrassment. That was one good thing to come out of this weekend; she definitely understood a lot more about herself and what she wanted. Peggy had been wrong. Ignorant. There was a side to Melody that had been unexplored, ignored, until now.

Wriggling in Daddy's arms, jubilant glee rose up inside of her. She didn't need to think about her work. Didn't need to worry about her living situation. She knew he would take care of everything, and she could just have fun at the fair he'd brought her to.

"Can we try to win the tiger?" she asked hopefully.

Daddy laughed. "Of course, sweetheart." Then his voice lowered, whispering into her ear. "But you're still being punished for your earlier behavior when we get home."

Darn it.

IT HAD TAKEN way too much money—and finding an easier game—but Kawan had eventually managed to win Melody a tiger. Granted, it was a smaller tiger than the massive once she'd first found, but she was happy enough with it.

"The other one would have been too hard to carry anyway," she told him, hugging the stuffie to her. She'd named it Tony, and Kawan had done his best not to laugh.

While Kawan would have been happy with her at any 'age,' he had to admit the one she'd chosen was his favorite. It was a good balance of allowing him to take care of her while she still retained independence. And although he'd enjoyed her bratty 'teenage' mouth, she was much sweeter like this.

Likely there would be times when she wanted to be a little 'older' or a little 'younger,' but she definitely seemed happiest around six to eight years.

They wouldn't always have time to spend a whole weekend like this, especially while she was still earning her PhD, but he would make the most of the time they did have. It helped that she was at his house. This relationship was moving faster than he'd thought it would, definitely faster than he'd planned it to, but it just felt so *right.*

He felt happier than he had in a long time.

They ate dinner out, her stuffed tiger sitting on her lap, and she was yawning by the time they got home.

Home. She made it feel like a home and not just his house. It was a feeling he was going to have to examine more closely later when he had the time to devote to it. Right now he needed to focus on his baby girl's discipline.

"Go upstairs and do whatever you need to before bed," he told her, slipping easily into his stern Daddy role. It wasn't hard, all he had to do was dredge up a memory of what a bratty 'teen' she'd been. "I want you waiting for me naked and bent over the side of my bed, ready to take your punishment for the evening. I'll be up soon to take care of your discipline."

"But..." She looked up at him with wide, pleading eyes, but saw the determination in his expression and immediately slumped. Even though her head was down as she turned toward the stairs, he could see the little smile on her lips.

The naughty little thing must have sensed that he wasn't actually upset. While she responded to his discipline on multiple levels, what really fueled her behavior was not wanting to disappoint him. Which was why she'd persisted in trying to please him by spending the full day in a role she didn't feel comfortable in, which had resulted in her acting out because she had been so uncomfortable.

She was everything he wanted.

For a long moment, Kawan stared at the window looking out onto his front yard. It was dark outside, so he could see nothing but his expression. Something felt strange. Different. Like there had been a shift in his world, but he couldn't quite put his finger on what it was.

I'm not worried.

That was it.

There was a part of him that had expected to fight his feelings for her. To compare her to Krissy, especially because she was living here with him so quickly, because she had *needed* him to help her, because she wasn't experienced... but Melody was real. Her inner sweet submissive little was exactly who she was, not a front she put on to play him.

Krissy would have had no problem playing any parts he'd asked of Melody this weekend. But that's because for her it had been just that—playing. She wouldn't have cared about his disappointment. She would have also used her role for everything she could get from him. If she'd decided she wanted a massive stuffed tiger, nothing but that would have satisfied her, no matter how much money he'd had to spend to make it happen.

For Melody, this weekend had been about self-discovery. She cared what he wanted, more than she cared about her own satisfaction. Wanted to please him, more than she wanted to please herself. She was sweet, smart, and sexy, as both an adult and as a little. If there were such a thing as the perfect woman for him, she'd be it.

He was falling in love, faster than he would have thought possible and enjoying every minute of the trip.

For now, though, he needed to focus on ending this magical weekend with a bang. Kawan knew exactly how he wanted to wrap things up. Grinning, he headed for the stairs.

CHAPTER 22

*T*he silence was deafening.

Melody had rushed upstairs, hurried through going to the bathroom and brushing her teeth, before practically throwing herself over the side of Daddy's bed. Butt up in the air, hands and cheek pressed against the mattress, she waited.

And waited.

And waited.

Every second seemed to stretch as long as an hour.

Was waiting part of the punishment? Because if it were, it was really working.

She'd already felt ashamed of how she'd behaved as a 'teen'. She couldn't even really explain *why* she'd gotten so mouthy. Teenage rebellion maybe? The urge to be a good girl just hadn't been strong enough against her urge to do what she wanted and say what she wanted. The snark had been strong this morning.

Too strong.

When she finally heard Daddy's footsteps coming down the hall, she was already so wound up, she tensed even more.

What was he going to do?

The creak of the door opening made her want to whimper as her very exposed, very vulnerable position slammed home.

"Good girl." Daddy's smooth tone made her relax slightly.

At least she'd managed to do *this* right.

She peeked over her shoulder to see Daddy standing a few feet behind her, hands on his hips, obviously admiring the view. Melody turned beet red, because her current bent over position, with her legs spread to make it easy for her to rest her upper body on the mattress, showed *everything*. Her feet started to inch inward.

Smack!

She squealed, the stinging spot on her thigh throbbing.

"Keep those legs nice and wide, baby girl," Daddy said sternly.

Now her thigh wasn't the only part of her that was throbbing. Even though she knew she was about to be punished, she was already getting turned on. Fingers stroked down over the small of her back, right down the center of her crease to her anus. Instinctively, Melody tried to clench her cheeks as Daddy massaged her little hole, but the widespread position made it exceedingly difficult, if not impossible.

"A plug first," Daddy murmured, and Melody bit back a moan as her arousal surged.

A few moments later, something hard and slick pressed against her rosebud. Melody pressed her forehead against the back of one hand, breathing deeply and trying to relax as Daddy worked the thick plastic back and forth. It felt so much *bigger* than before. The stretch was starting to burn painfully, her muscles protesting against the thickness of the plug.

"Daddy, it's too big," she protested, trying to move forward, away from the plug. Of course she was trapped by the bed, with nowhere to go and the plug continued inexorably deeper, making her whimper as she was stretched even further open.

The slick lube meant the plug easily kept pushing past her clenching muscles. While it helped ease the rubber toy's entry, it did nothing to help her with the burn from being forced open so wide.

"No, baby, you can take it." His hand massaged her lower back. "Just relax and bear down."

A white hot burst of painful pleasure ricocheted through her as the thickest part of the plug pushed past her entrance. She gasped and rocked forward on her toes at the sensation. The plug nestled inside of her, thick and uncomfortable although the stinging burn was thankfully subsiding now that her sphincter was securely clenched in the plug's notch.

It felt huge inside of her and she panted for breath as her body adjusted to the invasion. While it didn't feel bad, exactly, she wasn't sure that she could say it felt good either. Yet the discomfort, the feeling of being so intimately invaded, totally turned her on.

"Good girl." Daddy's praise warmed her. She moaned when he twisted the base of the plug, turning it inside of her. The little nerve endings around that particular entrance felt exquisitely sensitive right now. Her toes tried to curl in reaction to the sensation and she fisted the sheets on the bed, panting even harder for breath as pure lust shot through her.

THE THICK BLACK plug was firmly lodged inside Melody's tight hole, but Kawan couldn't help but play with it. He loved her little reactions: the hitch of her breath, the way her bottom cheeks moved when she clenched, and the squirming movements as she became more aroused.

His cock was rock hard, ready to replace the plug, but punishment before pleasure.

"You were a naughty girl this morning, weren't you?" he

asked, continuing to toy with the plug, pulling on it. She gasped as her little hole began to stretch again and then sighed with relief when he let the plug go.

"I was being a teenager," she said, a little sulkily, sounding a bit like she had that morning.

Kawan chuckled, tapping the base of the plug and making her squirm. "Not all teenagers are little sassboxes all the time you know. And even when you weren't being sassy, you weren't following directions either. You deliberately wandered off rather than meeting me where you were supposed to after using the restroom."

There was a moment of silence, since she couldn't really argue with that.

"I'm sorry, Daddy," she said, her voice sincere.

"I know you are, baby, but that doesn't mean your behavior can go unpunished." It wasn't going to be a very harsh punishment, more of an attitude readjustment. And then some fun for both of them.

His hand caressed her ass, sliding over the soft curve down to her pussy. With her legs slightly spread, he could see all the delicate pink folds, glistening with her arousal. He traced his finger through her sensitive flesh, teasing her wet heat, and grinned as he circled her clit and she moaned in response.

The cheeks of her ass clenched and then quivered, releasing, and he could hear her panting for breath again. If she'd tightened around the plug, it would have made it feel even bigger, and this was already the largest he'd used on her.

"I think a count of twenty is appropriate," he mused, as if he was just making up his mind on the spot, his finger still sliding around her swollen clit, teasing the little bud. Melody moaned in response, her bottom lifting up slightly, like an offering. "If you're a good girl and don't move out of position, it'll just be twenty with my hand. If you're a naughty girl and try to cover your bottom or stand up, I'll add five with the hairbrush."

"Yes, Daddy." Excitement threaded through her answer and Kawan wondered if she might be naughty just to see what the hairbrush felt like.

His mouth quirked. It was likely she thought he was going to go easy on her with his hand.

Well. It was simple enough to disabuse her of that notion.

SMACK!

She gasped, jerking forward, and then shuddering when she inadvertently clenched around the plug in response to the hard swat. Kawan didn't wait for the sting to sink in, he immediately drew back his hand and landed another stinging slap to the other side of her ass.

SMACK!

"Ow! Daddy, that hurts!"

"That's the idea, baby girl," he said, somewhat amused. "Naughty girls get real spankings."

SMACK! SMACK! SMACK!

Although her feet danced in place a bit, making her bottom jiggle even more, she didn't stand or try to cover herself. The sound of palm meeting flesh was interspersed with her little gasps of pain. Dark pink splotches bloomed on her creamy skin, giving him nice pale targets to aim for next.

Kawan pressed his free hand against his throbbing cock as he watched her buttocks turning pinker and her pussy becoming even more swollen and creamy under the painful assault. He loved the way a well-spanked bottom looked, and Melody's was certainly a beautiful one.

Now Melody *really* wished she'd been better behaved at the fair. At the very least she could have told Daddy that she didn't want to be a teenager. Her hips began to move up and down, trying to relieve some of the aching burn and also seeking out stimulation for her needy pussy.

Despite the plug filling her bottom, she felt achingly empty, and after Daddy had teased but not actually touched her clit, she wanted to rub herself against anything that she could. The angle at which she was bent over the mattress wasn't quite right but it was so close.

SMACK!

SMACK!

She'd already stopped paying attention to the count, too wracked with rising lust and the growing burn from her spanking to care. Heat and need flared inside of her as Daddy spanked her, the punishment fueling her passion. It hurt; he wasn't giving her a gentle spanking by any means, but it turned her on too.

The throbbing burn, the plug filling her most intimate area, made her feel decadently naughty and deliciously depraved. It didn't matter that it hurt; she was lifting her hips to meet each swat, the pain fulfilling her in a way that pleasure alone just couldn't satisfy.

When she moved to meet the next swat and it didn't come, she whimpered in disappointment.

"Good girl," Daddy said, and his palm came down to rest on her hot bottom. Not with a slap, but with a caress that made her moan as the pleasure and pain spun together inside of her. "We're almost done."

The slight sting of his hand squeezing her punished cheek contrasted sharply with the sudden, arousing stir of sensations when she felt him pulling at the plug again. This time he didn't just tease, he pulled until her anus was forced back open around the thickest part, making her cry out and shudder. Her toes curled; the feeling of being emptied, of the toy receding, stimulating her in an entirely different way than before.

Just as the plug had made her feel fuller than ever, the lack of it made her feel emptier than she would have thought possible.

Something softer but thicker pushed at the slightly gaping hole the plug left behind, and Melody instinctively knew it was Daddy's cock.

"Oh, please..." She choked out the words, halting because she couldn't possibly beg him to put his cock *there.*

"Please what, baby girl?" he asked, dropping a kiss to her spine, the position pushing him deeper in her ass. She gasped at the burn, the way his cock widened her already stretched muscles. There was no comfortable notch for her sphincter to settle into though, there was nothing but the burning stretch as he sank deeper into her.

Her soft pants as she was stretched, filled, his cock creating a burning path between her roasted cheeks, did little to help ease the discomfort. Yet she didn't ask him to stop. It was so filthy, so raw, so wonderfully *perverse* to have his cock sliding into that intimate space. Melody had never felt more submissive or more aroused.

"Please, Daddy, more..."

Daddy groaned, his hands gripping her hips, and he withdrew slightly before pushing in even deeper. Her pussy pulsed in response, her delicate muscles clenching around him in hot spasms that did nothing to ease the uncomfortable ache of his invasion or her growing arousal.

"Oh it hurts..." She moaned the words, pressing her face against the mattress, gasping for air as Daddy pushed deeper.

"I know it does, baby girl, but you're going to take it for Daddy, aren't you?" Daddy's voice was smooth, his fingers tightening on her hips. Despite his words, his forward momentum slowed, leaving her hot and throbbing around him but not yet entirely filled by him.

Melody had the insane urge to push back against him, until her roasted bottom was pressed against his body and his cock was fully embedded inside of her... but she had no way of knowing how much further he had to go.

"Yes, Daddy," she said, gripping the sheets beneath her even tighter. She peeked over her shoulder, but Daddy wasn't looking at her face, he was watching his cock slowly disappearing between the reddened cheeks of her ass.

"Good girl." Daddy's hands pressed down, holding her in place, before he pulled back and then pushed forward again, sinking another couple of inches into her hot hole. Crying out, she shuddered underneath him, clenching and squirming. Daddy massaged her lower back muscles with his thumbs, helping her to relax as he murmured again that she was a good girl. Flexing his hips, he thrust forward, finally burying himself completely inside of her, and making her gasp as his body pressed against the hot swells of her buttocks.

Then he began to pull away and the sensation of his cock dragging out of her body, rasping against her sensitive nerves, made her writhe. Somehow it felt even more intense than the insertion had. Then he reversed and began to fill her again.

Melody could only whimper and moan as Daddy began a long, slow ride of her ass. Each thrust went deep before pulling out almost to the head, and then sliding back in again. The sensory overload of the invasively pleasurable strokes combined with his body pressing against her sensitized cheeks every time he buried himself inside of her was overwhelming.

Then his hands slid up her sides, pressing underneath of her so he could cup her breasts, adding to the confusing mix of sensations whirling through her. Discomfort, pleasure, pain, the stinging burn and the erotic heat... he wasn't even touching her pussy and she could feel her orgasm growing inside of her.

"Oh, Daddy!"

"Do you like it?" he asked, pinching her nipples, thrusting his cock back into her a little harder now. It sank easily inside of her, her muscles had adjusted to his thick length, although the sensations were still uncomfortably intense.

"Yes! Yes, Daddy, I love it!" She practically sobbed the words out.

As if in reward, Daddy began to move harder, faster. Flinging her head back, Melody arched her back as strange ecstasy curled her body. It burned, far more than the spanking had, as his rougher thrusts increased the friction. Her nipples throbbed between his fingers and her pussy pulsed emptily in response.

"Oh, Daddy.... oh, Daddy..." she began to chant, over and over again as his cock drove her closer and closer to a deep, powerful orgasm. The faster movements made his balls slap against her pussy, sparking pleasure in her sensitive lips and clit.

Daddy's warm breath flowed over the back of her neck, her hips lifting to meet his hard thrusts, his cock pressing against a pleasure point she hadn't even known existed, deep inside of her body. Ecstasy coiled, a deep, implacable throbbing that left her gasping for air as it swelled inside of her.

As if sensing that she was on the cusp, one of Daddy's hands left her breasts and moved downward, thrusting between her thighs. The sharp pinch to her clit was all she needed to push her over the edge. She wailed as almost painful ecstasy flooded her system, unraveling all the coiled tension that had been wound so tightly inside of her.

She felt tears rolling down her face at the intensity of her climax, which only increased when she felt Daddy's cock begin to pulse inside of her. The thick length felt even thicker, harder, and she screamed in glorious bliss, rippling around him, as her clenching muscles milked hot jets of fluid from his pulsing cock.

~

"SUCH A GOOD GIRL," Kawan groaned, his grip tightening on Melody's hips as he emptied himself into her tight ass. He rubbed her clit in slow, methodical circles, feeling her jerk underneath him, and slowly brought her down from her intense orgasm.

With his body covering hers, he could feel each contraction, each shudder of her muscles as she spasmed in hot rapture. The sensations were sinful and her tight grip around his cock, pulling at him, had given him one of the most intense orgasms of his life.

Finally, she slumped beneath him, her muscles languid, the tight grip of her ass easing around him. Kawan kissed her shoulder.

"*Such* a good girl," he repeated.

She made a small little sound of contentment, and then moaned when he began to pull his softening erection from her ass. The little hole was left pink and swollen, gaping slightly from use. Kawan lowered his lips to press a soft kiss to one hot red cheek, smiling as she quivered slightly at his touch.

Pulling her upward, he lifted her in his arms. Her head lolled sleepily against his shoulder.

"Okay, baby girl," he said, heading for the bathroom. "Let's go get you cleaned up."

"Okay, Daddy," she said, snuggling into him with a sleepy sigh.

CHAPTER 23

*M*elody thought that the transition back to work and the real world would be weird, and she was surprised at how easy it was. Maybe because work was part of her usual routine, while the weekend had been like stepping out of the real world and into a magical place for a little while.

The magic still lingered though, bringing a little smile to her lips over all sorts of things. Inappropriate things. Like, she really shouldn't be smiling over the careful way she had to sit down, and yet she couldn't stop the edges of her mouth from curving upwards in remembrance of *why* she was so sore.

She'd also worried about being distracted, worried that she might not be able to focus when she had so many other things to think about, but if anything, she got more work done than ever. It reminded her of how she'd felt after being at Black Light —like something had settled inside of her. She felt refreshed, more grounded, and like she could take on the world.

Of course, all she needed to take on was blood and stool samples, but she was super on top of it. Even Colin noticed how much work she was getting done, and she actually managed to leave the lab early, feeling like she was floating on top of the world. Lisa told her that McCready's noxious presence had pretty much disappeared. All the women in the department were talking about how he'd suddenly been making himself scarce which was a huge relief to everyone.

The best part was getting to go home to Daddy.

Although he'd told her she could call him Kawan when she was 'big,' and especially if they were in a social situation where she'd feel more comfortable doing so, she doubted she'd be able to think of him as anything other than Daddy after this past weekend.

Even though she'd hadn't been staying with him for long, it felt like she'd been there forever. In a good way. Like she'd finally come home.

Then they went out to dinner with Alexander and Sienna. Which was fun. She really liked both of them, and she really loved being out with a couple who had a similar dynamic. Sienna even called Alexander 'Daddy' right in front of their server who, to his credit, didn't blink an eye. The problem came up when she and Sienna went to the bathroom together after ordering dessert.

"You and Kawan seem to be getting along really well," Sienna said as they walked back. She winked at Melody. "Even though some people might think you moving in with him so fast was a mistake, anyone who looks at you can tell it was a good decision."

Melody glanced over her shoulder, to see him leaning back in his chair and saying something to Alexander. Going by the smile on his face, it was something he found amusing. "It's moving fast, but it feels good. Right."

"I'm glad." Sienna smiled at her, holding the bathroom door open so Melody could precede her. "We were worried about him for a while. His ex really did a number on him. She was a total user. Alexander likes to give Kawan a hard time, but I know he was relieved when Kawan decided to move up here and away from that whole scene. He was worried Krissy might be able to play her damsel-in-distress card again and suck Kawan right back into her black hole."

Shaking her head in disgust, Sienna went into one of the stalls, completely unaware that she'd just tilted Melody's world on its axis. Of course, she knew that Daddy had a serious ex and the breakup had been bad, but he hadn't really gone into details. A damsel-in-distress and a user... that sounded uncomfortably like Melody herself, although she definitely didn't mean to be either.

"Her damsel-in-distress card?" she asked, as casually as she could, thankful to be going into her own private stall that hid her expressions.

"Oh yeah, Krissy was a master manipulator," Sienna answered immediately. "She figured out immediately that Kawan likes to be the hero and she totally used that against him to get whatever she wanted. Mostly what she wanted was for him to pay for everything. She wanted a sugar daddy, not a *Daddy* if you get my meaning."

Melody did, and she felt a little sick inside. Even though she didn't want a sugar daddy, she wanted Daddy, that didn't change the fact that she had definitely been a damsel-in-distress when they'd first met and that hadn't changed much after their second meeting. He'd offered to let her stay with him immediately... and she hadn't exactly been proactive about looking for a new place.

He didn't act like he wanted her out, but despite what Sienna had said, maybe it was too soon for them to actually be living together. Maybe he assumed she was looking for a new place on her own time, but she hadn't been. She'd gotten so caught up in how good, how right, everything felt that she hadn't really *wanted* to look for a new place.

But that wasn't fair to him.

She didn't want to use him like his ex had.

She was going to have to start looking for a new living situation as soon as she could. There was no way she wanted him to start feeling like she was taking advantage of him, and, in a way, that was exactly what she'd been doing. Well, that was going to end as soon as she was able to manage.

～

SOMETHING WAS WRONG.

Having made a study of Melody's facial expressions and body language, he picked up on it right away although he doubted anyone else would have. There was just something a little too tight about her smile, a little shadow on her brow that said she was worried about something.

She'd been just fine before she and Sienna had gone to the bathroom.

Kawan almost wanted to demand to know what Sienna had said to upset her, but he managed to hold back. For one, he seriously doubted Sienna had purposefully upset Melody. For two, Melody obviously didn't want anyone to know she was upset, and until he knew what was bothering her and why, he would respect that.

She did seem to relax a little over dessert, but on the drive home, she was quiet and contemplative, and not very forthcoming about what was on her mind.

"Are you okay?" he asked, squeezing her hand a little to emphasize his worry.

Turning her head, she smiled at him. "Yes! Sorry, I'm just a little distracted. And tired."

"You've been working hard." Some days she didn't get home from the lab until after dinner, although he always made sure to have a plate to heat up for her. He'd thought being a lawyer meant long hours, but she worked just as much as he did, if not more.

"I've been getting a lot done though. And now I have a good amount of play to balance out all my hard work," she said teasingly, squeezing his fingers back.

Kawan grinned. That she did—he made sure of it.

In fact, tonight he was thinking that a fun Disney movie, popcorn, and cuddling on the couch would be a good way to end the evening. Unfortunately, Melody had other plans, and when they got home, she said she had some things to do on the computer for a bit.

It wasn't suspicious in and of itself, but the *way* she said it made him think that something was up. He knew he was right when he sat down on the couch to watch some television and, instead of settling in next to him the way she normally did when she needed to use the computer, she put her laptop down on the dining room table and sat there. Screen facing away from him.

Fighting the frown that wanted to form on his face, he made himself focus on the television when he saw her glance over her shoulder... as if she was looking to see if he was watching her. He was, but the surreptitious way she checked on him was suspect.

Everything about her body language screamed guilt, but he couldn't figure out why.

She practically jumped out of her seat, her head jerking up, when he got up a few minutes later to go to the bathroom, only relaxing when she saw he was headed in the other direction. Something was definitely up and he was going to get to the bottom of it.

Rather than using the bathroom, he stealthily moved through the house, taking the roundabout way back to the dining room so that he could come up behind her and see what she was doing on the computer. He didn't think it would be nefarious, but something had her acting out of the norm, and he was determined to discover what it was.

While the instinct to text Sienna and ask her what she and Melody had talked about in the bathroom was still present, he'd prefer to talk to Melody directly. Well, direct in a sneaky way, since she was trying to hide whatever was wrong from him.

Creeping up behind her from the darkened hallway—and trying not to feel *too* much like an actual creeper as he did so—he peered over her shoulder to look at the computer screen.

His brow furrowed when he realized she was browsing apartment listings. Why was she looking at those?

"What are you doing?"

HER HEART JUMPED from her chest into her throat, stifling her scream, when Daddy's deep voice suddenly came from behind her. And it was definitely *Daddy's* voice. The particular intonation he used in the bedroom, when he was dominating her, and not his usual speaking voice.

Immediately, her hand shot out to try and close the laptop, but it was too late. He had her by the wrist before her fingers even touched the screen.

"What are you doing, little girl?" he asked again. This time he sounded even more displeased, the way he did right before she got a spanking. He was looming over her, looking at her like she'd been naughty.

But she wasn't doing anything wrong!

"I… just… I…" she stammered out the words before tugging her hand away from his and finally turning to face him. The dark expression on his face didn't help bolster her courage at all, but she managed to get herself together anyway. "I was just looking for apartments or rooms for rent."

"Why?" His expression flickered. "Are you unhappy here?" The second question was asked in a very different tone, a much less certain one. Melody didn't at all like the change in his demeanor, as he went from confident Daddy to insecure and slightly hurt man. That was *not* how she'd meant to make him feel.

"No!" She was horrified that he might think so. Now it was her turn to grab his hand "I'm very happy! But... well, it's so early in our relationship, and I know this wasn't meant to be a permanent thing..." Her voice trailed off nervously as he began to look very thoughtful.

"It is early, but it's been working. At least it has for me; are we moving things too quickly for you?"

For some reason, and she wasn't sure why, she felt like the reasonableness of his tone was a trap. Especially when his hand flipped hers around, so that he was the one holding on to her again, his thumb making little circles around the center of her palm. Melody did her best not to fidget in her seat.

"No... I mean, it's a little quick, but it hasn't felt that way."

Daddy's eyebrow quirked upward. "Then why the rush to leave? And why are you being so sneaky about it?"

"I don't know," she said, starting to feel irritable. "Why the inquisition? I just thought I should look at what's out there, so you don't end up thinking I'm using you for housing or anything."

His dark eyes sharpened, focused, and Melody felt a little bit like a mouse, caught by a cat.

"Sienna said something about Krissy to you," he surmised.

"So what? It just made me realize that you offered me a place here, but it wasn't supposed to be permanent, and then we haven't talked about it since I started staying here—"

"That's right, baby girl," he said silkily. "We *haven't* talked. Instead, you decided to sneak around behind my back and start doing things without talking to me about it at all."

"I haven't actually done anything yet," she protested. But he had a point. She hadn't wanted to bring it up to him because she hadn't wanted *him* to think that she was using him for housing, but that wasn't fair to him either. Deep down, she'd known that she should just talk to him.

Otherwise she wouldn't have felt so guilty about looking online.

∾

OH, his sweet little baby girl.

There was a protective streak there that he very much enjoyed, since it was directed at him, but he couldn't condone her making important decisions without talking to him. Especially decisions that affected him.

"Which is good, because I'd like you to stay." While it was soon—far sooner than he would have anticipated—he thought they had a good thing going and he didn't see any reason to change it.

She blinked at him, like she didn't quite understand what he was saying, and once she *did*, her expression turned disbelieving.

"You don't mean that."

Kawan felt his lips quirk. "I assure you I do."

"But... you can't. I can't." Now she was beginning to look rather stubborn and she tried to tug her hand away from him again, but Kawan didn't release his hold.

"Why not?" he asked, honestly curious. It seemed clear to him that she wanted to stay.

"Because I'm not going to use you that way!"

"You aren't using me, I'm offering," he pointed out with some amusement. "Besides, users don't try to reject offers. I already know you're not using me." Something flickered across her face, an emotion too fleeting for him to pin down, but he had a feeling he knew its source. "I think the problem is you're worried that *other* people might think you're using me. Which is unlikely, but even if they did, I don't care. What matters is that you and I know."

Surprisingly, rather than give in, her expression became even more mulish.

"Just because you're willing to be used doesn't make it right." She tugged on her hand again.

Kawan studied her for a long moment, pleased when some of her stiff demeanor slid away under his heavy perusal. She began to look more uncertain the longer he remained silent. Perhaps it was time to stop being so logical and start being her Daddy, since she wasn't willing to listen to reason.

Rather than giving up her hand, he used it to pull her up out of her seat and flipped her over his shoulder. Squealing, Melody's leg's kicked as she ended up with her bottom in the air.

"What are you doing?"

"Reminding you who's in charge." He slapped her upturned ass for good measure, making her shriek. "You couldn't make me do anything I don't want to do, baby girl. Now, this is only going to end in one of three ways: you can either give me a good reason why *you* don't want to live here, you can say your safe word, or you can agree to live here with me until such time as our relationship ends."

"What? You're... Daddy! We need to talk about this!"

"One of three ways, baby girl." Carrying her over his shoulder like a prize he'd won, he headed for the living room.

DADDY WAS EVIL.

Melody had heard about a Hitachi before, but she'd never used one—or had one used on her—before Daddy strapped her wrists to her ankles, set her literally hanging off the edge of the coffee table with her upper body supported by the hard wood, and then pressed the fat head against her clit and turned it on.

The intense vibrations were like nothing she'd ever experienced before, and she went from curious, mildly aroused, and stubbornly refusing to agree to live with him, to crying out from an almost painfully fast and intense orgasm within seconds.

Then, when she was still gasping for air, he gave her four hard swats—two on each cheek.

"So, are you going to keep living with me, talk to me, or say your safe word?" Daddy asked, and she could hear the amusement threading his voice.

He thought this was funny?

She gritted her teeth. "I shouldn't stay here!"

"That's not one of the options, baby girl." Before she could say anything more, the whirring noise of the Hitachi filled the air again and the rubbery bulb pressed against her open pussy lips. Daddy moved it down her slit and back over her clit and Melody screamed as she came again, her toes curling as her body jerked and spasmed.

These weren't like usual climaxes, they didn't build and release. No, they were being *ripped* from her, an involuntary reaction that both turned her on and infuriated her.

It also demonstrated her Daddy's absolute control over her body, and her complete inability to make him do anything he didn't want to do. But he had to realize how it looked—how it would look to everyone. Melody hadn't even told her parents about her housing switch-up, although she knew she would have to eventually.

Four more hard smacks landed on her upturned bottom while she panted and gasped for air. Tears had sprung up into the corners of her eyes, and she felt like she was splintering apart into little pieces.

Hanging off of the coffee table, the corner pressing against her elbows and waist, her mind whirled. *Did* she really even want to leave? Did she care more about what other people might think than about what would make her happy?

"Three options, Melody, which one would you like to take?"

She hesitated a moment too long and was left screaming and sobbing again as the Hitachi drove her to another blistering orgasm.

"I'll stay!" She practically screamed out the words when he finally pulled the vibrating wand away from her poor, overstimulated clit. Tears leaked down her cheeks and on to the wooden tabletop beneath her. Her arms and legs were beginning to ache —not from the position so much as because her movements were so restrained while she was orgasming.

"I'm so pleased to hear that, baby girl," Daddy said, his voice warm. A large palm cupped her bottom, squeezing it firmly but not roughly. "Now let's talk about why you should have had a conversation with me instead of sneaking around."

Melody whimpered.

Four orgasms later, Daddy finally felt the message had been driven home—that or he was taking pity on her. He undid her restraints, which were totally unnecessary at that point because her muscles felt so weak and watery, flipped her onto her back and then drove his cock into her.

At that point she was so sensitized that every bit of extra stimulation made her feel like her body was being drowned in pleasure, one long, relentless orgasm flooding her senses. She barely even remembered being put to bed or the soft lips pressing a kiss to her temple as the quiet peace of sleep slipped over her.

CHAPTER 24

"Ooo, let's look at the lingerie! I need something naughty for the weekend." Sienna's eyes lit up as she veered toward the section full of lace, silks, and corsets.

It kind of surprised Melody because she would have assumed that Sienna would shop online or at a kinkier store... but then she remembered that Daddy had mentioned something about Black Light doing a theme night this Saturday. She hadn't been paying much attention, because he'd said he'd pick her clothes.

Unfortunately, she couldn't ask Sienna to remind her what the theme was because...

"Ugh, I wish I needed something naughty for the weekend," Lisa said, sounding envious as she followed Sienna toward the lingerie.

The three of them had gone out to happy hour, Melody nervously braving trying to bring two of her friends together again. She didn't exactly have a lot of free evenings, so it had seemed like the best way to spend time with both of them. Thankfully, Lisa and Sienna got along much better than Lisa and Peggy had.

It was a little weird, bringing her work world and her kinky world together, but it also made getting to know Sienna outside of club stuff a lot easier. If it had been just the two of them, they probably would have spent most of their time talking about the sexy stuff. Sienna was really good about answering Melody's questions, and it was really nice having someone else to talk to who understood what it meant to have a Daddy.

But with Lisa there, they ended up talking about work, life, past experiences, and all sorts of things that she hadn't actually talked to Sienna about before. Which made her realize how much she really liked the other woman, outside of all the kinky stuff they had in common.

"Ooo, this is pretty," Sienna said, picking up a silky blue baby doll and holding it in front of herself. There was white lace over the blue silk on the bust and a little bow that tied the sides together. The silky empire skirt would go down to about mid-thigh, but plenty of skin would be visible since there was only the one tie between the breasts.

It also finally reminded Melody of the theme for the weekend—Silk and Seduction night!

She wondered what Daddy was going to get for her.

"I love it," she said, rather enviously. Maybe Daddy would pick out something like it. There was a faint little voice in her head though, Peggy's derisive tones: *Oh sweetie, not with your body.*

It would be really nice if she could get Peggy's voice out of her head one day.

Then she realized, it wasn't just in her head. She could actually hear Peggy's voice.

Melody whipped around and her heart sank when she realized she was right. Coming into the section, although she didn't seem to have noticed Melody yet, was Peggy and another woman. Her ex-friend looked the same as ever, put together and laughing, her red hair pulled back in a curly bun.

For one long moment, she felt a kind of yearning, as she watched Peggy laughing with abandon. She *missed* laughing with Peggy. Missed the camaraderie and the late nights and the gossip sessions. Yes, she had new friends, but that didn't stop her from missing her old one, no matter how it had ended. There was still a little part of her wondering why it had to end.

Then Peggy's eyes met Melody's and the laughter slid away to a sneer... oh yeah. That's why it ended. Because that was the same expression Peggy had on her face when she'd told Melody to get out. Because she hadn't been able to handle that Melody might want to make her own choices about her own life. Because Melody had finally bucked Peggy's control.

Looking at Peggy now, feeling herself shrinking back as Peggy's eyes narrowed in displeasure, it suddenly hit home how much she'd allowed Peggy to control her life just because she hadn't wanted to make waves. Which made the fact that she liked handing control of her life over to Daddy sound strange, but it was *different.*

Daddy still listened to and respected what she wanted and needed. Peggy had always bulldozed through any of Melody's protests. Daddy accepted the decisions Melody needed to make for herself. Peggy had kicked Melody out of the apartment as soon as she hadn't liked one of Melody's decisions—about something that had been none of her business. Daddy's control was something Melody willingly gave him. Peggy had taken it. Melody had let her. But not anymore.

It didn't stop her from missing her friend, but she knew she was better off with Peggy out of her life.

If she'd had any doubts, she didn't anymore... not with Peggy looking at her with such antagonism. A hot feeling of shame flushed through her, followed by fear, because Peggy never minded making a scene. Peggy was all about confrontation. And looking at her right now, all the feelings of missing her and wishing things hadn't changed between them melted away, and all Melody wanted to do was run.

"Pretty sure women pretending to be babies aren't supposed to be wearing lingerie," Peggy called out, her voice full of censure and mocking. Melody froze in place, the hot shame rushing up from her chest to her cheeks, and she could feel them turning red.

"Ew," said the woman next to her, wrinkling her nose. "She pretends to be a baby?"

"And calls her boyfriend 'Daddy.'" Peggy's voice went higher on the last word, like a little girl's, but full of malice.

It felt like everyone in the store was suddenly staring at them —at Melody. Judging her. Although the strangers didn't bother her as much as her friends being there. She could only imagine what Lisa must be thinking. And poor Sienna, she had to be freaking out, worried she was about to be outed.

She wanted to run, but her legs wouldn't move. She wanted to snap back at Peggy, but her mind had gone utterly blank and she couldn't think of a single thing to say. All the times she'd imagined running into Peggy, she'd never imagined anything like this... if it were just her, she could run, but she was with Sienna and Lisa. If they even wanted to admit they were with her right now.

"So what?" Sienna's voice rang out just as loudly as Peggy's did. "I call my fiancé Daddy too. It's hot. A lot of men like to be called Daddy."

The utter lack of shame in her tone penetrated the humiliated haze that had gathered around Melody. Not only was Sienna *not* embarrassed about Melody being outed in public, she was joining her. Someone else somewhere in the store laughed.

"It's not just that though," Peggy said, sounding scandalized, but her eyes flared with temper. She didn't like that Sienna was standing up for Melody, the same way she hadn't liked it when

Melody stood up for herself. It occurred to Melody that Peggy wanted to embarrass her, wanted to watch Melody run away. Because she was a bully. "She acts like a *little girl* when she calls him that. Like a baby."

"Well, if only I had some pearls to clutch, I'm sure I'd be able to react appropriately." Lisa said with a snort, sounding completely unfazed by the revelations being tossed around her. In fact, when Melody looked at Lisa, the other woman was actually rolling her eyes. She didn't care at all. Melody could feel the coil of tension inside her begin to unwind.

Sienna and Lisa were on her side. And Peggy was looking somehow smaller. Less threatening. Less important. Melody had already decided that she didn't care what Peggy thought, weeks ago, so why was she letting Peggy affect her now?

"It's perverted!" Peggy sounded outraged, but the woman standing next to her was no longer laughing with derision. The other customers within earshot weren't even pretending not to listen anymore and none of them seemed horrified, they just looked like they were enjoying the show. No one was staring at Melody like she was a freak. No one except Peggy.

"It's none of your business," Melody said, finally finding her tongue. Sienna and Lisa's reactions—well, their lack thereof—had given her strength. She straightened, facing down her ex-friend in a way that she hadn't before, even when she'd defied Peggy's demands. "We're two consenting adults, and we're not asking you to play with us. I don't know why you ever thought you got a say in what I do."

"Because I'm your friend! Or I was, until you turned out to be a shitty friend." Peggy's face was starting to turn red with frustration and anger. "I was supposed to look out for you!"

"By kicking me out of the apartment because you didn't like who I was dating?" Melody's temper, which had been smothered by her embarrassment, started to rise. "By trying to control my sex life? By mocking me and issuing ultimatums? By trying to embarrass me out in public when you could have just walked on by?" She looked at the woman standing next to Peggy, who was looking increasingly uncomfortable with the way the conversation was going. "If you're getting close with her, this is what you have to look forward to when she decides you're not friend material anymore."

Peggy flushed even brighter red, her fists clenching at her sides. "Fuck you, Melody! Go play your perverted games, but don't come crawling back to me when he dumps you for someone younger because you don't look like a little girl anymore!"

Glancing down at her breasts, which were by no means small or hidden, Melody had to laugh. "I'm pretty sure I don't look like a little girl right now."

Making a disgusted noise, Peggy spun around and stormed off as a sense of triumph welled up inside of Melody. Peggy's companion hesitated, glancing after Peggy and then looking back at Melody before finally turning and walking off—in a different direction than Peggy had gone.

Melody let out a long breath, shaking slightly from the adrenaline still coursing through her.

"Holy shit, girl!" Lisa's arms came around Melody from behind, giving her a huge hug and eliciting a surprised gasp from Melody. "I'm so proud of you!"

Another small impact rocked them both as Sienna came in from the side, hugging both of them. "I am too! Who the hell was that?"

They broke apart, so that Melody could turn around and face both of them. She felt rather sheepish, embarrassed again but for a different reason this time.

"That was Peggy." She'd told Sienna that she'd had a falling out with her former roommate and had to move out, but they hadn't gone into why and Sienna hadn't pressed. Lisa knew more about the situation, because she'd met Peggy and knew they hadn't just been roommates, but Melody hadn't told her exactly why they'd had an argument either. Just that they'd had one and Peggy had told her to move out. Lisa hadn't exactly been surprised.

"Ugh. Thank goodness you don't live with her anymore," Sienna said, wrinkling her nose.

"Right?" Lisa chimed in, shaking her head. "I never understood how you could put up with her. She's completely toxic."

"She was a good friend at one point..." Melody started to say and then her voice trailed off, because the truth was that it didn't matter how Peggy had come through for her or been a good friend at some point. In the end, she'd turned into a terrible friend and, Lisa was right, a very toxic one.

"Well, no one's *all* bad," Sienna said, sympathetically. "I stand by what I said though. She sucks. And not in the fun way."

Kind of hard to argue with that and Melody felt her lips tugging up in a reluctant smile. She wished that Peggy was different and their friendship had gone differently, but that wasn't up to her. And maybe Peggy hadn't been all bad, but she hadn't been good for Melody either.

"So..." Lisa drew out the word, her eyes sliding back and forth between Melody and Sienna. "Daddy, huh?"

This time when Melody blushed, it didn't feel like a bad thing. Lisa looked more curious than anything else, and she'd already demonstrated that she didn't care.

"Yeah. Um..." She groped for words but Lisa held up her hand, palm facing Melody, to stop her.

"You don't have to explain. Not my thing, but I'm not the one being asked to call my boyfriend Daddy." Lisa sighed, dropping her hand. "Not that I have a boyfriend anyway."

"Do you want one?" Sienna asked, in the same tone she might ask if Lisa wanted ice cream. Like, if she answered yes, then Sienna would take them to the part of the store where they could just pick one out for her.

"Eh. Maybe later." Lisa shrugged. "I'm too busy with school right now. I don't know how Melody manages to balance it all. I'd be going nuts."

"Who says I'm not?" Melody teased.

As the other two laughed and moved back to the lingerie, she couldn't help but glance over her shoulder. There was no sign of Peggy though. She had disappeared from Melody's life as quickly and fully as she had the first time. It was probably for the best.

Melody had real friends now. The kind who supported her and didn't try to manipulate or coerce her. Heck, she and Lisa might have been better friends sooner if it hadn't been for Peggy. Being friends with Peggy had made her so isolated, and she had a feeling that was how Peggy had wanted it.

She was better off now. She hoped that Peggy would find happiness, but she could do it without Melody in her life.

WHEN MELODY CAME HOME, Kawan was sitting on the couch reading through his latest case file. Looking up, his whole chest felt like it loosened when he saw her coming through the door. Of course he'd known it was her, but seeing her coming in with a bright smile on her face, made his home feel complete. She beamed as soon as she saw him, dropping her purse and the shopping bag in her hand as she bounded toward him. Chuckling, he set the file aside just in time for her to jump onto his lap.

"Hello there," he said, tilting his head back and pulling her down for a kiss.

Ever since they'd decided she was staying with him, she'd finally really started settling in. Her pictures had joined his on the walls and shelves, her books side by side with his, and her little decorations were out. Seeing how happy and settled she was gave him a sense of satisfaction every time he looked at her.

And having her delicious curves pressed against his lap gave him a hard on. His hands dropped down to her bottom, digging his fingers into her soft flesh.

"Daddy!" she squealed, pulling away from the kiss and wriggling on top of him in a manner that did absolutely nothing to allay his desire. "I was just saying hello."

"I'm just saying hello too," he replied innocently, giving her another squeeze with both hands. "And hello again."

She giggled, but there was some tension in her body and her happiness didn't quite go all the way through her eyes. Tilting his head to the side, he changed his grip to a softer, more soothing one, shifting her on his lap so that she was straddling him and facing him directly.

"Is everything okay? Did Sienna and Lisa get along?" He knew she'd been a little worried about getting them together, but her time was often at a premium. Which was why he hadn't minded eating alone tonight while she went out with her friends. He hoped she wasn't stressing about that though; she could take her determination not to 'use' him a little too far— which was part of how he knew she never would.

If anything, he had to watch her to make sure she didn't give too much of herself, something she was all too capable of doing. It was why he'd suggested introducing Lisa and Sienna rather than running herself ragged trying to spend time with them separately. She was a people pleaser, and as her Daddy, it was his job to make sure no one took advantage of that, even unintentionally.

"They did, they liked each other a lot." She perked up for a moment but then deflated a little. Reaching up, Kawan brushed her hair back from her shoulder, waiting for her to say something. Sometimes she just needed a few minutes to put her thoughts together and he didn't want to rush her. "I—we—ran into Peggy."

It was all he could do to keep his expression blank. While he might despise his baby girl's former friend and roommate, she'd been more wistful the few times the woman had come up in conversation. Running into her must have been tough, and she didn't need his opinion of the woman making it harder for her to talk about the encounter.

"And how did that go?" he asked, carefully adopting a neutral tone. The little look she gave him said that she saw right through the attempt, but at least he'd tried.

"She announced, very loudly, that I'm a pervert who acts like a baby and calls my boyfriend Daddy."

Another time, that might have enraged Kawan. But Melody seemed more annoyed and sad than hurt or distressed, and since he knew she'd been with Sienna, he could only imagine how well that had gone over.

"Did you tell her you're more like a five-year-old than a baby, unless you've been particularly naughty?" he asked, teasing her gently, hoping to make her smile.

She narrowed her eyes at him, but her lips did curve up against her will. "No. But Sienna told her that she also calls her fiancé Daddy. And Lisa made a pearl clutching reference. And then I told her that it wasn't any of her business... and then she ran away when she realized no one cared about my sex life, and that I wasn't backing down."

Pride swelled inside of him. He'd honestly expected to hear that Sienna had handled the situation. Melody had gotten better about speaking up when she wanted something—especially since the day when she'd experimented with being 'teenaged'— but it would have been easy for her to fall back into her old habits when faced with her former best friend.

"Good girl," he said warmly, his fingers caressing her hips. She flushed with happiness, smiling back at him as arousal began to stir in her eyes. "I'm very proud of you for standing up for yourself."

Immediately she brightened, her expression turning impish. "Does that mean I get a treat?"

He had to laugh.

"Absolutely, baby girl, what do you want?"

She eyed him slyly. "Orgasms."

"Then orgasms you shall receive."

She squealed with delight as he turned, rolling them off of the couch and taking her down to the floor in a controlled fall. It didn't take him long to strip her down to nothing and administer the first orgasm with his mouth while she tugged on his hair. Then he picked her up and carried her off to the bedroom for round two, which ended in a treat for both of them.

Cuddling her sleeping form in his arms afterwards, he stroked her hair and stared up at the ceiling in the darkness, completely struck by the knowledge that sometime during the past few weeks, he'd fallen head over heels in love with her.

CHAPTER 25

*H*olding Melody's hand, Kawan moved through Black Light toward the table where he could see Alexander, Sienna, Connor, and Ella already sitting. The latter two were back in town and had wanted to come out to the club tonight to see everyone. His baby girl bounced at his side, excited to be at the club and to see her friends.

It was Silk and Seduction night and he'd dressed her in an adorable pink silk chemise and shorts trimmed with white lace, with two white bows adorning her pigtails. She was adorably sexy, as the neckline dipped low to show off the rounded tops of her breasts and the short shorts barely covered her bottom. When she bent over, they rode up high enough that he could easily spank her sit spots without even adjusting them. Not that he'd needed to yet, but he was sure he could find an excuse before the night was over.

He felt a little odd walking through the club in his own silk outfit, but he'd bowed to the theme and put on a pair of silky pajama pants and a top, which he'd left unbuttoned. To his amusement, he saw that Alexander had decided to keep to his usual pants and dress shirt, although the shirt looked like it might be very expensive silk. He was the odd man out though; Connor was wearing nothing more than a pair of silky boxers.

Both Sienna and Ella were dressed in silky lingerie as well, although Sienna's was more of a very short blue dress and Ella's was a sumptuous red robe with black lace that went all the way down to her ankles. Likely she was completely naked underneath, but the very fact that she was so covered did make one wonder...

"Perfect timing!" Ella said as Kawan and Melody reached them. "We were just about to go to the ladies' room; you can come with us."

Connor's lips quirked, lifting his hand to curve his fingers around the back of Ella's neck. "Try that again, sweetheart, and this time remember where we are."

Ella's eyes flared, as if she wanted to argue with her dom. She could brat with the best of them, but she kept her focus. "Sorry." She smiled sweetly at Kawan. "Can Melody come to the ladies' room with us, Master Kawan?"

Leaning in, Connor whispered something in her ear, and her cheeks flushed with pleasure.

"Yes, she may," Kawan said. Ella couldn't know it, but he was grateful for the brief separation. He'd been hoping to talk to his friends privately at some point this evening.

"Come right back," Alexander ordered as Sienna stood up.

"Yes, Daddy." She leaned over to kiss him, grinning widely, her tone on the border of sassy.

Kawan patted Melody's bottom as she joined her friends, making her giggle, before he took one of the empty seats. The trio immediately linked arms, already chatting and laughing as they walked away.

"I swear, there's something in the water tonight," Connor murmured, turning slightly to watch them go, as if he didn't quite trust they'd behave themselves. "Ella's been toeing the line like she's looking for a spanking but isn't quite ready to commit."

"I think it's all the silk," Alexander said, shaking his head. They all looked around the room, and Kawan had to admit that there did seem to be a different feel in the air, a slightly softer one. As if the lack of leather and latex had changed something intangible.

Or maybe it was just Kawan who had changed. Since he didn't know how much time he had, he just went right into what he wanted to talk to them about.

"How did you know that Sienna and Ella were 'the one'?" he asked.

Two heads swiveled around to face him, like owls zeroing in on their prey with laser focus. Alexander's eyes gleamed with amusement, while Connor seemed more surprised than anything else. Of course, he and Ella had been traveling a lot the past weeks, so they hadn't been around to see the admittedly fast growth of his and Melody's relationship.

The swiftness with which everything was happening was the cause of his concern. He'd been sure about Krissy too, and while he knew Melody was nothing like Krissy, he was starting to think that maybe *he* was the problem. Falling too hard, too fast. Which was especially scary this time because he already felt far more for Melody than he ever had for Krissy.

Did that mean that she was the one though? Or did it just mean he was the kind of guy who jumped into the deep end without thinking, and someone needed to smack some sense into him? If it was the latter, he couldn't think of anyone better suited to the task than Alexander and Connor. And, conversely, he couldn't think of anyone better to ask about love. They'd both fallen hard, fast, and successfully. So far he had two out of three and he'd really like to add the third.

"Isn't it kind of soon to be asking that question?" Connor asked.

"That's exactly what I'm concerned about," Kawan admitted. He shrugged with one shoulder, the corner of his mouth tipping up in a rueful smile. "But... I can't imagine time changing my mind."

Alexander nodded. "I think I knew the night I met Sienna. At least, I knew she was special. The potential was there, even if I wasn't about to propose immediately." Now it was his turn to shrug. "I just can't imagine my life without her, and I don't want to. Even when we're arguing or hit a rough patch, I'd still rather work things out than lose her. She makes my days worth waking up for."

"Oh, now she's going to be sorry she missed hearing you say that," Connor teased, grinning. He turned to Kawan. "He's not wrong though. I feel the same way about Ella. Well, now I do." He rubbed his chin. "That actually happened pretty quickly too. One night at Black Light and I saw her completely differently."

That made Kawan smile. "So, you're saying that in comparison to you two, I'm going slowly."

"I understand why you're hesitant," Alexander said, smiling although his eyes were serious. "After Krissy, you should be. But Melody's different. You're different with her, in a good way. With Krissy you always seemed on edge, a little anxious, and you frowned a lot more than you smiled. Now you're always smiling, you're settled, and you seem fulfilled."

Slowly, Connor nodded his agreement. "It might be fast, but Alexander's right. You look good. And I like Melody." He shrugged. "I knew Ella for years before anything happened between us, but that was our timeline. Everyone's is different. If it's right, then there really is no such thing as 'too soon,' is there?"

Well, that was a very good point.

∼

Going to the bathroom with Ella and Sienna was actually the first time Melody had wandered through any part of Black Light without Daddy next to her. She felt a little odd and a little more vulnerable without him right by her side. Although, her friends were also protection in and of themselves, as was the silky pink ribbon Daddy had tied around her neck in lieu of a collar.

"I love the shorts and camisole look," Ella told her, eyeing Melody's outfit as they walked through the club. "I wish I'd thought of that."

Melody had to laugh. "I wish I'd been able to talk Daddy into letting me wear something more like what you have on."

The silky robe was nearly floor length and made Ella look like she should be lounging on a chaise somewhere, sipping a cocktail. Possibly while someone fanned her with a gigantic palm leaf. Probably not Master Connor though. Melody couldn't imagine him being the one to fan her.

Ella's eyes lit up with mischief. "I'm actually in a wee bit of trouble for wearing this... Connor was running late so we met here instead of at home."

"Brat," Sienna teased, laughing, as they walked into the ladies' room. Melody giggled.

As things went, wearing something that followed the letter—although not the spirit—of the theme night wasn't exceptionally bratty. She was sure Ella would pay for it in a mutually satisfying manner.

She'd have to remember that for the future, if she was ever in the same position to choose her own outfit without Daddy changing her before they even got out the door.

They all exchanged greetings with the other women they knew who were in the room and then Sienna and Ella went into their respective stalls. Since Melody didn't actually have to go to the bathroom, she primped in front of the mirror, messing with her pigtails and the bows Daddy had put in them.

"So, you and Kawan are officially living together now, huh?" Ella asked, emerging from her stall. She grinned at Melody, which helped relieve some of Melody's immediate tension at the question. Even though Daddy had made it clear that he wanted her there, she still worried a little bit about what other people would think. Especially his friends. "That's exciting."

"It is," she replied, leaning her hip against one of the sinks as Ella went to wash her hands. "I didn't really think I'd have time for a new relationship right now, but he's made it easy. And it feels right."

"Have you said the 'L' word yet?" Sienna asked, coming up to one of the other sinks. Her eyes were bright with interest.

"No." Although she felt it. Had felt it. But it was so soon, and she was afraid to say it in case he didn't say it back. Or worse, if he said it back because he didn't want to hurt her feelings but didn't actually mean it. Not that she thought she could gather the courage to say it first anyway.

"Oh, don't look so down." Ella wrapped her arm around Melody's shoulders. "He totally does. It only takes one look at him to know that. It's the way he looks at you."

"It's true." Sienna smiled at her reassuringly. "I've never seen him happier than he has been since he met you."

"That might just be the rampant sex," Melody pointed out, making the other two laugh.

"I'm sure that doesn't hurt either," Ella teased, steering her back to the door to the club.

On her first step back into the club, a flash of something bright caught Melody's eye. Was that... *fire*? Holy crap it was! A submissive was tied down to a table, arms above her head, and the Dom—holy shit, it was Elliott. Elliott!—was setting her on *fire!*

"Ooo, never seen fire play before?" Sienna asked from behind her, startling Melody and making her realize she was just standing there, staring, and blocking Sienna and Ella's exit from the bathroom. "Want to go take a closer look?"

She did, she *really* did but... "Aren't we supposed to go right back?"

All three of them turned to look as one at the bar where their dominants were sitting. The men appeared to be deep in conversation, none of them paying attention to their immediate surroundings, much less keeping an eye on the restroom.

"We'll just go take a little peek," Ella said, her tone a little wheedling. "I've always wanted to see one of the demonstrations. We'll be so quick, they won't even notice."

As much as Melody wanted to be a good girl, she had to admit, she felt a little rush of excitement at the idea of being a teensy bit sneaky. It wasn't like they were going to hurt anyone by taking a tiny detour, after all.

"Okay," she heard herself saying, taking another quick glance over at her Daddy, who was listening earnestly to something Alexander was saying. "Real quick."

THE GIRLS WERE TAKING TOO LONG.

Frowning, Kawan turned his head over toward the restroom. No Melody, Sienna, or Ella. Seeing his movement, Alexander and Connor looked over too.

"They might just be talking, like us," Alexander murmured, but his tone had hardened. Deepened.

Like hawks, all three of them swept their gazes around the room, seeking out their prey.

In her soft pink lingerie, Melody was easy to spot, even if the fire play demonstration hadn't drawn his eye. The moment he found her, he relaxed slightly, although he also had to shake his head. Naughty baby girl. If she'd wanted to watch the fire, she should have come and let him know, not walked over by herself.

"Well, I believe that ends the talking portion of the evening," Connor said, pushing back his chair and getting to his feet. "It looks like I now have *two* good reasons to punish Ella tonight."

Kawan didn't ask what the other reason was, although he suspected it had to do with the long, covering robe Ella was wearing. He grinned though, standing and moving quickly enough that he was leading the pack of them as they strode across the club floor, heading for their naughty little girls. As if sensing the danger, Sienna's head turned. Her eyes widened and she grabbed the other two by their hands.

They looked at her and then immediately jerked around to see their doms—their Daddies—bearing down on them. Three pairs of wide eyes in three excited but fearful faces.

Perfect.

"Fire, hmm?" Alexander asked, as soon as he reached Sienna, one hand wrapping her ponytail around his fingers and using her hair to draw her closer. "I believe I know what puts fire out."

"Daddy, no!" But he was already dragging her away.

Connor didn't even bother saying anything to Ella, just lifted her up over his shoulder in one swift movement and kept going. She let out a little squeak as she was carried off like a barbarian's prize.

Standing in front of his own baby girl, Kawan put his hands on his hips and lifted his eyebrows at her. He didn't say anything, just waited. Master Elliott had only paused for a moment to see what was happening, but now he was continuing his demonstration. Melody didn't look back as the flames flared behind her again.

"Sorry, Daddy," she said, teeth scraping over her plump lower lip like a nervous tic. "The fire just looked really neat and..." Her voice trailed off when his expression didn't change one iota.

"I'm sure it did look neat," he finally said. "But you should have come right back to the table the way you were supposed to and then we could have come over and watched together. Instead..." She squealed as he flipped her over his shoulder, mimicking Connor's move, but he added to it by smacking her bottom right on the tender sit spot which was revealed by her shorts riding up. "You're going to get a demonstration on what it's like to have Daddy set his naughty little girl on fire."

"Pretty sure I already know," she muttered, and by happenstance there was just enough of a lull in the noise around the club that he managed to hear her.

SMACK!

She shrieked, wriggling, when he spanked her other sit spot.

Spotting a free alcove, Kawan adjusted his course. She hadn't been *very* naughty, but he was going to enjoy giving her a thorough spanking.

By THE TIME Daddy had wrangled Melody over his knee, the crotch of her silky shorts was soaked with her juices. The two swats she'd already taken to her backside had stung, but that heat had quickly morphed into arousal. Now her nipples were puckered buds, stimulated by the silken fabric of the camisole as her breasts swayed beneath her.

Her shorts were pulled swiftly down to her mid-thighs, baring her butt. Not that the thin fabric would have offered much protection anyway, but her face flamed because she knew anyone looking in this direction would now have a completely unobscured view of her upturned bottom and her creamy pussy. That kind of embarrassment wasn't enough to safe word over though, and she knew it was likely part of her punishment to be put on display like this.

Not exactly a harsh punishment, since the bit of exhibitionism also sent a thrill up her spine.

"Now, naughty girl," he said, his voice almost silky with the salacious threat. Melody's pussy clenched at being called a naughty girl. She liked being naughty just as much as she liked being good. "What do you have to say for yourself?"

Being questioned made her squirm uncomfortably. She was all too aware of his hand caressing her ass, drawing out the anticipation before her spanking.

"I'm sorry, Daddy," she said, wiggling her bottom enticingly.

"That wasn't very sincere, but don't worry, baby girl. We'll get there." The promise made her arousal spike. Then Daddy's hand lifted and she tensed just before his hand landed.

SMACK!

Ouch! Sometimes in between spankings she forgot how much Daddy's hand could hurt. The hard swat wasn't his full force, but it stung enough to not be purely erotic either.

SMACK! SMACK! SMACK!

As he began to pepper her bottom with firm, even swats, Melody squirmed on his lap, the heat in her skin beginning to build. He moved his hand all over, so that she couldn't antici-pate where each blow was going to land. Tears began to sting the back of her eyes as each smarting stroke added to the overall burn. His hand landed all over, from the top of her curves to her sensitive sit spots, making her writhe as she started trying to avoid the rain of painful smacks.

"Ow! Daddy, I'm sorry! I won't do it again!"

The spanking stopped, making her slump... but her relief was mingled with disappointment. A small part of her wondered *that was it?* Daddy's hand roughly caressed her bottom, making her whimper and her pussy spasm in response. The heat beneath her skin spread through her lower body and she moaned when his fingers dipped down to her slick pussy.

"That sounded a little more sincere, but I don't think we're quite there yet."

A quick dip of his fingers into her pussy and then he retreated. Melody was ready for the next swat. What she *wasn't* ready for was where it landed.

She shrieked, the fiery sting shooting through her, her pussy throbbing from the unexpected strike. While Daddy hadn't used the same amount of force as he had on her bottom, her swollen nether lips were far more sensitive and the stinging bite much more severe.

A second swat followed the first, so quickly that it took her breath away. It wasn't until the third painful slap was applied to her puffy, aching pussy, his fingers snapping against her pulsing clit, that she managed to cry out.

"I'm soooorry, Daddy!"

Two more hard slaps to her pussy left her writhing in lustful agony, panting for breath at the intense sensations, and closer to orgasm than she would have thought possible.

MELODY'S sweet juices coated Kawan's fingers. He'd never spanked her pussy before, but he'd wanted to see how she reacted to it. The apology she uttered was far more sincere than the first, impish one she'd offered, and yet she became wetter and wetter with each swat. Her sensitive, swollen lips were now dark pink and glistening with her juices, her bottom was rosy from her spanking, and she was wriggling on his lap with arousal. His cock pressed against her soft side, aching and ready to take her.

It took but a moment to tug her shorts completely off and drop them to the floor. Pulling her up, he had her straddle his lap, leaving her pussy spread and vulnerable. Tears were gathered in her eyes and the moisture trickled down her cheeks in the new position, making her look very much like a sorry little girl. Sliding one hand between her thighs and the other hand around her neck, Kawan drew her in for a kiss, simultaneously pressing his fingers against her wetness. She moaned as he slid two fingers inside of her heated pussy, stroking her gently, his hand rubbing against her sensitized flesh.

Muffling the small noise with his lips, Kawan deepened the kiss, thrusting his tongue into her mouth and mimicking the movement with his fingers. Melody squirmed, her pussy clenching around his fingers. Her hands came down on his shoulders, helping her to hold position while he began to fingerfuck her.

When she mewled against his mouth, he pulled away, ending the kiss and slowing the movement of his fingers.

"Daddy, please," she whimpered, tightening her pussy around him and arching her back, seeking the stimulation she needed to come.

"Please what, baby girl?" he asked, languidly pumping his fingers. His thumb circled her clit but didn't touch it, and she shuddered, arching again in desperate need.

"Please, may I come?" The plea was appealingly heartfelt, but Kawan shook his head.

"Not until you're on my cock, baby girl." Pulling his fingers completely free from her body, he grinned wickedly at her whimper.

It took just a small amount of shifting to free his dick from the silky confines of his pants, and then he pulled Melody forward by her hips. They both groaned in unison as she sank onto him, her pussy tighter than usual in this position, although she was slick enough that it didn't matter. Gravity pulled her down, until his cock was fully embedded in her body.

Holding her hips tightly, he moved her atop him, making her grind down on him, and she cried out, arching her back.

"Ride me, baby girl," he commanded, moving his hands from her hips to her hot bottom, giving her some control over her movements.

~

OH MY GOODNESS...

Daddy didn't often put her on top, but she knew it didn't matter that she was now in the 'position of power'. She still didn't really feel like she was leading the show because she knew he could take back control at any moment. Hard hands gripped her bottom, bringing the burn from her spanking back to life. Her pussy felt more sensitive than ever, the lips swollen and hot, his body hair tickling her skin. The discomfort was already fading, turning the pain into her pleasure.

Moaning, she moved up and down, clenching around the thick rod of his cock, impaling herself on him and rocking her hips back and forth. It felt so good. The sounds of the club filled her ears—noises that somehow always became dimmed when she was being spanked, but now returned to full volume, enhancing the experience. Slaps, moans, cries, and even screams. Pain and pleasure. Like she was a tiny part of something larger, a small piece of the seductive microcosm of Black Light.

"Oh, Daddy..." She shuddered, feeling his fingers pressing into the cleft of her bottom cheeks, seeking out the tiny hole there. Immediately, everything felt naughtier, dirtier, and more lewdly charged than before.

His fingers sank into her at the same time as his cock and Melody sobbed at the deliciously filthy sensations. Her thighs flexed and she moved harder, faster, her climax rushing toward her as Daddy filled her completely.

"That's right, baby girl." His voice was hoarse, rough, and she felt his cock surging upwards, his body rubbing against her sensitive pussy. "Come for me."

Her muscles clamped down around him and she threw her head back, crying out and grinding down atop him. Heat, need, ecstasy all rushed through her. She was stuffed so wonderfully full, every inch of her humming and buzzing with all the titillating stimulation she could handle. The orgasm drew back like a massive tidal wave and then crashed over her, through her, drenching her with the hot pleasure.

Daddy's lips covered hers, his fingers pumping into her ass, his other hand on the back of her neck, holding her in place as she moaned and sobbed for him. She felt him swell inside of her, hardening, and then the hot, wet heat as he throbbed inside of her. The kiss ended, and she was left panting and clinging to him, perfectly, wonderfully satisfied.

Head resting on his shoulder, she whimpered a little as he rocked her back and forth atop him, sending small aftershocks of pleasure through her body. The hand on the back of her neck stroked the soft skin on the edge of her jaw and a feeling of utter contentment swept through her.

"I love you, baby girl."

The whispered words shocked her to her core. She jerked back to see his expression, and Daddy smiled up at her, his adoration clear in his dark eyes.

"You aren't supposed to tell a woman that right after sex!" she protested.

Laughing, Daddy slid his fingers from her bottom and gave her already roasted cheek a little slap, and she squealed, although it didn't really hurt. It was just an automatic reaction.

"It's true no matter when I say it," he told her. "And I will tell you again and again, as often as needed, in as many different circumstances as I can. I love you, Melody Williams, my baby girl."

She blinked, but the tears springing into her eyes weren't from pain, but from sheer, euphoric happiness.

"I love you too, Daddy."

The End

ABOUT THE AUTHOR

About me? Right... I'm a writer, I should be able to do that, right?

I'm a happily married young woman and I like tater tots, small fuzzy animals, naming my plants, hiking, reading, writing, sexy time, naked time, shirtless o'clock, anything sparkly or shiny, and weirding people out with my OCD food habits.

I believe in Happy Endings. And fairies. And Santa Claus. Because without a little magic, what's the point of living?

I write because I must. I live in several different worlds at any given moment. And I wouldn't have it any other way.

Want to know more about my other books and stories? Sign up for my newsletter! Come visit my website! I also update my blog at least a couple times a month.

You can also come hang out with me on Facebook in my private Facebook group!

Thank you so much for reading, I hope you enjoyed the story... and don't forget, the best thing you can do in return for any author is to leave them feedback!

Stay sassy.

OTHER TITLES BY GOLDEN ANGEL

Standalone Romances

Mated on Hades

Marriage Training

Domestic Discipline Quartet

Birching His Bride

Dealing With Discipline

Punishing His Ward

Claiming His Wife

Bridal Discipline Series

Philip's Rules

Undisciplined (Book 1.5)

Gabrielle's Discipline

Lydia's Penance

Benedict's Commands

Arabella's Taming

Venus Rising Quartet

The Venus School

Venus Aspiring

Venus Desiring

Venus Transcendent

Stronghold Series

Stronghold

Taming the Tease

On His Knees (book 2.5)

Mastering Lexie

Pieces of Stronghold (book 3.5)

Breaking the Chain

Bound to the Past

Stripping the Sub

Tempting the Domme

Hardcore Vanilla

Masters of the Castle

Masters of the Castle: Witness Protection Program Box Set

Tsenturion Masters

Alien Captive

Alien Tribute

Big Bad Bunnies Series

Chasing His Bunny

Chasing His Squirrel

Chasing His Puma

Chasing His Polar Bear

Chasing His Honey Badger

Chasing Her Lion (coming April 2020)

Night of the Wild Stags – A standalone Reverse Harem romance set in the Big Bad Bunnies World

Poker Loser Trilogy

Forced Bet

Back in the Game

Winning Hand

Poker Loser Trilogy Bundle (3 books in 1!)

THERE'S MORE TO DISCOVER IN THE WORLD OF BLACK LIGHT!

Black Light is the first series from Black Collar Press and the response has been fantastic, but we're not done yet. There are many more books to come from your favorite authors in the Romance genre! Including some continuations from the characters in Valentine Roulette, but we won't spoil anything...

If you're new to the world of Black Light, be sure to catch up with the books already released in the first two seasons of Black Light, so that you're ready when the next stand-alone BDSM fueled book is released! Keep in mind that all books in the series can be read as a standalone or in any order.

And be sure to join our private Facebook group, Black Light Central, where fans of the series get teasers, release updates, and enjoy winning prizes. If you are brave enough to become a member, you can find us at Black Light Central.

BLACK LIGHT SEASON ONE

Infamous Love by Livia Grant is the prequel that started it all! It explains how Jaxson, Chase, and Emma get together, fall in love, and fight to stand for their relationship against the forces that would keep them apart.

Black Light: Rocked by Livia Grant is Book 1 in the world of Black Light that begins on the opening night of the club, it follows a rockstar named Jonah "Cash" Carter and his love interest Samantha Stone. Misunderstandings and a dark history have turned this sweet, childhood romance into a dangerous situation – and when Cash and Samantha finally meet again there's only one thing on his mind: revenge.

Black Light: Exposed by Jennifer Bene is Book 2 in the world of Black Light. Thomas Hathaway and Maddie O'Neill would have never met if it weren't for the reporter opening at The Washington Post. But with her dreams on the line Maddie only has one focus: get the story, then get the job. When she lies her way into Black Light on Thomas' arm, everything seems perfect, except that she enjoys the belt and the man who wields it a little too much. Before time runs out Maddie will have to make a tough choice... to follow her dreams, or her heart.

Black Light: Valentine Roulette was the first boxset in the series where for the first time dominants and submissives came to the Black Light BDSM club to spin for their chance at a night of kinky fun, and maybe even love. With eight stories from eight *USA Today* and international bestselling authors, it's sure to heat up your Kindle! Featuring: Renee Rose, Livia Grant, Jennifer Bene, Maren Smith, Addison Cain, Lee Savino, Sophie Kisker, and Measha Stone.

Black Light: Suspended by Maggie Ryan is Book 4 in the world of Black Light. Charlize Fullerton is a tough DEA agent who has worked hard to prove herself, and when she meets Special Agent Dillon MacAllister on a joint task force to take down a drug ring sparks start to fly. When their mission ends he's sure he's lost his chance with her, until they run into each other at the Black Light BDSM club, and Dillon refuses to let her go a second time.

Black Light: Cuffed by Measha Stone is Book 5 in the world of Black Light. Sydney is a masochist that doesn't stick around for Doms who don't push her to the edge. Tate knows exactly what Sydney is after and he's intent on giving it to her, just not until she begs for it. One snag, there's a murderer in town and it's their job to make sure they get the right guy and keep him behind bars. But when the case starts to hit a little too close to home can Tate and Sydney work side by side without losing each other in the fray?

Black Light: Rescued by Livia Grant is Book 6 in the world of Black Light, and we're right back with Ryder and Khloe from Black Light: Valentine Roulette. Saying goodbye after Valentine Roulette had crushed them both, but Ryder Helms is a realist. He knows his CIA covert career will never allow him to be with a superstar like Khloe Monroe. But when things go sideways for both of them, it's not just their lives at risk, but their hearts as well.

BLACK LIGHT SEASON TWO

Black Light: Roulette Redux by eight talented authors was Book 7 and our second boxed set in the Black Light world. Our couples are back to their naughty shenanigans on Valentine's Day by being randomly paired and made to play out scenes decided by the turn of the wheel. Are you brave enough to roll?

Complicated Love by Livia Grant is the follow-up to the prequel, Infamous Love. It gives Black Light fans another look into the complicated lives of the trio, Jaxson, Emma, and Chase as they try to live their unconventional love in a sometimes uncompromising world. This book is a must read for MMF menage fans!

Black Light: Suspicion by Measha Stone is Book 8 in the world of Black Light. Measha is back with another fun dose of suspense and sexy BDSM play combined Sophie and Scott work together to solve crimes by day and burn up the sheets by night. When Sophie is in danger, there is little her Dom won't do to keep her safe, including warming her bottom when she needs it.

Black Light: Obsessed by Dani René is Book 9 in the Black Light world. Dani's first story in the series is also the first Black Light book set on the West Coast new club. He might just be a little obsessed with his new submissive, Roisin. Does he go too far?

Black Light: Fearless by Maren Smith is Book 10 in the Black Light world. The talented BDSM author, Maren, is very familiar to Black Light fans since she has had short stories in both Roulette boxes sets. In fact, fans of her short story Shameless will recognize the beloved characters in this full-length follow-up novel. This is a must read Black Light book!

Black Light: Possession by LK Shaw is book 11 and the final book of season two. It brings the action back to the East Coast and gives us a glimpse of another fantastic menage relationship set in the middle of danger and intrigue. It is the perfect ending to our second season as we move forward into season three with Celebrity Roulette.

BLACK LIGHT SEASON THREE

Black Light: Celebrity Roulette by eight talented authors is Book 12 and our third annual Valentine's Day boxed set in the Black Light world. New couples are back to their naughty shenanigans on Valentine's Day by being paired, this time with a celebrity auction, and made to play out scenes decided by the turn of the wheel. Come see how the celebrities play on the West Coast!

Black Light: Purged - A Black Light Short by Livia Grant is a bit unique in the Black Light world. It is a short glimpse into the lives of some of our beloved recurring characters, Khloe Monroe and Ryder Helms. It is a dark and realistic view into the lives of someone living with an eating disorder and how having someone who loves you in your corner can make all the difference in the world.

BLACK COLLAR PRESS

Black Collar Press is a small publishing house started by authors Livia Grant and Jennifer Bene in late 2016. The purpose was simple - to create a place where the erotic, kinky, and exciting worlds they love to explore could thrive and be joined by other like-minded authors.

If this is something that interests you, please go to the Black Collar Press website and read through the FAQs. If your questions are not answered there, please contact us directly at: blackcollarpress@gmail.com

WHERE TO FIND BLACK COLLAR PRESS:

- Website: http://www.blackcollarpress.com/
- Facebook: https://www.facebook.com/blackcollarpress/
- Twitter: https://twitter.com/BlackCollarPres
- Black Light East and West may be fictitious, but you can now join our very real Facebook Group for Black Light Fans - Black Light Central

Made in the USA
Middletown, DE
03 March 2020